"YOU THINK YOU KNOW SO MUCH ABOUT WOMEN," ANNIE SCOFFED.

"I know what they want, and I know how to give it," Brett replied calmly.

It wasn't a boast, just a simple fact that had the power to kindle a fire in the pit of her stomach. "And what does the woman get out of it?"

"She gets to feel needed. Cherished. Desired." Each word fell in tempo with her heartbeat. "Think about it, Annie."

She did. In excruciating detail. Worse, she remembered seeing him in the creek. All that muscle. All that power. All that . . . utter and absolute *maleness*. And it could be hers with a crook of her finger. She could hardly remember the last time the blood in her veins felt so hot.

"Is bedding women all you think of?" she demanded.

Brett looked at her. "Bedding *you* is all I can think of."

Other **AVON ROMANCES**

Rachelle Morgan

Mustang Annie

AVON BOOKS

An Imprint of HarperCollinsPublishers

This is a work of fiction. Names, characters, places, and incidents are products of the author's imagination or are used fictitiously and are not to be construed as real. Any resemblance to actual events, locales, organizations, or persons, living or dead, is entirely coincidental.

AVON BOOKS
An Imprint of HarperCollins*Publishers*
10 East 53rd Street
New York, New York 10022-5299

First Avon Books paperback printing: August 2000

Avon Trademark Reg. U.S. Pat. Off. and in Other Countries, Marca Registrada, Hecho en U.S.A.
HarperCollins® is a trademark of HarperCollins Publishers Inc.

Printed in the U.S.A.

WCD   10   9   8   7   6   5   4   3   2   1

This book is gratefully dedicated to Micki Nuding and Lucia Macro, for saying yes; to the incomparable "Avon Ladies," for their spirit and generosity; and always, to my very own Mr. Morgan, who never fails to amaze me.

This book is a work of fiction. Names, characters, places and incidents are products of the author's imagination or are used fictitiously. Any resemblance to actual events, locales, or persons, living or dead, is entirely coincidental.

Prologue

West Texas, Early 1870s

They'd come for the horses.

Choking dust still haunted the earth torn up by a thousand hooves. The stench of pillage and desolation twisted around a cold March wind. Blackened embers smoldered from what remained of a home that only hours before had rung with the promise of a future filled with laughter, adventure, and a love so powerful that nothing had existed outside it.

Ashes to ashes, dust to dust . . . never had a phrase been more fitting.

Annie Harper rose from where she knelt in front of a freshly dug grave, dropped the rock she'd used to pound a crude wooden marker into the ground, and pulled the edges of her shredded blouse together over her naked skin. If

1

the mustangs had been all they'd taken, Annie could have dealt with it.

The loss of her husband, though . . .

She shut her gritty eyes and bowed her head. Why'd they have to kill him? He'd only been trying to protect what belonged to him. His horses. His home.

His wife.

It was hard to believe that only yesterday they'd been planning another excursion into the canyon. Only yesterday they'd made wagers on which of them would spot the herd first, and who would capture the most profitable mares to take to auction, and whether or not they'd see the lead stallion.

And only yesterday she'd celebrated love, success, and happiness in her beloved's arms, never imagining that come dawn, yesterdays would be all she'd have left to hold.

A coldness invading Annie's breast, she backed up several paces from the grave, turned away from the rising sun, and walked, neither knowing nor caring where her legs took her.

When she reached the edge of the property she looked backward one last time, first at the empty, broken corrals, then at the smoldering mound of rubble beneath the cottonwood trees, then at the plain wooden cross sticking up through the prairie grass like a brittle bone.

They'd come for the horses . . . but they'd taken so much more. They'd taken everything worth living for.

Chapter 1

Four years later . . .

"That no good, dirty, rotten son-of-a-bitch." Brett Corrigan stormed into his study, toward the walnut cabinet across the room.

His foreman followed at a slower pace, wisely saying not a word. In the year since Brett had first taken over the ranch and made it his own, Wade Henry had learned that when his boss's temper let loose, it was safer just to keep his distance until it ran its course.

With the strength of the fury building inside Brett, it might be awhile. He loosened his kerchief with a single jerk, sloshed three fingers of bourbon from the decanter into a cut-crystal glass, and downed the liquor in one swallow.

3

"You want me to round up the men, Ace?" Henry finally ventured.

"And spend another month chasing a shadow?"

"We gotta do somethin'. That devil thinks your ladies are free for the takin'."

"I know!" Brett slammed the empty glass against the cabinet top. "I know." This wasn't the first time that cunning rogue had slipped onto the Triple Ace and stolen his stock. Over the last two months, Brett had lost almost a dozen horses to the wild black stallion they'd taken to calling Blue Fire. And last night he'd managed to lure away two of Brett's best Arabian fillies.

The timing couldn't be worse, either. Those fillies were just about to go into season, and he had a prime Thoroughbred stud waiting in the wings to service them. Albert Moore, a Kansas cattle baron with interests in racing, had already claimed the foals, and extended a promise of more contracts to come if the bloodlines were kept clean.

"Damn that rogue!"

Brett poured himself a refill, then strode to the vast window overlooking the bald landscape of the Triple Ace. He wondered again why he'd chosen this God-forgotten place to settle. There was nothing to boast about—just twenty thousand acres of sand and sagebrush, with a few juniper shrubs thrown in to break up the monotony. If the land hadn't come to him fair and square, he'd never have ventured onto it, much less decided to raise horses again.

What the hell had ever made him think he could take a handful of bony nags and turn them into valuable breeding stock? His father was probably laughing his fool head off. *Think you're so high and mighty, don't you, boy? You couldn't raise a good horse with a windlass.*

Brett's grip tightened around the glass. No, he wasn't going to fold his hand yet. Call it pride, call it arrogance, call it simple greed. This piece of Texas might not look like much now, but by God, it belonged to him, along with everything on it. One day the Triple Ace would be the most prosperous horse farm in the territory. No wild mustang with a fancy for his fillies was going to cause its failure before it even had a chance to succeed.

But how did he stop the wretch? And just as important, how did he get his fillies back before the stallion ruined them?

Brett glanced over his shoulder at the bowlegged man standing between matched black and burgundy-striped armchairs. Wade Henry looked like a hundred other veteran horsemen Brett had seen in his lifetime: gaunt cheeked, bristly haired, skin beaten into bronzed grooves by more than half a century of relentless Texas sun. What's more, he had exceptional horse sense. That alone made him worth keeping on. What would *he* do if he stood in Brett's boots?

He folded the temptation to ask Henry for advice almost as soon as the notion formed. Bosses gave the orders; hired hands took them. The rule had been bred into Brett so deeply that crossing that boundary had never entered his mind before, and probably wouldn't have now if he didn't feel so damned helpless. But the word of a leader was second only to God's, and allowing a hireling to influence his authority eroded the workings of the whole outfit. As with every other decision that affected the Triple Ace, this one rested solely on his shoulders.

Brett swirled the bourbon, and as he watched the amber liquid lap against the rim, he considered his options. Angry as he was, he'd castrate the stallion if he could get his hands on him. Unfortunately, his men couldn't get close enough to rope him, much less bring him in.

Chasing him off hadn't worked, either; he'd just come back again and again, slipping past the guards under the cover of darkness, collecting a couple more missies for his harem, then disappearing the same way.

Maybe he should just hire a sharpshooter to solve the problem once and for all, Brett thought with a sigh. No one would fault him for it; he wasn't the only rancher in the area to have lost valuable horses to the wild herds. Still, he had a hard time with that idea. As infuriating as it was to have his stock stolen right from under his nose, a part of him couldn't help but respect— even admire—the stallion's boldness. Hell, if half the Triple Ace colts had that kind of gumption, he'd make a fortune.

Brett's head slowly lifted. *Arabian grace and speed . . . Mustang stamina and grit . . .* Why hadn't he thought of it before? Not everyone could afford Thoroughbreds. Local ranchers and the military were just as hungry for good mounts as wealthy businessmen. Breeding a couple of his mixed blood mares with the stallion could produce foals worth quite a tidy sum. . . .

All it would take is someone smarter and more cunning to bring him in.

Brett abandoned his drink and headed for the door, for once not giving a gator's hide that his spurs might chip the flagstone floor. "I want the patrol doubled on the boundaries," he instructed Henry. "Have the men rotate in eight-hour shifts. Do anything you have to to protect those mares."

"Where are you goin'?"

Brett grabbed his hat and duster off the rack by the front door. "To find someone to catch that devil," he said, jamming on his Stetson. "If he wants my horses, he can have them—on *my* terms."

Hire a thief to catch a thief.

The phrase repeated itself in Brett's mind several hours later as he flipped through the ring of wanted posters in the jailhouse lobby. Dead. Dead. Captured. Dead.

The door opened, sending a wedge of light

across the pocked plank floor. "Afternoon, Sheriff," Brett said without glancing up.

"Corrigan." Ike Savage hung his hat on a wall peg near the door, then lowered his lumpy frame behind a scarred desk cleared of everything save a dented tin can of pencils. Long black sideburns framed the sheriff's bloated cheeks and a thick mustache drooped low over his puffy lips. "Don't tell me you've developed an interest in the law."

"Only when it suits my purposes," Brett answered evasively. He'd met Savage a year ago in the poker game that had won him the Triple Ace. Brett hadn't had much use for the man then, and didn't have much use for him now. Whether because of the badge he wore or a distrust of the man himself, Brett couldn't say, but he'd learned a long time ago that the less said around Ike Savage, the better.

He flipped over another page. The sketches contained some of the most plug-ugly desperadoes he'd ever set eyes on. Cheats. Murderers. Bandits. "You've got quite a collection here." He thumped his finger against the stack of posters. "How many of these are still on the loose?"

Ike withdrew one of the pencils and tapped it against the desktop in a swift, hollow rhythm that set Brett's teeth on edge. "Two. Maybe three." Ike shrugged a meaty shoulder.

"Losin' your touch, Sheriff."

Savage stiffened at the jibe. "What's this all about, Corrigan?"

Brett smiled. "Just passing the time till your deputy shows up." A familiar burst of robust laughter outside put a genuine smile on Brett's face. "Ah, speak of the devil. . . ."

A second later, a tall, lean figure swaggered through the open doorway. Favored with long, sandy blond hair, piercing blue eyes, and a careless charm that seemed to draw women to him like dew to wild rye, Jesse Justiss was probably the only man in town who gave Brett a run for his money when it came to the ladies. He was also dependable, discreet, and a damn fine poker player—not to mention the closest thing to a friend Brett could claim.

Spying him, Jess grinned. "Well, look what the dogs dug up! What brings you to Tascosa?"

"Actually, you do." Brett tipped his hat in the Sheriff's direction, then walked out onto the weather-warped boardwalk with Jesse. If anyone could give him the answers he sought, Jess could. Though at least ten years his junior, the man could find a needle in a haystack before it even got there. Brett had always wondered why Jesse was wasting his time working for a worm like Savage when he could be putting his sleuthing talents to better use.

In silence, Brett fired up a cheroot, offered one to his friend, then pocketed his container of matches.

"Store-bought smokes," Jesse said, popping the end into his mouth. "Must be serious."

Brett took a deep pull of the tobacco and

squinted into the sunlight. "I'm looking for a thief."

Jesse grinned. "Someone run off with one of your women?"

"No, something more irreplaceable," Brett said. "I had a couple more horses turn up missing."

"Ah, so that's why you were rifling through the wanted posters. I take it you didn't find the crook who took them."

"Actually, I know who took them. I was looking for a crook to steal them back."

Jesse threw back his head and laughed. "I should have guessed."

"Unfortunately, I couldn't find a decent horse thief in the bunch. Most of them have either been hanged or sent to prison."

"Or hightailed it to greener pastures," Jess added. He inhaled, then exhaled a stream of smoke. Around them, a warm wind kicked up balls of dust and sent them rolling down the street like tumbleweeds. A pair of hawks circled high above a thicket of sagebrush, waiting for an unwary rodent to emerge.

"You know, it's too bad Mustang Annie isn't around any more," Jess said after a spell. "This sounds like something right up her alley."

"Who's Mustang Annie?" Brett asked, his interest snared.

"Hell, Brett, have you been living under a rock? I didn't think there was a man alive who hadn't heard of her!"

"Who is she?"

"Only the most notorious con artist and horse thief since Joe Flick."

Brett had never heard of Joe Flick, either, but chose not to further reveal his ignorance.

"Shame, too. She used to be a hell of a mustanger. Every horse trader and rancher in four territories would have sold his soul to have her join his outfit. There wasn't a maverick she couldn't catch or a bucker she couldn't settle. Between you and me, I think that only played to her advantage."

"How so?"

"Well, she had herself quite a scam going there for a while. She'd get herself hired on with some outfit, tame the wildest broncs for the boss, and collect her fee. A couple weeks later, the horses would turn up missing."

Brett's mind began to whir with possibilities. He hadn't considered hiring a woman. Females were put on earth to grace a man's arm and warm his bed, not sling ropes and chase horses. But if she could recover his fillies. . . . "What ever happened to her?"

Jesse shrugged. "Your guess is as good as mine. She disappeared about five years ago. Nobody's seen hide nor hair of her since."

It seemed awful strange that such a notorious woman could just up and disappear. Of course, if she were responsible for the disappearance of freshly broken broncs, as Jesse had implicated, it was highly likely that she'd finally gotten caught and wound up being the guest of honor at a necktie social.

On the other hand, if she was just lying low. . . .

"You won't find her, Corrigan," Jesse said, as though reading Brett's mind. "Even Savage hasn't been able to pin her down."

With a sly grin, Brett loosened Fortune's reins from the hitching rail and swung into the saddle. "Maybe he hasn't been looking in the right places."

Chapter 2

❧

It took him a week to track her down.

Shorter than he'd expected, yet longer than it should have taken, considering she'd hired on to one of the biggest ranches in the Nevada Territory.

Assuming she'd taken the same direction as most fugitives, Brett had headed west. He knew he'd hit pay dirt when the mere mention of "Mustang Annie" had normally loose lips locking up tighter than a chastity belt on a million-dollar virgin. Even the substantial reward he'd offered for information hadn't been much of an incentive—until he'd made the acquaintance of a pretty little widow at a roadside way station who remembered that a woman named Annie Harper had been hired onto the Bar 7, due north. He wasn't sure Mustang Annie and Annie Harper were one and the same, yet it seemed too much a coincidence to ignore.

His hunch became a gut-tight certainty the instant he set eyes on her. And, observing in awe from the corral fence, Brett could now understand why she'd become the best kept secret in the west.

The woman was amazing.

She sat the coffee-and-cream paint beneath her as if it were a natural extension of herself. The horse made it clear that she was not welcome on his back; he crow-hopped and twisted in ways that would have loosened the teeth of any seasoned bronc rider—yet the hundred-and-twenty-or-so-pound woman kept her seat. Each time the horse bucked, she arched; each time it bowed, she curved forward, her slender body flowing with the powerful motions like a cottonwood in the wind.

No wonder everyone had been so close mouthed. He'd held more than a few doubts about her legendary skills, and traveling five hundred miles to offer someone work based on hearsay seemed a foolish venture at best, when he was needed back in Texas.

But Brett had made fortunes taking risks, and damned if it didn't feel like he'd struck the mother lode. If she joined his outfit, he wouldn't be too quick on making it public, either. Every rancher with a bronc to break—not to mention bounty hunters after a quick buck—would be converging on his property, trying to snatch her away.

He didn't know how much time had passed before the horse finally began to wear down, then settled in a quivering, defeated stance, head low, girth heaving. She remained on the horse's back, bending low over its neck, caressing every inch of its sweaty flesh within reach, as if praising him for his surrender.

Lucky beast, Brett thought, watching her lavish attention on the animal. Any time he'd been stroked like that, it had wound up costing him—one way or another. He couldn't remember a single time he'd been rewarded simply for a job well done, and it struck him as odd that he might even want it.

He'd been cured of wanting what he'd never get years ago.

Finally she dismounted and handed the reins to a young wrangler. He must have told her that Brett was waiting to speak with her, because she glanced over her shoulder in his direction. A long moment passed while she studied him from under the brim of her dusty dun Stetson. He felt her reluctance. Her wariness.

Finally, she headed toward him. Leaning his shoulder against the fencepost, Brett treated himself to her approach. He knew from experience how badly the snapping back and forth could batter a body, yet it didn't seem to faze her in the least. Her hips swayed from side to side in an utterly provocative, utterly feminine walk that heated his blood. The fringe on her leather chaps

slapped against legs as perfectly formed to strad-
dle a man, as a saddle.

She came to a stop a couple of feet away. The
top of her low-crowned felt hat barely reached
his nose. "I'm told you're lookin' for me." Her
voice, brisk and smoky, carried a distinctive
Texas brand.

For a moment Brett couldn't breathe, much
less speak. This definitely was not the leather-
faced, weather-skinned rope spinner he'd antic-
ipated. The brim of her Stetson cast her eyes in
secret shadows, but didn't hide the fact that she
was younger, softer, and much, *much* prettier
than he'd ever expected. An oval face, small
nose, and lush mouth just ripe for kissing. And
that bleached corn silk braid falling to her waist
would tempt any red-blooded man to unravel
the bound strands and feel them dragging across
his bare skin. . . .

Brett forced himself to remember the reason
for seeking her out had nothing to do with an
affaire de cœur, and everything to do with reclaim-
ing his fillies. "I am if you're Annie Harper."

"And if I am?"

She tilted her hat back and Brett stilled. Staring
up at him from a circle of thick, golden lashes
were a pair of eyes so flat and expressionless that
it chilled his blood. Not a speck of emotion, not
a flicker of life showed in the dull blue depths.
Brett gave himself a mental shake. "Then I have
a proposition for you."

"I'm not interested."

To Brett's surprise, she turned away and started walking back toward the barn. He'd never chased after a woman before—it had never been necessary—and he wouldn't have started now if his entire enterprise wasn't at stake. He caught up to her in two long, loping strides. "You haven't heard it yet."

"I've heard it a hundred times."

He stepped in front of her and gave her his most persuasive smile—the one women claimed to find charming and irresistible. "Not from me."

Faster than he could say howdy, a pocket six-shooter appeared in her hand and leveled itself at his mid-section.

His smile faded; his hands lifted. It struck Brett in that instant that they were talking two different brands of beef: he meant business; she thought he meant—Well, he had a damned good idea what she thought he meant, and she couldn't be further off the mark. Not that the idea didn't have its merits, he decided, taking in the trim figure standing on the other side of the Smith and Wesson. Annie Harper had a body that could convert a saint to sinning. The leather vest she wore over a loose cotton shirt hardly disguised the womanly swells straining the tiny buttons.

"Mister—"

"Corrigan." He licked his dry lips. "Brett Corrigan."

"Unless you want a hole in you the size of a pie tin, move out of my way."

The glint in her eyes told him she'd do it in a heartbeat and probably dance on his grave afterward.

"Look," Brett said, holding her gaze. "I don't doubt you've received your share of propositions." Some undoubtedly more honorable than the one streaming through his mind, which involved bare bodies, slick skin, and wild rides. "But let me assure you, mine is strictly a business venture."

The barrel lowered a notch. Winged brows dipped together over the bridge of her nose. "What kind of business venture?"

Pleased that he'd snared her attention, he slid his thumbs under his lapels and cocked his hip to the side. "A year ago I . . . acquired a modest ranch in Texas." A dry grin touched his mouth at the image of the broken down heap of boards he'd found waiting for him. Folks in Tascosa had assured him the then Bar 7 was one of the finest spreads south of the Canadian River, and he'd bought into it like a greenhorn at a hustler's table. "I say modest because the only thing of any value turned out to be a handful of Arabian fillies."

One slender brow lifted.

Brett chuckled. "I know. I'm sure you can imagine how popular that makes me." Arabians were about as welcome in mustang country as rats in a flour mill. "But I plan to breed the fastest Arabians in the territory for competition—or I *did*, until a wild stallion took it in his head to claim my ladies for himself."

"So what is it you want of me?"

"To catch the fillies—and the stallion who stole them."

If Brett hadn't spent over half his thirty-four years studying people's reactions, he might have missed the slight tensing of her spine.

"Then you've wasted both our time."

The unhesitating answer didn't register until she turned and started walking away, her spurs making a staccato ringing against the packed earth. Brett saw the hand of his future spread wide, the success of his ranch slip through his fingers like sand. "I'll make it worth your while."

Halfway across the paddock, Annie came to an abrupt stop.

I'll make it worth your while.

Six little words. They should have meant nothing. But those six little words spoken in a husky bayou drawl drove shards of splintered memories through Annie's breast.

"I'll make it worth your while, sweet Annie."

"Oh, yeah? What'll you give me?"

"The moon on a silver platter."

The words came from a place deep inside, laughing, teasing, with such familiarity that it nearly brought her to her knees.

She closed her eyes. One deep breath. Two. Her emotions tightly held in check, she slowly turned to face Corrigan.

He stood against a backdrop of hot sun and

ice blue, looking more suited to a fancy Carson City casino than a horse ranch. A tailored green coat and fine linen shirt of starched pearl stretched across the breadth of his shoulders, a black silk tie loosely circled his neck, and a shimmering green vest lay open over a flat abdomen. His trousers fit snugly around his waist and buttoned down one side of his pelvic bone. The woolen fabric tapered down muscled legs to just below the knees, where they disappeared into fashionable glossy brown stovepipe boots with fancy stitching from knee to ankle.

His face wouldn't crack any mirrors, either. Deeply tanned skin and creases at the corners of his eyes carried the mark of the outdoors. Hair the color of liquid amber was slicked back from a high forehead and curled around his ears to toy with his nape. Silvery green eyes—the same swirling shade as his fancy waistcoat—studied her through thick, spiky lashes in a manner that had a long cold ember flickering to life in her belly. She recognized that look. Had encountered it and spurned it more times than she cared to count. But it had been years since it had stirred any sensation inside her beside nausea.

"Why?" she asked in a tight voice she hardly recognized as her own.

"Why?" he echoed. "That stallion stole my fillies and I want them back."

"No; why me? There are plenty of other mustangers—"

"But none of your caliber," he smoothly interrupted. Broad hands slid back the frock coat and came to rest on his hips. "You're an impressive woman who has earned herself quite an impressive reputation. When I want a job done right, I hire the best."

Annie didn't deny it. She was the best. At least . . . she used to be.

For the briefest second, she was tempted to take him up on his offer. It awakened a restlessness inside her she hadn't felt in years. To feel the thrill of the chase, to ride with the wind, to pit her skills against nature and beast, just to see if she still could. . . .

Annie squared her shoulders and said, "Find someone else, mister. I don't chase horses anymore."

She didn't wait to see if he left; she didn't care. Mouth tight, movements precise and efficient, Annie disappeared into the barn, tossed a saddle on her buckskin mare, and rode hell for leather across the desert. Wind tore her hat from her head and sent it slapping against her back. Churned grains of sand ripped across her cheeks. The stench of a charred past filled her nostrils.

Chance finally stumbled, jolting Annie to awareness. She pulled on the reins until the winded animal came to a stop.

Her upper body dropped forward; her head fell against Chance's sweaty neck. Damp horsehide pricked her wind-chapped cheek, and her heart pounded with such force that she wondered how it kept behind her ribs.

She slid down the mustang's heaving side to the ground and pressed her forehead to its mane. Her hands smoothed the quivering withers. She'd caught this animal after she'd been abandoned by her herd and raised her from yearling. How could she have pushed her so hard?

Damn Corrigan! If he hadn't approached her with his stupid proposition, if he hadn't stirred up memories from the grave. . . .

She fished in her pocket for makings and tried rolling herself a cigarette, spilling more on the ground than in the fold. In frustrated despair, she flung the tobacco and papers and wrapped her arms around her middle, cradling the unexpected pain. It had been years since she'd heard his voice, and eternity since she'd felt his touch. "Oh, Koda," she whispered.

"Buck up, girl, it's time to ride."

"I can't do it, Sekoda. I can't do it anymore."

"You're Mustang Annie. You can do anything."

Not this, she couldn't. Not this. Not now. Not ever.

Mustang Annie didn't exist anymore.

Chapter 3

⎯⎯◦○◦⎯⎯

Ten days later, Annie held tight to Chance's reins and stared at the rambling adobe house visible beyond the arched gateway. A trio of entwined T's and A's had been burned into a pine board above the drive, broken up by the symbols of a deck of cards: a spade, a diamond, a club . . . no heart, though. How appropriate.

What was she doing here? Why had she come back? Four years ago, she'd walked away from this area and vowed never to return. Yet here she was again. Had she lost her last ounce of common sense? She must have, otherwise she wouldn't have set foot back in Texas, much less shown up at Brett Corrigan's ranch.

She should turn around. Corrigan would never be the wiser, and she'd still have some dignity left.

Too bad dignity didn't keep the hang man's noose at bay.

Her hand went to her vest, where an old folded poster lay in the inside pocket. Rotten timing, rotten luck. Usually Annie could smell danger a mile off. She supposed anyone who'd spent over half their adult life staying one step ahead of the law would develop the sense. If she hadn't been so rattled by Corrigan's visit that day, her instincts would have warned her against going back to the ranch. Instead, she'd returned to the Bar 7 and found herself face to face with a trader she'd rustled from in the old days, who'd come to do business with her boss.

Her years of making an honest living training mavericks shattered in the split second it took him to recognize her.

With Chance winded from their earlier run, Annie had no choice but to break the promise she'd made to Sekoda all those years ago: she had stolen a horse.

Chance eventually caught up to her at the border, and Annie had considered returning the horse she'd taken. But she knew from experience that the only chance she had of saving her neck was to put as much distance between herself and the Bar 7 as possible, in as short a time as possible, and to find someplace to lie low for a while. Unfortunately, she'd left before collecting her fee for settling the stallion. With no money and no quick means of getting any, she sold the paint for a fraction of its worth and hightailed it out of Nevada—as a wanted woman.

Well, Corrigan had claimed to make it worth her while, and by God, she'd hold him to it. Since he was partly to blame for throwing her back into a life of crime, he could provide the means to get her out of it. Those fillies of his must be worth a pretty penny or he wouldn't have traveled a thousand miles to try and convince her to recover them. She'd recover them all right, along with the stallion, and he'd pay for the service.

Handsomely.

She flicked the reins, feeling her heart tighten and her stomach twist with each step that brought her closer to the house. She had to admit that he kept a fine spread. X-style fencing wearing a fresh coat of whitewash encompassed the front pastures, where dozens of Quarter horses grazed on Texas grama, along with a breed she'd often heard of but hadn't seen before now—Arabians. No self-respecting horse rancher in the territory would be caught dead raising such a blue-blooded breed. But then, Brett Corrigan hadn't struck her as a man who gave a tinker's damn what folks thought. He could obviously afford not to.

Just as she halted Chance at a hitching post by the wrap-around porch, a bow-legged man in his early fifties wearing faded britches, worn cowhide chaps, and a matching vest emerged from the house. Spurs jangled against the planked gallery.

"Can I he'p ya?"

"I was told I'd find Brett Corrigan here." Just saying his name left a bitter taste on Annie's tongue. Lowering herself to go to him for work chafed her as badly as a week in the saddle.

"Good Glory—Annie? Is that you, little filly?"

The pet name threw Annie off balance. It had been so long since she'd heard it that she'd almost forgotten it. She squinted, then her eyes widened in amazement. "Well, I'll be horsewhipped—Wade Henry?"

Annie dismounted. Before her feet even hit the ground, she found herself enveloped in a bony embrace. "You're the last person I expected to see," she told him after he set her down.

"I'm surprised you remember me. The last time I saw you, you was still in ponytails."

"How could I forget? Granddaddy talked about you all the time."

"How is the old cowpoke?"

Annie's delight at seeing the old wrangler dimmed. She pulled back and let her arms fall to her sides. "He died, Mr. Henry. About five years back."

Surprise skittered across his features. "How?"

Annie averted her eyes and let her silence speak for itself.

He passed a veined hand down his face, then turned away to absorb the news. They'd been close once, Wade Henry and Clovis James. Annie had lost count of the stories her granddad had told of their adventures, most of them so incriminating they couldn't be repeated in public. What Annie remembered the most, though, was Grandad telling her that his and Wade's biggest fear was being betrayed.

Wade Henry had escaped that fate.

Clovis James hadn't. And there was a grave on Boot Hill to prove it.

When Henry looked at her again, his eyes were moist with sorrow but he managed a smile for her anyway. "Well . . ." he cleared his throat. "It's good knowin' there's still a piece of him left behind. You growed up right pretty, Annie."

She managed a weak smile.

"Made quite a name for yourself, too."

Annie stilled at the faint censure in his tone. They both knew he wasn't referring to her skill at taming horses. Quietly, she replied, "I never planned it that way."

"What are you doin' back here, little girl?"

Little girl? Once upon a time, maybe, she'd been a little girl, with big hopes and even bigger dreams. But things changed. Little girls grew up. Hopes fell. Dreams died. Sometimes all that was left was survival. "I expect I'm here to see your boss."

Concern clouded his solemn brown eyes, but thankfully he didn't press for reasons and Annie didn't offer. Instead, he stepped aside and gestured for her to lead the way up the steps.

The instant she passed through the doorway, the breath left her lungs. Nothing on the outside of the house had prepared her for the magnificence she discovered within the adobe walls. It was definitely a man's domain, decorated in colors of the earth—deep blues, hunter greens, autumn rusts. A curved staircase with a polished pine balustrade led to a second floor landing, while the main floor remained open and airy. Each doorway boasted painstakingly detailed archways, the elaborate grooves and swirls scorched a rich chestnut tone to give the appearance of age and wear. Elongated windows of real glass, set two feet apart, allowed the sun to flow freely onto a red flagstone floor polished to a high sheen. The Navajo rugs strewn about showed an appreciation for southwestern design, and paintings framed in gnarled mesquite complemented the textured whitewashed walls.

Mr. Henry gestured to a striped medallion-backed sofa and two matching chairs in the center of the main room, which seemed to invite anyone who passed through to relax and enjoy a crackling fire from the granite fireplace. Hurricane lamps with prism fringe sat idle on nearby tables, waiting for dusk to display their painted glory. On each wall, glass fronted cabinets with wooden fixtures and heavy walnut shelves displayed glazed pottery and priceless trinkets. Two plush burgundy chairs with matching footstools waited in a nearby corner, inviting someone to read an almanac, journal, or classic novel from the cabinet behind.

The smell of wealth hung in the air, thick as the humidity outside. Forcibly containing her awe, Annie remarked, "He isn't subtle, is he?"

Mr. Henry responded with a toothy grin. "Ace always surrounds himself with the best life has to offer. I expect that's why you're here." He walked farther into the room. "Ace? You got a visitor."

At the far end near a bay window, a shadowy figure at a desk glanced up from the stack of papers beneath his hand. "I'm not receiving call—" The sentence broke off abruptly.

The tension in the room went as taut as a pull rope, and Annie wrestled with the urge to turn on her heel and run. Only the belief that Corrigan owed her this job kept her from doing so.

Mr. Henry cleared his throat. "Think I'll mosey on down to the stables and see if those lazy good-fer-nothin's fed the horses before taking off for town." He tipped his hat in Annie's direction. "Nice seein' you again, Annie."

She gave him a short nod, then returned her attention to Corrigan.

"You know my foreman?" he asked.

"He was a friend of my grandfather's."

Setting down the quill in his hand, Corrigan rose from his chair, then all six feet two inches of him rounded the desk.

She remembered the last time she'd seen him, standing near the corral fence at the Bar 7, looking for all the world like a dandy out for a Sunday buggy ride. But a woman would have to have been blind not to notice how well the broadcloth coat and trousers flattered his brawny build.

Much to her dismay, he cut just as fine a figure in working duds. The dark chambray blue shirt he wore open at the collar emphasized the stretch of his shoulders. His sleeves were rolled up to reveal corded forearms liberally sprinkled with golden hair. Faded blue jeans hugged his legs from hip to ankle like a second skin, and from beneath the hem of his britches peeked out a pair of—

White wool socks.

Annie might have laughed if the sight didn't surprise her speechless.

"So . . . Miss Harper." He leaned a hip against the desk corner, crossed one ankle over the other, and hooked his thumb into his front pocket; his fingers splayed downward along his groin, drawing her attention to the impressive bulge between his thighs. "To what do I owe this honor?"

Annie's head snapped up. One look at the smug grin on his face squashed any hope that the direction of her gaze had gone unnoticed. Her gaping mouth shut with a click, then she drew back her shoulders and tilted her chin. "You still want a mustanger to go after those horses?"

Green eyes twinkled from beneath thick brows. "I might."

He wasn't going to make this easy, was he? "I've been reconsidering your offer."

"I'm flattered."

"Don't be. It's going to cost you."

"I didn't expect you'd work for free."

Annie walked toward him. "Five hundred for each mare, a thousand for the stallion, and the first colt produced. And I run the show. I don't take orders; I don't put up with anyone telling me how to do my job."

He didn't speak for several long seconds, just stared at her with the same unnerving intensity as he had done back in Nevada. Annie stared back, uncompromising.

Finally, he moved back behind the desk and stroked his jaw. "Those are some mighty high demands."

"Take it or leave it."

"How do I know I'll be getting my money's worth?"

"You don't."

Annie wondered if maybe deep down she'd hoped he would reject her price. If so, she was disappointed.

"You're right. I expect that's a gamble I'll have to take." He pointed toward the curving staircase. "There are a couple of spare rooms upstairs. Choose whichever one strikes your fancy."

"I'll sleep in the stables."

He looked as if he'd argue, but pressed his lips together and conceded with a nod. "As you wish. Henry will see that you're settled in. The rest of my men have gone into town for the night, but you'll meet them before we ride out in the morning."

"We?"

"You didn't expect I'd let you go after those horses without protection, did you?"

Annie bristled. "I don't need protection."

"You may not think you need it, Miss Harper, but you've got it anyway."

Annie flattened her hands on his desk and leaned forward. "I work alone, Mr. Corrigan."

He mimicked her stance and smiled implacably. "Not this time."

Annie stomped into the sparsely furnished six-by-six room Henry had assigned to her, threw her saddlebags on a narrow iron-framed cot and slammed her hat on a wall peg, then moved to a square of a window set shoulder-high into the wall. She hadn't dared let Corrigan see how much his announcement had disturbed her, but in the privacy of her temporary quarters, she gave her frustration free rein.

Having him along—let alone his men—had never been part of her plan. There was no predicting how long it would take to track down and capture the horses. Sometimes she and Sekoda had spent weeks following the bands, observing their daily habits, discovering their hideouts, and the best way to capture them. Of course, back then, time had been their friend, a treasure never to be squandered. . . .

"You're playing with fire, Annie."

She ran both hands through her tangled hair, stunned to find her fingers trembling. There was no way she could let Corrigan go with her. Yet how the hell could she stop him? He'd agreed to every other term she'd set, but every man had his limit, and he'd clearly reached his. If she refused his company into the canyon, she might as well say adios to this job.

She was damned tempted to anyway. Every instinct inside her warned her against working with Corrigan. She couldn't trust the man. She couldn't trust *anybody*, but especially not him. He had the eyes of a gambler: scrutinizing, assessing, and much too unsettling.

And she had the distinct feeling that pulling this job off wasn't going to be as easy as she'd first believed.

Long after the light in the spare tack room went out, Brett stood at the bay window in his study, savoring a nightcap of bourbon, thoughts of Annie lingering in his mind.

He didn't know what to make of her. Ten days ago she hadn't given his offer a passing thought. He'd never been a man to give up on something he wanted, though, so he'd gone back to the Bar 7 the next morning, only to discover she'd skipped town with one of the owner's finest horses.

He'd briefly considered joining the search in progress, but delaying his return to the ranch any longer was out of the question. He'd been away too long as it was. So he'd come back to the Triple Ace and begun planning his own excursion into the canyon. Mustang Annie or no Mustang Annie, he had horses to catch.

Then out of the blue, she shows up on the Triple Ace with her stiff spined demeanor and dead-sea eyes, demanding outrageous prices no sane man would even listen to, much less agree to. He'd agreed to them only because, as much as it galled him to admit it, he had neither the time to waste nor a better chance of getting his fillies back before the stallion ruined them.

The question was, what had changed her mind? Desperation? The illusion of easy pickings?

His immeasurable charms?

The last thought made him grin. For a woman who so obviously wanted nothing to do with him, she'd developed quite a fascination with his nether region. He hadn't seen anyone turn so red since Melanie Haverson had gotten caught in the swamp with his brother, Adam.

Brett had to give Annie credit, though; she'd recovered much faster than he had. If ever a woman had given him such a swift and painful arousal with just a look, he couldn't remember it. If she'd stared at his crotch any longer, he swore he'd have busted a seam. She'd really have blushed then.

"You wanted to see me, boss?"

Startled, Brett swung toward the door where Henry stood, his ten-gallon hat gripped in a gnarled hand. He cleared his throat, then strolled toward the cabinet and refilled his snifter. "Is our guest settled in?"

"I tried to put her up in my cabin but she wouldn't budge. Insisted on taking up in the stables, so I put her up in the spare tack room."

"She refused one of the rooms upstairs, too."

"Sounds like Annie," Henry replied with a yellow-toothed grin. "Stubborn as on old cayuse."

Brett returned to the window overlooking the dark stables. "Tell me everything you know about her."

Through the reflection in the window, Brett watched Henry shove a plug of chaw into his mouth and work it around to his cheek. An unspoken "why" hung in the air.

"Not much to tell," he finally said. "Me and her granddaddy used to work with the same outfit till I hired on with Durham. Ole Clovis owned a bitty spread down south of here and took up sheep. Annie was just a girl back then. Perty as a sunflower, but good glory, she was a wild one. When she wasn't stirring up mischief, she was out chasin' the horses."

"So that's how she got her name," Brett said with a smile.

"Her name?"

The old man looked genuinely puzzled, yet a strained note in his voice put Brett's suspicions on instant alert. Did Henry not know what had become of his old friend's granddaughter? Or did he know, and just wasn't saying? Loyalty had always been one of the traits Brett respected most about Wade Henry—so long as it wasn't misplaced.

Well, he'd let the man keep his secrets for now. He'd be spending the next couple of weeks with the infamous horse thief. By the time they caught his horses, he'd know everything he wanted to know about her—and more.

Chapter 4

Dawn crept softly over the tops of the sagebrush, drizzling the woody shrubs with
gauzy pink. Steam rose from the sea of dew-
tipped buffalo grass surrounding the house and
outbuildings, giving the land an ethereal appearance.

Brett stepped out onto the shaded gallery, saddlebags draped over one shoulder, and paused
at the railing to savor the view. Mornings had
always been his favorite time of day. Even as a
kid, he could remember waking up long before
the trainers on his father's farm, just to watch the
sun rise. The habit had stayed with him through
adulthood. No matter where Lady Luck led him,
no matter how late the stakes kept him awake,
he'd wait until the blushing sky gave way to orange and blue before dropping exhausted into
whatever bed he'd found available.

But there was no more beautiful a sunrise than those he'd seen here on the High Plains. And no more beautiful a woman than the one emerging from the stables.

Brett watched Annie lead her horse, a fine buckskin with a java brown mane and tail, and a mustang's distinctive stocky build, to the series of blocks and sawhorses his men used to tend their equipment.

They'd gotten off to a rocky start, he and Annie Harper, but new days brought new beginnings.

Adjusting the saddlebags to a more comfortable position, he strode down the steps and across the yard. " 'Mornin', Miss Harper."

She didn't so much as glance at him.

"I trust you slept well?"

Continuing to ignore him, she grabbed a coiled lariat off an up-ended barrel between the horse and the corral fence. Beside it waited a bulging pair of well-used saddlebags, a cowhide canteen, and a gray bedroll. Packed and ready. Brett wondered if she'd been planning on leaving without them.

Keeping his thoughts to himself, he circled the mare. "Nice piece of horseflesh here," he complimented, running his hands across her sleek hide. "You catch her yourself?"

Still no response, and Brett had to chuckle at her refusal to acknowledge him. "Nobody could ever accuse you of talking a man to death."

She finally turned toward him. "Let me make

one thing clear, Mr. Corrigan. You're paying me to catch your horses, not chit-chat, so save the small talk for someone who might appreciate it. It's wasted on me."

His smile faded. Her words held no inflection, yet they stung like nettles. "Would you like a cup of coffee before we head out or is common hospitality wasted on you, too?"

She actually had the grace to look chagrined. "Coffee would be welcome, thank you."

So she had manners after all. Hard to tell. The woman was as temperamental as an old cayuse.

Hoping a good, strong cup of Arbuckle's would soften her disposition, Brett entered the main room of the bunkhouse where he knew a fresh pot would be brewing. He'd just passed the bunk room door when raised voices—one voice in particular—made him pause.

"All we need is a woman getting underfoot."

He took two steps backward and perked his ears just outside the bunk room.

"Women got only two uses far as I'm concerned—lying on their backs or standing at the stove."

Brett's jaw tightened. The remark might as well have come straight from his father's mouth.

Time swept him back over twenty years. *You think you can do better than me, Maggie? You should be thankful I married you, because sure as shootin' no other man wants you. Only things you're good for are baking and breeding, and you can't even get those right.*

Never had he felt more powerless than he had as a twelve-year-old boy, listening from the top of the stairs to his father degrade his mother.

He wasn't powerless anymore, though.

He stepped through the doorway, his shadow casting a long length of intimidation on the hardwood floor. A half dozen men froze next to the iron bunkbeds stacked along both walls.

Brett leaned his back against the frame and slid a cheroot out of his shirt pocket. He took his time lighting it, purposely letting the tension build. Finally he targeted his gaze on the tallest man, a twenty-year-old wrangler who had shown up at the Triple Ace nearly a month ago with a gunshot wound to the shoulder. To Brett's knowledge, no one had ever broken the code and questioned Rafe about it, but it quickly became apparent that his newest hand was still young enough and audacious enough to rile up a pile of goose feathers if he had a mind to.

"Is there a problem in here?"

For a long time no one spoke. A couple of the men averted their faces, a couple more shuffled their feet.

"You hired a mustanger to bring in the horses," Rafe finally said, his tone bordering on belligerent.

"That's right."

"But she's a woman!"

"I'm aware of that." Sorely. Despite her masculine duds, no man with eyes could fail to notice the curves under the simple cotton shirt and loose denims. "It seems to me that you've forgotten who deals the cards at this table. But you'll have plenty of time remembering over the next few weeks, while you're constructing the breeding pen."

Rafe's tan gave way to ruddy indignation. "You're leavin' me behind over some skirt?"

"That *skirt* happens to be the best mustanger alive, and it wouldn't have been necessary to hire her in the first place if you hadn't let that stallion steal my fillies."

Rafe's complexion grew even more mottled. For a second there, Brett thought he'd press the issue. It would be a shame to lose one of the best wranglers he'd ever had, but one thing he never tolerated was having his decisions questioned, and every hand on the ranch knew it. If any one of them didn't agree, he could pack up his spurs and head down the road. There were plenty of others willing to keep their mouths shut and their minds on their job instead of in the boss's business.

That thought must have occurred to Rafe, too, because he shoved his hat on his head, grabbed an ax from the wall by the door, and strode out the door without another word.

Brett turned to the rest of the men watching the scene with a mix of wariness and discomfort. "Anybody else got a beef with the way I handle my business?" he challenged in a quiet tone that belied the anger simmering in his blood.

Not a one spoke up. Obviously they valued their jobs.

"Then Emilio, Flap Jack, and Tex, load up your gear. We're heading out in fifteen minutes."

The men he'd chosen scrambled out the door faster than he could say tumbleweed.

Brett followed, drawing in deep, even breaths in an effort to calm his temper. He didn't know what angered him more—the slurs against Annie or the blatant disregard of his authority.

The trouble with cutting Rafe from the crew was that it left him short a wrangler to tend the extra mounts each rider would bring. He already had every man he could spare—eleven in all— divided between himself and Tex.

The only wrangler left was. . . .

Brett closed his eyes and cursed. He had no choice. He'd have to bring Dogie.

"I can't believe it!"

Startled by the exclamation, Annie spun on the ball of one foot to face a lantern-jawed boy in his early teens wearing the loudest purple shirt she'd ever set eyes on. She'd been so preoccupied with eavesdropping on the conversation drifting through the bunkhouse window—and rattled at the way Corrigan had come to her defense—that she hadn't heard anyone approach.

"I just can't believe I'm standin' on the same spot of ground as Mustang Annie!" The boy grinned widely.

Annie's heart stuttered. Hell, did everyone

know who she was? And why was he hollering at her? She pushed past him to fetch her saddle-bags from an up-ended barrel. "You've got me mixed up with someone else," she muttered.

"What?" He smacked the side of his head a couple times. "Sorry, since the explosion I don't hear so good."

She raised her voice a notch. "I said, you've got me mixed up with someone else."

"Oh, no, I'd recognize you anywhere!" he insisted. "You probably don't remember, but I met you a few years back, after you broke a mustang down by the Tongue River."

The Tongue River? She hadn't been there since—oh, God, now she remembered. How could she have forgotten? She and Sekoda had gone down to trade a few mares and discovered a contest in progress. She never should have let Koda coax her into entering the competition, for it had made public her talents on horseback that she'd much rather have kept a secret.

"I'm Dogie." The kid swiped a sweat-and-soil-stained hat off his head. A shock of curly wheat-brown hair tumbled past his ears. "I tend the horses and tack."

She'd guessed that. Most wranglers started out young, learning the trade, building their skills. He seemed a little younger than most—no more than thirteen—but ranchers often employed their own relatives, and there was enough of a resemblance between him and Corrigan to hint at a kinship.

"Wade Henry says you're gonna help us catch Ace's fillies," he said while she flipped her saddlebags across Chance's rump. "I'd give my right arm to be going with ya, but Wade Henry says I ain't seasoned enough yet. How's a man supposed to put any cracks in his chaps if nobody ever lets him sit in a saddle?"

She didn't have an answer for that one. She'd been sitting in a saddle since the beginning of time. A hazy memory of riding in front of a tall, blond cowboy lingered in the back of her mind to this day, the only memory that she had of her late father.

"Here comes the rest of the crew now."

Annie looked across the yard at a trio of men emerging from the bunkhouse. The first had black hair and brown skin, the second was lean and wiry, and the third was as burly as a buffalo and twice as tall.

"The Mexican is Emilio. He's the best roper I ever saw. Can lasso a dragonfly at full gallop. Hope you know some Mexican, though, cause he can't speak a lick of English."

The only Spanish she knew couldn't be spoken in public.

"And that there's Tex in the middle. He can break a horse like nobody's business. I once saw him take a mustang down in seven seconds. Flap Jack there is the big feller on the end. He can track a hoot owl in a snow storm. Wait here— I'll bring 'em ov—uh, I just remembered there's somethin' I gotta do."

Dogie hadn't skulked more than a few paces away before the cutting call of his name stopped him in his tracks.

Annie turned and spotted Corrigan emerging from the stables. It had taken every ounce of will power she owned to ignore him earlier. After the way he'd manipulated himself into her life, she hadn't trusted herself to look at him, much less carry on a polite conversation with him.

He wasn't an easy man to ignore, though. With a voice like thunder and eyes like lightning, Corrigan could make stout-hearted women wilt and fierce-tempered men cringe. Even now, as he strode toward them in a loose-limbed walk, he carried an aura of authority that commanded notice as much as respect.

And Annie definitely noticed. Damn. She tossed the forgotten saddlebags over Chance's rump. No man should look so devastating this early in the morning, and wearing simple work clothes to boot! Yet the gray shirt and leather vest he wore stressed the broadness of his chest, and tawny chaps fit over his faded blue jeans with glove-tight perfection. Polished silver spurs banded a pair of dark brown box-toes that had seen plenty of days in a pasture.

And with that rolled-brimmed, crown-creased "Boss of the Plains" Stetson completing the outfit, the gambler could almost pass for a seasoned horseman.

A pang of guilt assailed her for the uncharitable thought when he held out a steaming mug of coffee.

"Are you the one making all the noise around here?" he asked Dogie.

The boy's face went ashen white. "Just havin' a chat with Miss Annie," he said.

"Your chatting can be heard clear across the Mexican border."

Annie looked first at Dogie, then at Corrigan.

Both were speaking in perfectly normal tones.

Realizing that Dogie wasn't hard of hearing after all, Annie tightly remarked, "It seems I've been made the day's entertainment."

Corrigan's eyes twinkled. "If it makes you feel any better, he once pulled the same prank on me."

It didn't make her feel better. After the restless night she'd spent, then the confrontation with Corrigan, she was in no humor to be played with.

Just then, the men joined them. Though they seemed harmless enough, she couldn't stop herself from retreating a few steps—directly behind Corrigan's solid back. Annie silently cursed her cowardice, and sidestepped out of his shadow. She thought she'd gotten that weakness under control years ago.

When he introduced each crew member, Annie returned their nods of greeting with one of her own.

Corrigan then addressed the youngest of their

gathering. "Dogie, are the extra horses rounded up?"

"Yessir," the boy replied, running his sleeve under his nose. "All five of 'em."

"Then what are you doing standing here?"

He looked stumped for an answer. "Sir?"

"You've got five minutes to get a horse saddled and your gear loaded, or we're leaving you behind."

The boy's eyes glittered with surprise and disbelief. "I'm going? I really get to ride with you?" He punched the air, then like a colt with its first taste of freedom, leaped into a full gallop toward the bunkhouse. "Yee-haw!"

Annie's mouth fell open, unable to believe her ears. "You're letting him ride with us?"

"I'm one man short."

Annie crossed her arms over her front and retorted, "So you replace him with a boy?"

Corrigan's expression went rigid. The men around him looked thunderstruck. An instant later, they mumbled a few excuses, then left her standing alone with six feet, two inches of simmering anger.

Quietly, he told her, "You laid your cards on the table; now I'm laying mine: if you have any objections to the decisions I make, take it up with me in private. Never do so in front of my men."

He spun on his heel strode toward the corral, where Henry and the other men were studying a map spread out atop an upended barrel.

Overbearing ass, she thought, glaring at his

back. The last thing she needed on this trip was a barely weaned kid. What if the marshals caught up to her? Bad enough she had Corrigan's men riding along—now she had the added responsibility of seeing that a kid didn't get hurt. Unfortunately, pushing the argument with Corrigan would do nothing but raise suspicion.

Still, if Corrigan thought she'd put up with his attitude the entire trip, he had another thought coming. She'd take it only so long before she told him what he could do with his horses.

With jerky movements, she finished loading her gear onto Chance's back. Just as she fastened the last buckle, the men's conversation drifted toward her.

"We'll head northeast toward the Canadian and follow the river south. The men lost him here, just south of McClellan Crick. My guess is he's takin' them into the canyon. There's plenty of places to hide there."

Annie's hand went limp as she listened through a growing fog. The Palo Duro? Corrigan had never mentioned the Palo Duro. Not once. Not even a hint. Of course, it was logical that the stallion might head into the canyon. The steep ridges and deep ravines offered plenty of safe havens for grazing and roaming and breeding. . . .

But logic didn't stop the stuttering of her heart or the sweat from breaking out on her palms. If she'd known. . . .

"Somethin' wrong, Annie?"

Her gaze snapped to Mr. Henry. "That's Comanche land."

"Not anymore," Corrigan stated. "The Rangers rousted them out last year."

The news came as a surprise to Annie. She'd expected it might happen one day, but it still seemed impossible that the Indians could no longer call this area home.

"We'll still keep our eyes peeled for renegades, though," Henry said. "No use gettin' caught off guard. If we're lucky, the stallion will have found himself a paradise along the river and we won't have to go that far."

Corrigan nodded in deference to Wade Henry's judgment. "Emilio, Flap Jack, and Dogie, you'll ride south with me and Henry to the north end of the canyon. Tex, you take your crew along McKenzie Trail, then cut west at the South Fork. Whoever finds the herd first will get a message to the saloon in Sage Flat. Otherwise, we'll meet up there."

Nodding in agreement, the men claimed their horses.

Corrigan folded the map and slipped it into his vest pocket. "Annie, you ready to ride?"

She could handle it, she told herself. Just a quick trip into the canyon. Knowing the Palo Duro as well as she did, she'd have the task done in no time, then be on her way to Mexico. Managing a strained smile, she replied, "As ready as I'll ever be."

*   *   *

Brett tried his damnedest to keep his eyes on the land as they rode through the knee-high grasses, yet time and again, his attention strayed toward Annie. Riding well ahead of him, she sat the buckskin with the straight-spined confidence of a woman well seasoned to the saddle, her figure moving to the motion of the animal, her long flaxen braid swinging down her back like a bell-pull.

She hadn't said a word since leaving the ranch. That in itself didn't strike Brett as odd; he could sum up their conversation since meeting in one paragraph. But the set of her posture told him how she resented the company of his men and the protection he'd imposed upon her.

Or maybe it was just his company she resented.

The thought grated as much now as it had the first time he'd met her. Gaining the attention of a woman hadn't ever been a problem, and the thought that Annie would give a pile of dung more notice than him frosted his chaps.

Well, she could fuss and fume all she wanted, but damned if Brett would let her venture off on her lonesome, no matter how reputable her skills.

He had an investment to protect.

Even the reminder of Annie's criminal history didn't stop Brett's gaze returning to her yet again, despite his best effort. What was it about her that he found so compelling? Sure, she was pleasing to look at—her honey-toned features strong-boned and natural, wide sapphire eyes set under arched blonde brows, a straight-bridged nose and stubborn chin.

The rest of her wasn't so hard on the eyes, either, he admitted, his attention dropping to her legs.

The image of those shapely limbs wrapped around him sent the temperature of his blood rising, and made him painfully aware that hard leather and even harder flesh did not make a comfortable match. He shifted, trying to ease the discomfort, but it didn't help.

If she had any clue where his thoughts were heading, there was no doubt in his mind that she'd bust his jaw.

Brett grinned. God, what a woman.

Urging Fortune into a lope, Brett closed the distance between himself and Annie until their horses were neck and neck. They traveled in silence for a while, and Brett realized this was the first time he'd ever ridden with a women beside him. "So, what do you think of my little dynasty?"

She shot him a startled look. "We're still on your land?"

"Yep. Quite a spread, isn't it?"

"I had no idea Durham owned so much property."

"I had no idea you knew Levi Durham."

"Our paths crossed on occasion," she replied absently. "This place doesn't look anything like I remember it. I almost didn't recognize it."

"I'll take that as a compliment."

"Take it any way you want. Durham wasn't one much for orderliness and it showed in the way he kept his spread. Still, I never thought I'd see the day he'd sell."

"He didn't. My hand beat his."

"Ah, now that makes sense."

Brett almost laughed at the sudden clarity in her tone. "What's that supposed to mean?"

"You don't strike me as the horse rancher type."

Was it that obvious? "What type *do* I strike you as?"

She gave him a good once over. "The type who will take advantage of any situation where you'll come out the winner."

"I'm glad you think so highly of me," he said dryly.

"I call a spade a spade." She shrugged. "So what was the hand? Royal flush, joker's wild?"

Brett grinned at her astuteness, both of his character and his means of acquiring the Durham spread. "Aces—three of a kind. Hence, the Triple Ace."

"Where was the fourth one, up your sleeve?"

Brett chuckled. "Darlin', the only thing up my sleeve that night was the hand of a comely Frenchwoman—"

"Spare me the details."

"Can I help it if women find me irresistible?"

"It's a wonder you can sit upright, with the weight of your conceit."

He let out a full-bellied laugh. "To tell the truth, Durham got off easy. This place nowhere near covered his bet. He was in debt up to his eyeballs. Took almost everything I had just to get this place in decent shape."

"So you won not only his land, but his hired hands as well."

"In a manner of speaking. Some came with the deal, some came later. It seemed foolish to replace the men here when they already knew their business."

"You made a good decision. Wade Henry could ramrod a horse ranch blind. I'd ride shotgun with him any day."

At the time Brett had just thought it a convenient decision, but Annie's backhanded compliment warmed his insides. He couldn't remember the last time his actions had met with approval, and he savored it like a kid with a piece of horehound candy. "If you'd known he worked for me, would it have made any difference?"

She shrugged. "Probably not."

The answer didn't surprise him. Annie struck him as the kind of woman who wouldn't let personal ties influence her decision. "Then what did change your mind?"

Long seconds passed before she answered. "Unfinished business."

The remark hung in the air long after she rode ahead. Usually by the end of a conversation with a woman, Brett knew everything from her favorite color to the size of her corset. Yet Annie left him more puzzled than the day he'd met her. She had a way of answering a question without revealing a thing, and he wondered if it came naturally or if it took a concentrated effort.

They reached the southern border just after dusk. After they unsaddled and brushed down the horses, the men went about setting up camp. Dogie scoured the ground for whatever fuel he could scrounge up, Henry brought out the makings for coffee and supper, Flap Jack fetched water, and Emilio examined the tack.

None of them required Annie's help, so she found herself a spot beneath a mesquite tree, cleared the ground of pods and thorns, then sat on her rolled-out bedding and unraveled her hair.

Brett knew he should be doing something more productive than standing by the horses, gaping at her, but for the life of him he couldn't think of what. Hypnotized, he could do nothing more than watch as the flaxen ropes came apart beneath her nimble fingers. He'd imagined what she'd look like with her hair unbound, but imagination came nowhere near the actual sight of glossy strands falling over her shoulder and over one breast in waist long waves.

When she brought out a brush from her pack, Brett thought for sure he'd died and gone to heaven. Each stroke was a no-nonsense swipe that nonetheless grabbed him by the vitals. How could so ordinary and artless a task send all the blood in his body shooting straight to his groin?

His hands begged to touch her hair, to draw the strands through his fingers and carry them to his nose so he could inhale the Eden of her scent. The outside glossy and tangle-free, she flipped the mass over her head and started the process all over again.

Brett closed his eyes and groaned.

A forceful nudge to his arm knocked him off balance. Brett regained his footing, and found Fortune staring at him, vexed at being ignored.

Brett cursed and strode away from camp. It was going to be a helluva long trip.

Chapter 5

The gentle strum of Emilio's guitar flowed around Annie like a warm prairie wind as she packed away her brush, then rested against the peeling trunk of the mesquite tree, her arm slung over one upraised knee. The odors of scorched coffee, burned beans and sweaty skin hovered in the cool evening air, as much companions to her as the packed ground beneath her bottom, the glitter of stars overhead, and the taste of grit on her tongue.

A few feet away, Dogie and Flap Jack lay on their sides on their wool soogans, the cow chip campfire shedding light on the cards each held. Emilio sat closest to her against his saddle, and Wade Henry lay opposite them, in his hand a worn edition of the Good Book.

Some things never changed. He'd had a Bible in his hand for as long as Annie could remember.

Granddad once told her that Wade Henry had found religion after a job gone bad. A bullet shattered his thigh, and he'd nearly bled out before they got him to a doc. According to Clovis James, Henry had made a bargain with the Almighty: let him live, and he'd never rustle another horse. The Lord lived up to his end of the deal, and so, apparently, had Wade Henry.

As for Corrigan, Annie had no idea where he'd disappeared off to. Nor, she told herself as she closed her eyes, did she care. The farther she stayed away from him the better. She didn't know how much he knew about her or her past, but the man asked too many questions. Worse, he was too shrewd. If he didn't have suspicions already, he would before long. Annie hoped she could track down and catch his horses before U.S. Marshals picked up her trail, and he learned the truth of why she'd left Nevada.

At the rate they were traveling, that didn't look too promising.

He'd surprised her today, though, she'd give him that. She wouldn't have thought he'd last an hour in the saddle, much less ten. Hell, he wore silk vests and drank bourbon. Even his horses were high class. Why would a man whose tastes ran toward the more refined go through all this trouble for a rangy mustang?

No, she didn't want to know. Corrigan's reasons were none of her concern. As long as he stuck to his end of their bargain, there'd be no problem. This job would be over soon. When the money she earned ran out, she'd move on to the next job and load up her pockets again.

Yeah, the next job, she thought with unaccustomed bleakness. The next bronc. The next dollar. The next sunrise. One of these days she might get lucky enough to see an end to it all.

The sharp crack of Dogie's name sliced through Emilio's rendition of "Laredo." Annie opened her eyes and sought out the source. On the fringe of the campfire's glow, Corrigan stood beside the first horse in the string, his hand on the animal's forelock.

Dogie glanced in his boss's direction, then quickly at the men. From their shrugs, none had any more idea of what had riled their boss than he did. Dogie dropped his cards face down, rolled to his feet, hitched his droopy britches, and swaggered with false courage toward his boss.

"What burr got under *his* saddle?" she asked Wade Henry.

He glanced briefly toward the remuda, then returned his attention to his reading. "Nothin' to worry your perty head about. Ace is just bein' Ace, is all."

Flap Jack drew a card from the deck. "The boy's probably just gettin' his hide chewed a bit."

That was obvious, but for what? Corrigan couldn't be finding fault with the way Dogie took care of the horses; he cared for them as tenderly as a mother with a new babe.

Then again, what concern was it of hers? If Corrigan felt there was cause to upbraid the boy, that was between the two of them.

"How long do you think it will take to track down the horses, Miss Annie?" Flap Jack asked. For such a giant, deep-chested man, he had an incongruously mellow voice.

"Tracking them down won't be the hard part," she told him. "If they've gone into the canyon, and if renegades haven't already claimed them for themselves, we should find them in a few days. It's catching them that'll be tough."

"That's been our problem all along," Wade Henry commented. "That bandit won't let us get close enough to the herd to rope 'em."

Annie nodded. "A lead stallion is naturally territorial. He's worked hard to build his harem, and he won't let them go without a fight."

"Maybe, but that devil don't stand a snowball's chance against you."

She frowned at Wade Henry's confidence in her. What if she didn't get the stallion? It had been years since she'd gone after mustangs. What if she'd forgotten everything Sekoda had taught her?

Dogie returned then, distracting her from the image of her neck in a noose if she didn't accomplish the task she'd taken on. Despite the grin on his face, his brown eyes carried a shadow of dejection that pulled at her heartstrings.

"What the matter, kid?" Flap Jack asked him

as he sat cross-legged on his blanket. "Forget to brush down one of the horses?"

"Naw. Ace just didn't like the halter I put on the pinto."

"Don't let him get to ya."

"Heck, he don't bother me none."

None seemed inclined to challenge the bald-faced lie.

Wade Henry closed his Bible. "Come on, boys, time to hit the sack. We got an early day ahead of us."

Emilio packed away his guitar, Flap Jack pocketed his cards, and everyone settled into their bedrolls. Within minutes the peacefulness of night descended, broken only by the song of cicadas and the bark of a prairie dog.

Despite her fatigue, Annie couldn't make herself relax. Corrigan still hadn't returned and she couldn't help wondering what kept him. Damning her curiosity, she rolled to her feet and strolled toward the edge of camp. The spotted horse Corrigan had been inspecting earlier blew a greeting through his nostrils as she passed the remuda. Annie paused, then cupped her palm over the animal's velvety nose. He nuzzled her collarbone for a moment before losing interest in her.

Moonlight shed a dim glow to see by as she examined the tack closely for whatever flaw Corrigan had found. It was almost unnoticeable to an untrained eye. If Annie hadn't been braiding halters since God was a baby, even her keen eyes might have missed the tiny knots threaded into the rope. Knots that eventually would have chafed against the horse's tender cheek.

Was this the boy's great crime?

A muffled curse drew her attention beyond the campfire's glow, where a lone silhouette stood head bowed amidst the billow of buffalo grass.

Leaving the horses, she crossed toward the figure, knowing it could only be Corrigan.

A moment later it was her turn to curse. He'd stripped himself of his shirt and chaps, and the quarter moon outlined his broad shoulders and narrow torso. Even the dim lighting couldn't disguise the impressive expanse of bare arms and back.

Annie's heartbeat suddenly picked up pace. She was no stranger to a man's nudity, but catching Corrigan alone and half naked seemed somehow . . . forbidden.

Just as she turned sharply away, a gentle whirring sound made her pause. She looked back. He'd set the lasso circling above his head, and Annie was drawn to the sight of his body in motion. Tendons flexed, muscles rippled . . . was there not an ounce of loose skin on the man?

He released the noose. It soared toward a saddle set on the ground about fifty feet away.

She'd had no intention of spying on him, and even less intention of alerting him to her presence. But when the lasso landed short of its mark, she found herself saying, "You aren't rotating your wrist enough."

He glanced over his shoulder. "What are you still doing awake?"

Neither hellfire nor wild horses would get her to admit she'd been checking on him. "It's all in the wrist," she said instead. "If you don't give it enough rotation, the noose won't build up enough speed to fly." She hesitated, then held out her hand for the rope.

He surrendered it with a smile and a bow.

Gripping the rope tight in her fist, Annie stepped in front of him, certain the heat of the day had baked her brain. She'd gone out of her way to keep her distance from this man, and here she was, strolling straight into the dragon's lair.

Annie pressed her lips together and tossed the coil in her hand, testing its weight and feel. "You start out with a slow circular motion," she instructed, swinging it first at her side, then above her shoulder. "Keep your elbow up. As it builds up speed, loosen your grip on the neck, letting the loop get bigger. Then release it." The rope fell directly over the horn. Annie gave a swift yank, tightening the noose.

She looked at him to gauge his reaction, only to find his heated gaze on her rear end.

"Very impressive." One eyebrow rose and he gave her a crooked smile that had her nerve endings tingling. "Care to show me again?"

Annie snapped her mouth shut and lurched forward to retrieve the rope. She hated it when he looked at her like that—as if she'd been put on this earth solely to satisfy his appetite. "I didn't learn overnight. And when I made a mistake, I didn't have someone tanning my chaps about it."

"Ah, so *that's* what this little lesson was all about. And here I thought you just wanted to be alone with me."

She ignored the dramatized sigh of disappointment. "There was nothing wrong with that hackamore that couldn't be fixed."

"It was shoddy braiding."

"I suppose you can do better?"

"This isn't about me—"

"You can't, can you?"

He stared at her for several long seconds. Then he took the lasso and began to coil it. "A person doesn't have to carry a tune to recognize good music. I was raised around horses. It's been a lot of years since I worked with them, but I haven't forgotten that sloppy work will cause unnecessary injury to the horse or the rider."

"Ah, and raking a child over the coals is such an effective way of teaching him."

He leaned in close enough to tease her with the musky scent of his skin. "Careful, Annie, I think your heart is beginning to soften."

He drew back, and Annie's fingers curled into her palms to keep from smacking the smirk off his face. But he was right, as much as she hated to admit it. She was acting as protective as an older sister against the town bully, and she couldn't think of a single reason why.

It had to stop. The kid was on his own. Let

him figure out that the world was a tough place and life didn't always play fair. And that there wouldn't always be someone to stand up for him, to shelter him, to protect him. . . .

Those who did wound up paying the ultimate price.

"Rise and shine and give God the glory!" Wade Henry called in the same cheerful tone as he did every morning.

Brett wanted to strangle him. If he'd gotten two hours of sleep last night, he'd count himself lucky—and it was all Annie's fault. Every time he closed his eyes, images of her taunted him— the erotic motion of her body on that bronc back in Nevada, the controlled defiance when she'd spouted off her terms in going after the horses, that mind-numbing display with her hair, and the fire in her eyes when she'd taken up for Dogie last night. . . .

Never had he met a woman who could so infuriate and amuse him at the same time. He didn't have to justify himself to her or anybody. How he handled his men was his business. At least they had jobs. And if they wanted to keep them, then by damned they'd better be willing to do the work he assigned them in the manner he expected.

Didn't it occur to Annie that going easy on the boy wouldn't do him any favors in the long run? That a stern hand built character? Obviously not, or she wouldn't have invented that little lesson.

Brett couldn't decide if he should thrash her for her meddling or applaud her for her mettle. Few men dared to talk to him the way she did, yet Annie stood her ground and spoke her mind as if *she* ramrodded the place. Hell, if he hadn't been so aggravated with Dogie, he might have thanked him for inciting the first bit of emotion he'd seen in Annie since they'd met.

If she displayed half as much passion in bed as she did out of it. . . .

Spanish curses provided a merciful distraction from his wayward thoughts. Brett glanced up from his coffee toward Emilio. Clad only in his long-handled underwear, the roper was tearing through his belongings like a Texas twister.

"What are you looking for, Emilio?"

"Mis ropas! Alguién me robó de mis ropas!"

Just then Brett spotted Dogie racing away from camp. A strip of something that looked suspiciously like a pant leg flapped behind him from the wad of material in his arms.

"Dogie!"

The boy stopped as suddenly as if a brick wall had shot up from the ground in front of him, then twisted around to face Brett.

"Give Emilio back his clothes."

Shoulders slumping, the boy did as ordered. "I was just funnin' with him."

Brett sighed in exasperation. He should have known bringing Dogie along would cause a stir. The thirteen-year-old had shown up at the ranch a few months back, scraggly and unkempt and looking for work. There'd been no reason to hire him on. They didn't need the help, and Brett sure as hell didn't need an inexperienced hand around his beauties. He found himself putting the boy on the Triple Ace payroll anyway, if for no other reason than Brett remembered what it had been like to be young and cold and hungry.

That should have been his first warning.

He shook his head at his own foolish impulses. They'd gotten him into more than one kettle of hot water over the years.

Just as he started to take a drink of his coffee, he caught sight of Annie over the steaming rim. The cup halted mid-air, and his mouth went as dry as rawhide.

She stood in a ray of saffron sunlight, wriggling into a pair of chaps. Inch by inch, soft leather worked its way up those never-ending legs, the outer length of each thigh decorated by five silver conchos.

As she cinched the buckle around her slender waist, his gaze centered on the V between her hipbones where tanned canvas trousers were revealed. He couldn't recall a pair of chaps looking as good as they did on Annie. But then, since the only chaps he'd ever seen were on men, he hadn't given them much notice before.

Then she turned and bent over to fasten the ties below her knees. Brett's stifled a groan at the sight of her heart-shaped ass outlined in snug leather. God, the woman was going to kill him. He'd always thought the most provocative part of a woman was her backside—the extension of the valley between the shoulder blades, the delicate structure of ribs, the hollow at the base of the spine, the swell of buttocks and flare of hips . . . just the sight was enough to make him rigid for hours.

The thought of seeing Annie wearing nothing under the chaps had an entire fantasy unfolding. Cupping each cheek in his hands, pulling her close, rubbing himself against her—

"What the hell are you lookin' at, Corrigan?"

Brett's head snapped up. Annie was glaring at him over her shoulder, her blue eyes flashing, scalding color staining her cheeks.

He lowered his cup and said, "I was just admiring your. . . ." His gaze took a leisurely journey to her rear, then rose back up to her flushing face. "Assets." His lips slid into a slow, sensual smile.

Her eyes narrowed. The color in her cheeks deepened. "I would think for a man so hepped up on catchin' his horses, he'd have more important things to do than sit around letting his gums flap and his eyes roam."

At the moment, Brett couldn't think of any. "More important, maybe." He saluted her with his cup. "But not nearly as pleasurable."

Her spine went rigid. She grabbed the buckskin's bridle, swung into the saddle, and wheeled her horse around.

Grinning at her hasty departure, he turned around, then came to a sudden stop at the sight of his men standing around in various stages of undress, their mouths agape, their lustful gazes on Annie's disappearing figure.

Brett's good humor died. He whipped his revolver out of its holster and fired a shot into the air. "If you men aren't on your horses in ten seconds, the next bullet will be between your beady little eyes."

No one called his bluff; within the ten allotted seconds, all hands were in their saddles and spurring their mounts out of camp.

Brett reholstered his revolver and kicked dirt over the embers. Maybe bringing her into the outfit had been a mistake. This was only the second day on the trail, and already she had his blood sizzling and his imagination running wild.

It had to stop. She wasn't a concubine brought along to indulge his baser needs. She was a hired horse thief, whose sole purpose was to save his fillies from ruin—and it was best he keep that uppermost in his mind.

Forgetting for an instant could mean the fall of the Triple Ace.

Chapter 6

As they headed south along the windswept plains, Annie kept as far away from Corrigan as possible. She didn't know what disturbed her more about the way he'd been looking at her—the smoldering fire in his eyes or her own reaction to it. No man had made her stomach flutter or her skin tingle in years. Yet every time Corrigan looked at her, strange things happened to her insides.

And every time she looked at him. . . .

Annie swiped her kerchief across her brow. God, it was hot out here.

"Is that true, Miss Annie?"

She swung her attention to the right and found Dogie staring at her, brows raised in expectancy. This morning, when she'd seen him match up that crimson red shirt with a pair of plaid britches, her first thought had been a hope that they wouldn't run into any bulls during the day's traveling. Strangely enough, she'd gotten used to the color. It certainly matched his sun-burned complexion. "Is what true?"

"Henry was just telling us that him and your granddaddy once drove a herd of longhorns clear into Montana Territory."

She could neither confirm nor deny the claim, for even if she hadn't been too young to accompany them, Granddad rarely told her and her mother where he went on his trips and it went against the grain to ask. "I expect if Mr. Henry said it, it's true."

" 'Course it's true!" Henry cried. "Me an' Ole Clovis had us plenty of adventures. Annie, did your granddaddy ever tell you about the time we had to drive a herd of mustangs from Dead Injun Creek to the rendezvous at Pease River?"

Before she could reply, he launched into the tale. "Danged sandstorm whipped up a good froth, stinging our eyes and plugging our noses. Got us so turned around we didn't know our As from our Zs.

"We ate dust for days. It was in our hair, our skin. We poured out boot-fulls of Texas at night. Finally we wound up at this tiny stream. Ole Clovis says he's got to see a man about a horse and he disappears behind a set of bushes. Not two seconds later, he comes runnin' through camp, hollerin' at the top of his lungs, 'Injuns! Injuns!' Well, I had me more hair back then, and no way was I gonna lose it to some Comanche buck, so I jumped on my pony and we skedaddled out of there.

"Next night we come upon another stream that looks a lot like the first one. We make camp. Clovis disappears behind the bushes, then comes runnin' out again, hollerin', 'Injuns! Injuns!' His face is pale as sourdough and he's shaking like a cottonwood in a windstorm. So I get on my pony, only this time I give the place a good scourin'. Not an Injun in sight.

"This goes on for three nights, and I was gettin' mighty furred up at Ole Clovis. I thought sure he was playin' a shine on me. So I decide I'm gonna get to the bottom of this once and for all."

"Was he playin' a shine on you?" Dogie asked with the eagerness of youth.

"Yer jumpin' ahead of my story, boy." Henry cast a ferocious scowl toward Dogie—at least, Annie figured he meant it to be ferocious.

"Where was I? Oh, yeah. The next mornin' I go exploring, and what do I find but a pair of ladies' unmentionables strung up in a tree? Turns out we'd been riding in circles, landin' at the same creek each night, and ever' time the wind blowed, the ruffles flowed out so it looked like a redskin's headdress."

The side of Annie's mouth curved into a smile. She'd heard the story a dozen times before, but it had always been Mr. Henry hollering "Injuns" and Clovis discovering the clay-stained petticoat in the huckleberry tree.

"I got lost in Forth Worth once," Dogie claimed.

"Good glory, boy, everyone knows *you* can get lost in a bath tub."

Annie bit the inside of her cheek to keep from laughing. She could hardly believe it. How long had it been since she'd felt like laughing?

A sudden shout interrupted her thought. Annie's attention veered toward the man galloping toward them, a thunderous expression darkening his face.

Corrigan reined in his mount so hard its hooves sent a spray of dirt. The blaze of fury in his eyes had Annie reining in, with Henry and Dogie following. What had set off his temper this time?

"Dogie, I thought I told you to keep a watch out for prairie dog holes."

"Yes, sir."

"Then what the hell are you doing back here?"

Dogie swapped a look with Annie. Despite her resolve not to soften, she couldn't help but feel sorry for him. The last time she'd been in Texas there had been no law against chewing the fat, but Corrigan obviously thought there was.

"Just keepin' Miss Annie company," Dogie answered.

"Keep her company on your own time. If one of these horses busts a leg, I'm taking it out of your hide."

Dogie dropped his gaze and, shoulders drooping, tapped his spurs to his horses's belly.

"Henry, start scouting for watering holes. I want to show Annie something."

"Sure, Ace." He tipped his hat at Annie. "Bye, Annie."

The instant Mr. Henry rode out of earshot, Annie turned on Corrigan. "Were you born a bully or is it an acquired talent?"

He deflected the question with one of his own. "Were you born a temptress, or is it an acquired talent?"

Annie glared at him.

"My men have a job to do, and they don't need you distracting them."

"I didn't want them along, as you'll recall."

"You didn't have a choice."

God, he was a bastard. "If I'm so much of a distraction, why in the hell did you ask me to go after your horses?"

"Because you're the best."

Annie didn't grace that with a reply.

"Take a ride with me."

She laughed humorlessly at his gall. "No thanks."

"You'll ride with a boy and cripple, but you won't ride with a man."

"I won't ride with *you*."

"Afraid?"

"Selective."

A grin spread across his face, creating deep creases in his tanned cheeks and crinkles at the corners of his eyes, transforming him from arrogant commander to irresistible rogue. "Oh, but

Annie, I could take you on a ride you'd never forget."

Somehow she didn't doubt that. The gleam in his gray-green eyes promised no less.

"Come on," he cajoled. "It's not far, I promise."

She felt herself weaken. What was this power he had over her? He was hard-hearted and pigheaded and quite the most conceited man she'd ever had the displeasure of associating with.

He could also be quite disarming when he put his mind to it. No doubt women all over the territory had fallen victim to that grin he flashed with such ease.

"What did you want to show me?" she asked irritably.

"Follow me." He clucked to the stallion.

Annie reluctantly flicked Chance's reins. She couldn't quell the feeling that she was making a big mistake, letting Corrigan lead her away from the rest of the outfit. She bent low and patted her boot, comforted by the bulge of her pocket revolver.

They rode for what seemed miles before Corrigan brought his horse to a stop and stared out across the land.

"Take a good look." He dismounted slowly, almost reverently.

She followed the direction of his gaze. Summer had hit the plains with a vengeance, sending waves of shimmering heat hovering above the surrounding buffalo grass, giving it the appearance of flickering green fire. And in the midst of it, two dozen hump-backed beasts lumbered across the terrain.

They were ugly, mangy creatures, yet there was something regal and awe inspiring about them.

"You're seeing the last of a disappearing breed."

It was hard to fathom that one day buffalo would no longer roam the plains, but she knew he spoke the truth. Prices for bones and hides were skyrocketing across the country and people were cashing in on the profits by the hoards; she'd even heard of men shooting at the beasts from train windows.

"Watch that bull. He's found himself a lady."

Annie focused on the biggest bison, a thick shouldered male with short gray horns curving out from his shaggy black head. His glossy, deep-set eyes were trained on a cow standing apart from the rest of the herd.

"Look at the way he preens in front of her," Corrigan said as the bull circled the cow, head high. "He's showing her his strength and prowess."

The cow retreated several paces.

"Doesn't look like she's much interested." Annie commented.

"She will be. He's just got to be patient."

"He'll be waiting till hell freezes over. She won't give in to him."

"Care to make a wager?"

Annie narrowed her eyes. "What kind of wager?"

His gaze dropped to her thigh, and she thought he was going to demand stakes that she'd not grant any man again for any price.

"If she submits, I'll buy you a new saddle."

A new saddle? Lord, she needed one badly! She'd had this one for over ten years now. The latigos were stretched, the buckles worn. She'd planned on buying a new one with the wages from catching Corrigan's horses, but if he wanted to purchase it and save her the money. . . .

"And if she doesn't submit?"

"You buy me a new saddle."

The image of a fancy new Mother Hubbard with Sam Stagg rigging was just too tempting to resist. "All right—it's a deal."

They continued watching the mating ritual, Corrigan cock-sure the cow would submit to the bull, Annie just as certain she'd let him know where he could put his seed. Sure enough, each time the male got too close, the female backed off, forcing him to repeat his courtship all over again.

Just when visions of breaking in a new leather seat began to play through Annie's mind, the bull closed in on the cow, and damned if she didn't lift her tail and let him mount.

With no more a desire to watch two animals rutting than listen to Corrigan gloat, Annie wheeled Chance around.

Corrigan caught the bridle in one gloved hand. "Looks like I won the wager, Annie."

She glared into his glittering eyes. "Enjoy the victory, Corrigan. It'll be the last one."

With twenty miles of arid earth and travel embedded in their skin, Brett signaled the party to dismount. Relieved sighs floated on the breeze, followed by collective moans as they slid from their saddles.

Brett probably would have moaned along with them if he could have found the energy. Rubbing his aching tail bone, he rounded Fortune to see how Annie was faring and found her leaning against her mustang's girth.

"Annie, go on and get yourself something to eat. I'll tend your horse."

She lifted herself off the animal and sighed. "No, I'll do it. You've got your own horse to tend."

He couldn't tell if she was still angry with him for winning the wager, or just plain tired.

Once the horses had been relieved of their saddles, he and Annie took stiff-bristled curry brushes out of their packs and set about grooming the dirty hides. Each stroke brought to Brett's mind the night before, when he'd watched Annie's own grooming. "How did you ever get involved with horses, Annie?" he asked in an effort to distract himself.

"Chance."

A logical answer—one that had landed him in

many an unexpected venture. "They used to scare the living hell out of me."

She shot a startled glance at him over the mustang's back. "Horses?"

He regretted the confession instantly. Next, she'd ridicule him. Or at least think him a coward.

Instead, she said, "I can't imagine you being afraid of anything."

"Not now, but when I was a kid. . . ." He ran the brush down Fortune's breast. "I was small for my age, and they were so big. So powerful. One on one they weren't so bad, but get in a herd of them. . . ."

The old hatred rose up without warning. *You ungrateful whelp! Those animals put the bread and butter on this table. Be a man. Just go in there and feed them.*

His father had known how terrified it made him to bring the horses their grain. Rolling the wheelbarrow into the paddock . . . the way the horses would crush around him the minute they caught scent of oats . . . kicking, biting, chasing each other away, caring not if a small boy got between them and took the blows instead.

"I suppose if anyone gets kicked enough times they'll develop a certain . . . apprehension. But this . . . this was more. It was the kind of fear that chokes off your air supply. I tried to pretend that they didn't make me feel completely defenseless, completely at their mercy, but. . . ."

"How did you get over it?" she asked quietly.

Brett shrugged as if it meant nothing. "I grew up. I learned to take control. Show them I was in charge."

"Is that what you were taught?" she asked, a note of anger in her tone.

"It worked," Brett stated in simple defense of himself—and yes, maybe of the way he was with those around him. If she understood, maybe her opinion of him wouldn't scale the bottom of the barrel. Not that he really cared one way or another. . . .

"Whoever taught you that should be shot. You don't tame mavericks by overpowering them; that'll break their spirit. You woo them. Win their trust. Once you've got that, they'll follow you anywhere."

Woo them. Win their trust.

Was that what it would take to tame Annie?

Scowling, Brett hefted his saddle into his arms and carried it to the campsite. He didn't want her trust, he wanted her body. And he wanted her giving it to him wildly, willingly, not with loathing in her eyes.

Brett's gaze followed her as she shook out her soogan. The men had fallen into their nightly ritual: Emilio brought out his guitar, Wade Henry his Bible, and Flap Jack a deck of cards, though all engaged in their tasks with only half-hearted vigor tonight. Annie's fragrance rose apart from the odors of stale sweat, horse, and earth. A little spicy, a lot alluring, utterly female.

Brett tried to concentrate on the beginnings of

a straight he'd been dealt, but when Annie began readying for bed, the last thing he wanted to look at was a bunch of painted numbers. Not when there were more . . . fetching views to enjoy. It amazed him how, even after two full days of travel beneath the relentless sun, she could still look as fresh and lovely as if she'd just stepped out of a bath.

He regretted the comparison when his imagination immediately conjured a picture of Annie wearing nothing but the skin she'd been born with, every luscious inch of her glistening with moisture. . . .

"I'll take first watch tonight," he announced abruptly.

The men looked up at him in surprise as he folded his cards and grabbed his rifle. Every last one of them knew he always took the three-to-six shift. Tonight he might just take full duty. Weariness didn't matter; he'd not get any sleep lying next to Annie anyway.

A short distance away from the remuda, Brett sank to the ground with a sigh, rested his rifle across his lap, and stared up at the stars. He didn't know how much longer he could take this torture—listening to the sounds she made, seeing her without touching her, smelling her without tasting her. . . .

Hell, if Annie gave him half a chance, he could show her pleasures beyond her wildest dreams. If there was anything Brett knew, it was women. Young, old, slender, plump, pale, dusky—they were all beautiful and all perfect and Brett hadn't met a one in fifteen years that he couldn't seduce or charm into his bed—often without even trying.

He'd gotten a late start down that road of delight. Most boys he knew got their first taste of pleasure at fourteen or fifteen. Brett hadn't been tall enough or strong enough or handsome enough. . . . His brow furrowed. In a sense, he'd been a lot like Dogie was now.

But all that changed in his twentieth summer, when two things had happened: his scrawny body had finally filled out, and he'd met the woman who'd made him a man.

Molly had been something, all right, he remembered with a fond smile. He'd won her contract in a game of faro, saving her from working one day longer in a slimy dock-side brothel. She'd returned the favor by teaching him ways of making love that would make even the boys back home blush. From that point forward, he'd perfected the art of seduction, and discovered that there was no more powerful a feeling than bringing pleasure to a woman, of watching her succumb to his touch, of making her feel cherished and adored.

The idea of introducing Annie to the skills he'd learned made his groin tighten and his imagination take a crazy spin.

Yep, there was only one way to end his suffering. He was just going to have to bed her.

Chapter 7

***

The deliciously sharp aroma of coffee and the sensation of being watched roused Annie the next morning. She slowly opened her eyes, only to find Corrigan crouched next to her bedroll, studying her through lowered lashes.

"Mornin', Annie."

His voice, husky with sensual undertone, came to her straight from midnight dreams. She sat up abruptly and ran a hand over her hair, strangely self-conscious of the tangles.

"Thought you could use this." He held out a tin cup, aromatic steam curling from the top.

"Thanks."

"Sleep well?"

Obviously one of them had, she thought sourly. She rolled to the side and grabbed her boots, shaking them upside down before pulling them onto her feet. Then she marched toward a thicket of sagebrush. It didn't offer much in the way of privacy, but since his lewd scrutiny of the day before, she'd taken to dressing behind whatever shield she could find.

When Annie emerged moments later and approached the remuda, she found Chance saddled and ready. She waylaid Dogie with a hand to his sleeve. "Did you saddle my horse?"

His glance flicked from her to Chance then back to her again. "No, Ace did it."

Corrigan? Corrigan had saddled her horse? What was going on? First the coffee this morning, now the tending of her mare. . . .

What had gotten into him?

The question plagued Annie as they made their way south. Every time she turned around, Corrigan seemed to be right there. Sometimes he'd wink. Sometimes he'd study her with that intense curiosity that set her nerves on edge. Always he'd be wearing that secretive smile. She felt it chipping away at her senses and her defenses.

Even now the memory of his shameless grin had the power to awaken sensations long dead—a lightness in her head, a fluttering in her belly, a thickening of her blood. . . .

What did he want from her?

They reached McClellan's Creek around midday and stopped to rest the horses. Annie dismounted, feeling stiff and sticky and covered with grit from head to toe. The sight of the creek was too inviting to resist, so after tending to Chance, she grabbed a piece of flannel and a chunk of soap from her saddlebags and headed upstream.

Blooming black-eyed susans, yellow-petaled broomweed and shady cottonwoods lined banks littered with rocks and natural debris. Annie pushed her way between two slender trunks—

And came to a sudden stop.

Her eyes slammed shut, and she spun away from the sight of Corrigan wading in the creek, stripped down to a pair of short-handled underwear.

Then curiosity got the better of her.

Hidden behind the cottonwoods and brush, Annie allowed herself to look at him—really look at him—without fear of getting caught. The water level reached just to the band of white cotton below his navel. A line of damp hair extended up the center of his lean, rippled abdomen and ended between chiseled pectorals. Slick with moisture and caressed by sunshine, each muscle, each tendon stood out in stark relief, making Annie painfully aware how long it had been since she'd felt a man's flesh beneath her fingers.

When he reached midstream, he sank into the waist high water and lay backward. As he backpaddled across the surface, water rippled beneath him and above him, clinging to the tanned cords of his arms.

Any man with a body like that should be outlawed.

"Hey, Annie."

Annie whirled around, her hand to her chest.
"Damn it, Dogie! Don't ever sneak up on somebody like that."

"Whatcha lookin' at?"

When Dogie tried to peer around her, she sidestepped and blocked his path. He slanted to the
right, and she blocked his path again. His brows
narrowed over the bridge of his nose.

"It's nothing—just a snake."

"Really?"

Annie should have known better than to dan-
gle such enticing bait in front of a young boy.
She caught him by the collar just as he tried
dodging passed her. "You're too late. It already
slithered into the water."

"Dad-gum it, I always miss the good stuff."

"What are you doing out here, anyway?"

"Lookin' for Ace. You ain't seen him, have
ya?"

More than she'd ever planned, she thought.
Sudden color rose in her cheeks. "Uh, no," she
stammered. "Maybe h-he went scouting."

"Naw, his horse is still here."

"Well, I'm sure he'll turn up." Clutching her
clothes in one arm, she used her free hand to
steer Dogie away from the creek. "Come on. We
better get back to camp before the master has to
come searching for us." Her bath would have

to wait; for certain she'd not get into that water now.

Even so, it took every ounce of willpower Annie had not to take one last peek through the trees.

The days passed in a blur, one blending into the other. In an effort to forget the scene at McClellan's creek, Annie poured all her concentration into watching the land for signs of the horses. Corrigan hadn't given any indication of knowing that she'd spied on him so shamelessly. Still, she maintained her distance from him. Unfortunately no matter how far she kept herself from him, she couldn't seem to escape his piercing eyes or knowing grin.

Damn it, what did he *want* from her?

A sudden thought had Annie's heart stammering. How did she know the horses they were chasing even existed? What if it was all a ruse? All she had was the word of a cardsharp and his cronies, and Annie knew good and well that Corrigan's men would follow him to hell if he ordered it. What if he already knew of the bounty on her head, and was using the horses as a ploy to lead her to the law?

But . . . why would a man of such obvious wealth go through all this trouble for a measly two-hundred dollars? It just didn't make sense.

Then, an even more horrid thought occurred— what if *they* had sent him?

"Señorita."

Jolted, Annie looked over at Emilio, who held a gloved hand up, bidding her to wait. He'd dropped back to ride with her earlier that afternoon. Until now they'd not exchanged a single word, and Annie suspected Corrigan had sent him to guard her so she'd not *distract* him.

She followed his gaze and recognized Corrigan loping toward them on Fortune. "Do you still have that little pea-shooter on you?" he asked, reining in.

For a moment Annie was tempted to keep the element of surprise on her side and deny the Smith and Wesson in her boot. But the set of his jaw warned her that it was a serious question that demanded a serious answer. "I always have it with me." Maybe it was better he knew up front that she'd never be caught defenseless. "Why?"

"Keep it handy. Emilio, *ven conmigo.* Annie, you wait here."

"What's going on?" she demanded.

"There's something up ahead. It's probably nothing, but I'd rather be safe than sorry."

Corrigan and Emilio rode ahead to investigate while Annie and the others stayed behind, weapons drawn, all senses on alert, none forgetting that Comanche could appear out of thin air. Though most of them had been driven north onto reservations, renegades still prowled the area.

Several heart thumping minutes later, a loud whistle rent the still air, the signal that it was safe to proceed. Corrigan met them halfway. "It's just a supply wagon."

"Injuns?" Flap Jack asked.

"Busted axle. We might as well pitch camp," Corrigan said. "It's early, but it looks like we'll be in for a gully washer before nightfall."

Annie glanced up. The sky was pure blue, not a cloud to be seen, but she remembered how quickly that could change. Granddad used to say, "If you don't like the weather now, little filly, wait five minutes."

"How are you holding up?" Corrigan asked of her after the men rode ahead.

Like she'd been put through the wringer and hung out to dry. But there was no way she'd admit that the heat was wearing her down fast. Taking in the rings of sweat under his arms, the lines of weariness around his eyes, she gained some satisfaction that he was feeling its affects as well. "I could outlast you in the saddle any day of the week."

"Why, Annie, that sounds almost like a challenge."

Annie frowned. It did, now that he mentioned it.

"How about it?"

"How about what?"

"A race to the wagon. Winner cooks supper tonight."

She shouldn't. She absolutely, positively should not let him goad her into accepting another challenge—especially after the outcome of the last one. Not only was it too damned hot, but Chance, for all her heart, wasn't built for speed the way his Arabian was. Yet if she *did* win ... well, the image of Corrigan eating crow was just too tempting to ignore.

"You're on, tenderfoot. Let's see if you can ride as well as you gloat." She lashed the end of a rein against Chance's flank. "Haw!"

The mustang immediately jumped to obey, then quickly extended into a full gallop. Muscles stretched and tightened, breaths blew hot and aggressive. Her hooves churned up prairie grass, patches of yellow flowers and sandy soil.

Annie tasted the heat of the race on her tongue, felt the sweetness of freedom in her blood. How long had it been since she'd raced for the sheer joy of it, and not to escape capture?

From behind, the vibration of the ground grew stronger, and she knew Corrigan was gaining on her. She leaned low over Chance's neck, adrenaline pumping through her veins like wildfire. Wind blurred her eyes and ripped at her hair, sending her hat sailing behind her.

In the periphery of her vision, she saw Corrigan's men draw their horses to a halt. Dogie stood in his stirrups and shouted something she couldn't make out, but that sounded like encouragement.

Chance kept pace with Corrigan's stallion for a good half mile before the Arabian started pulling ahead. Annie lifted her weight from the saddle and bowed closer to Chance's neck, urging her to greater speed. But the mare, for all her heart, just didn't have the fleetness of the other breed.

Rather than kill her horse over a stupid bet, Annie accepted defeat and allowed Chance to slow. She patted the mare's sweaty hide, giving praise for her effort, while around her cheers and whistles erupted.

With a disgusted frown, she watched Corrigan accept the congratulations from his men. "It's all right, Chance. You gave it all your heart," she consoled her mare.

At the wagon, Annie dismounted and walked Chance in a circle to cool her down, patting her neck, crooning her approval while the men scavenged through the spilled crates.

"Hey, look!" Dogie cried. "Canned peaches—and sourdough batter!" He held up a rusty tin can and a Mason jar half full of a thick, pasty substance. "We hit the jackpot here, Ace. Someone lost themselves a whole dad-gummed chuck wagon!"

She knew without looking the instant Corrigan came up behind her. The air fairly crackled. A tingle began at the base of her back, crept up her spine, spread across her nape. His musky scent caressed her like a warm prairie wind.

Bracing herself, she looked over her shoulder and found him standing too close, his golden brown hair tousled by the wind, his green eyes glittering with the same excitement that flowed through her veins.

"Looks like I won again, Annie."

"With me cooking supper? I wouldn't be so sure about that."

Emilio stirred his fork around his plate.

Flap Jack sniffed his meal suspiciously, then raised his head. His bushy brows lifted, his lip curled.

Wade Henry bravely tried a bit.

Only Dogie ate with gusto, obviously not minding the undercooked beans or charred chunks of salt pork swimming in the greasy film.

Annie chanced a glance at Corrigan. She might have been insulted at the sight of him chewing on a piece of jerky if it weren't so amusing. Oblivious to her study, he brought the strip to his mouth. Annie found herself mesmerized as he parted his lips, pushed the jerky inside, and tore off the tip with straight, white teeth.

Annie quickly looked away before he caught her watching him—again. Her face flamed anew at the memory of the last time she'd gotten caught staring at him. She still couldn't believe she'd looked at the front of his britches. Worse, that he'd seen her doing it. She'd never been so mortified in her life.

"That was some mighty fine supper, Miss Annie," Dogie said, setting his plate aside, then wiping his mouth with his sleeve.

She couldn't help but smile. "Thanks, Dogie."

"That was some race, too. Ain't seen so much

excitement around here since Flap Jack had the tro—"

"Dogie . . ." Corrigan warned.

The boy ducked his face. "I ain't seen anything like it in a long spell."

"I lost, Dogie," Annie reminded him. The point still rubbed her raw. She'd known better than to let him cajole her into a second wager, yet she'd accepted it anyway.

"I know, but . . . you were amazing! You looked like the wind. Where'd you learn to ride like that?"

Annie hesitated a second before deciding that the truth couldn't hurt. "My granddad."

"Did he race horses?"

She exchanged a look with Mr. Henry, then glanced at Brett. He lay on his side across the fire with one ankle crossed over the other, watching her, waiting.

"He had a talent for it," she finally answered. "I suppose I learned it from him."

"Did you learn how to bust broncs from him too?"

"No, that came later." Putting an end to his barrage of questions, Annie rocked to her feet, grabbed her plate and cup, and left.

"See what you did?" Flap Jack scolded Dogie. "You got her all upset."

"What? I was just curious!"

"You know better than to be asking so many questions."

The chiding faded as Annie moved to the edge

of the alkali puddle they'd camped by and plunged her dishes into the water, trying to keep her hands busy, trying to keep the panic at bay.

Damn it, why was this happening? Why was this sense of losing control creeping up on her now? First the memories of Sekoda, then this awareness of Corrigan, now the resurrection of her granddad. . . .

Why this sudden feeling that her past and her present were about to collide?

Wade Henry came up beside a few minutes later, knelt, and swished his plate in the water. "You okay, Annie?"

"Fine. Why?"

"You wash any harder, you're gonna scrub the tin off that plate."

Her hands stilled instantly.

"Dogie didn't mean no harm. He's just curious about you. I think he looks to you as some sorta hero."

A hero? Her? He'd be better off idolizing Jesse James. She resumed scrubbing. "Yeah, well, one of these days he's gonna ask questions of the wrong person and land himself six feet under."

Henry didn't deny the truth of that. Around them, the cicadas had begun their pre-nocturnal songs. In her younger years, she used to love listening to the sound. She remembered sitting on the front stoop with Grandad, making up stories about the locusts.

"Why didn't you come to me after your granddaddy died?" Henry asked quietly. "You know I would have taken you in."

She lifted her gaze to his wrinkled, sun-beaten face, and they shared a look born of a past that refused to rest. Everything Clovis James had been and had done had shaped her into the woman she was, and though she couldn't find it in her heart to resent him since he'd done his best raising her, she often wished things had been different.

She stared into the murky red surface of the watering hole. She tried to see in her reflection what Corrigan saw, but all that appeared was a hollow-eyed, gaunt-cheeked outlaw. "I thought about it once or twice." Or a hundred times. "Reckon I didn't know where to find you."

"As you can see, you didn't have to look far."

Annie turned away, hating the gentle censure. Even if she'd known Henry had been so close, she'd never have gone to him. Never would have dragged him into the life she'd chosen for herself—a life he'd left long before she'd entered into it. He'd been given a second chance and he'd made something of it; she'd been given a second chance and had it ripped away from her.

Deep in the distance, a grumble of thunder warned that it wouldn't be long before the skies opened up and let loose with a good soaker. They finished washing their plates in silence, then returned to camp. The men had already begun unloading crates, barrels, pots and pans and assorted cooking equipment from the flatbed wagon, and were stacking them in a horseshoe shape nearby.

Annie's suspicions toward Corrigan continued to haunt her. She wished he'd just tell her what in hell he was planning, why he was being so . . . amiable, because the not-knowing was driving her mad. The only thing that kept her from jumping on Chance's back and high-tailing it out of here was the possibility that she might be wrong—that she might be letting her own fears color her judgment. If Corrigan was playing straight with her and she fled prematurely, she'd be leaving behind her only chance for freedom.

"Well, g'night fellas," Dogie exclaimed, hitching up his britches in a boastful manner. "Reckon I'll be staying all dry and cozy while the rest of you slugs get to sleep in the mud." He started for the wagon.

Flap Jack snagged him by the back of his coat. "Oh, no ya don't. You got low rank in this outfit, pup. I'll be the one sleeping in the wagon."

"Why should *I* be the one getting wet?"

"You could use a little waterin', ya scrawny little sprout. It might make you grow."

"Why, you—"

Dogie charged at Flap Jack, lowering his head like a raging bull. Flap Jack's broad hand to Dogie's forehead kept the little scrapper at arm's length. His fists flailed like paddles in a wild current, never making contact with the burly man holding him in place.

"Knock it off, boys," Corrigan commanded. "Annie's sleeping in the wagon."

Flap Jack and Dogie snapped upright in surprise, then their heads ducked, as if in shame that they'd forgotten a female existed among them. Never had Annie felt so conspicuous—or so resentful of misplaced manly honor. How was she ever to have the respect of these men if Corrigan insisted on giving her special treatment all the time?

Still, she might have been touched by his care for her comforts if she hadn't spotted Wade Henry just then, lowering himself gingerly onto a crate. It didn't take a medical man to see that all their traveling was taking its toll on his aged body. "No, Annie isn't." She approached the stoop-shouldered man and knelt on one knee. "Wade Henry? You okay?"

"Oh, shore. Comin' rain is just makin' the rheumatism act up. I'll be fit as a fiddle once the weather clears."

"I want you to sleep in the wagon tonight."

"No, Annie. Your heart is in the right place, but I can't take your bed. It wouldn't be right makin' a woman sleep out in the rain."

"Don't worry about me; I'm not made of sugar. Come on." She hooked her arm through his and helped him to his feet. "Let's get you settled."

He resisted with a strength that belied his feeble stature. "No, Annie, it's a matter of honor for a man to put the welfare of womenfolk first."

"I can take care of myself," she interrupted.

"I know, but . . . sometime's all a man's got left is his pride. Even if I wanted to, Ace would never put up with it. I think it might be on account o' his mama dyin'."

Annie drew back in surprise. "His mama is dying?"

"No, she's already gone. Died in some sort of accident years ago, but some things stay fresh up here"—he tapped his finger to his temple—"and in here." He patted his heart. "I think he blames himself because he wasn't there to stop it. It does something to a man's innerds when he can't protect his own."

Somehow her mind couldn't wrap itself around the fact of Corrigan even having a mother, much less losing her. She did understand pride, though. Sekoda had been proud, and she'd seen what it had done to him when they'd stripped it from him. And by disagreeing with Corrigan in front of his men, she'd been no better. "Well, you leave Corrigan to me."

She left Wade Henry sitting next to the tailgate and strode past the rest of the men, who were dishing up the stew Wade Henry had cooked while they'd unloaded the wagon.

"Corrigan, I need to speak to you." Aware of his men's curious attention, she grit her teeth and added, "Privately."

She turned her back on his wicked grin and led him a short distance away from their audience. "I want Wade Henry sleeping in the wagon."

His grin disappeared. "I've already decided who will sleep where."

Any sympathy she might have felt for him over the loss of a parent vanished at his unhesitating answer. "Damn it, he's too old to be sleeping in the rain."

He turned away from her. "Boys, let's finish getting this wagon unloaded."

Annie glared at him, every nerve and muscle in her body quivering with fury. "How can you be so heartless?"

He twisted back around and looked at her through eyes as flat and unreadable as a block of stone, giving no clue to his thoughts. And yet, Annie sensed a struggle going on inside him. If he gave in to her, he'd lose face in front of his men—partly because she was a woman, partly because he would be showing preferential treatment toward Henry, a hired hand. If he didn't, he looked inhuman toward an old man.

"You're fond of him, aren't you?" she asked.

"Of course I'm fond of him. He was like a second grandfather to me."

"Fond enough to make a wager?"

Not another one. . . . "What kind of wager?"

He searched their camp, then pointed to a keg a hundred feet away. "If you can rope that barrel, he sleeps in the wagon. If I rope it, you sleep in the wagon."

A glimmer of admiration was born in that instant. He'd found a way to save face and still respect her wishes, for they both knew her skill with a rope far exceeded his. "What if we both rope it?"

"Then we keep throwing until one of us misses."

Chapter 8

$\sim\!\!\!\curvearrowright\!\!\mathcal{C}\!\!\mathcal{O}\!\!\curvearrowleft\!\!\!\sim$

Annie got Wade Henry settled beneath the bed of the wagon in a rawhide hammock normally used to carry firewood or prairie coal just as a thick layer of pewter clouds rolled in. Then, with a heavy heart, she headed toward the tailgate.

She couldn't believe she'd missed. She never missed! Because of one stupid slip of the lariat, an old man was forced to sleep under the wagon instead of inside it. Sure, he'd be elevated out of the mud and muck, but nights got cold on the plains, and with rain coming. . . .

She glanced at the wagon bed, then at the elongated mounds scattered about the ground. The few crates that had been salvageable were stacked in a half circle and the oilskins spread over them to make a lean-to, but it was pitiful shelter at best. Damn Corrigan. Why should *she* get to sleep inside the comfort of the wagon when everyone else was forced to sleep out in the elements? What made her so special?

Nothing, that's what.

With sudden decisiveness, Annie grabbed her own slicker and bedroll and headed toward the horses. She didn't know who was more surprised—Corrigan or her—when she stumbled over him. He sat against a tree trunk near the watering hole, his legs stretched out in front of him. Rain rolled off the brim of the hat tipped low over his eyes and onto the shoulders of his slicker.

"You aren't planning on sleeping out here, are you?" Annie asked.

He took a deep pull of the cheroot cupped in his hand. "Someone's got to keep watch. It would be just my luck that the stallion would try and filch a couple more of my horses tonight."

The remark had her suspicions surfacing once more. If the entire scheme to catch his horses was an act, it was a damned convincing one. He could be sleeping behind the windbreak with the shelter with the rest of his men. Or even in the cooney, instead of Mr. Henry. Corrigan was the boss, after all. Yet here he was, willing to give up his own comfort for those of his men.

And for her.

"You best get bedded down," he said, crushing out his cheroot.

Annie pushed aside the stab of guilt. He was right; morning came early. Clutching her slicker and bedding, she headed for the opposite end of the string of horses, as far from Corrigan as safety would allow. No sense in giving any of his men the wrong impression, should any of them wake up in the middle of the night.

Somehow it didn't surprise her when Corrigan came up behind her a moment later. "Annie, what do you think you're doing?"

A flick of her wrist sent the layer of slicker and quilt rolling open across the ground. "Bedding down."

"Out here?"

"I am not sleeping in that wagon when everyone else is stuck out in the rain."

"The hell you aren't. We made a deal, Annie. Now get your little fanny in the wagon."

She whirled on him and planted her hands on her hips. "Stop telling me what to do. I'm not one of your lackeys."

She saw his temper rise like mercury in mid-July heat. "Either you get into that wagon or I'll put you there."

"You and who else?"

She should have known better than to challenge him; the instant the words flew out of her mouth, she regretted them. But no power on earth could take them back before Corrigan reached her.

He tossed her over his shoulder so quickly she had no time to prepare. Momentum folded her over his shoulder; bone and muscle dug itself into the tender spot between her ribs; her head swam from the swift motion of flying through air. Despite her struggles, she couldn't free herself of the iron tight grip around her thighs. "Damn it, Corrigan! Put me down."

"Not on your life."

Annie continued to demand he let her go. He ignored her. Pounding on his back with her fists had about as much affect as hitting a steel keg with a feather. He slipped and slid down the slight slope next to the barracks, then regained his footing and strode without pause to the wagon, where he flipped up the canvass and dumped her inside.

A second later, he climbed in after her. The already cramped space shrank even further. Annie sat up and glared at him as he settled his frame against the tailgate. "What do you think you're doing?"

"Making sure you stay put. I wouldn't put it past you to sneak around me after I fall asleep just to prove some dumb point—and the last thing I need is for you to get sick on me."

Her hands clenched into fists. "We are not sleeping in this wagon together, Corrigan."

"Oh, yes, we are. Me on this end, you on that end. Keep arguing with me about it and I'll lay on top of you."

Annie didn't make the mistake of thinking he was bluffing.

Furious, she climbed across the wagon bed as far from him as the close confines would allow. Overbearing brute. God, she hated him.

Annie busied herself with spreading her soogan along the floorboards. Though the old canvas above was ripped and torn, it would give her more protection than the slicker she'd planned on huddling inside.

As she listened to Corrigan peeling off his wet clothes, she hoped he wasn't taking everything off. Sharing her quarters with a man was one thing—sharing her quarters with a naked man quite another.

He settled down with a sigh that made Annie grip her pillow and clench her eyes shut. Outside, the storm built. Wind rocked the wagon, raindrops splattered against the canvas, lightning sizzled across the sky; flashes of it glowed through the coarse white covering stretched over her head.

She knew Corrigan was watching her; she could feel it. The heat of his gaze chased off the chill seeping through the cracks of the side boards.

Annie brought the blanket up tighter over her shoulders and tried to ignore his presence. Easier said than done, though. The air seemed thicker, the heat seemed hotter. And there was something about the darkness that made the senses more acute. The scent of him, warm and musky, rose above the dampness of the rain and the staleness of the dust. The sound of his breathing spun a circle of intimacy, reminding Annie how comforting it could be, having a man beside her after a tough day or a lonely night. And she remembered the glory of being able to turn to the man beside her, feel his body pressed against hers, let his hands chase the loneliness away . . .

Thunder crashed above them, making Annie flinch in surprise.

"If the storm bothers you, I don't mind you snuggling up to me."

She pushed back an image of the two of them tangled together. "No thanks."

"Afraid you might enjoy it?" he teased.

That's exactly what she was afraid of. "I'm afraid *you* will."

"Don't you doubt it for minute."

Annie refused to rise to the bait. She had no wish to engage in any sort of conversation with him, much less one with sexual undertones. Maybe if she pretended sleep. . . .

"What's that scent you're wearing?" he asked softly.

She looked at him over her shoulder. He'd clasped his arms behind his head, and the heat of his stare had the air around her crackling. "It's saddle oil."

"No, the other. The flowery one."

Her lilac soap? "Why?"

"It's nice." Silence fell for a moment. Rain pattered on the canvas like little feet.

"There is nothing more evocative than the scent of a woman, did you know that?"

Wonderful. Now she wouldn't be able to use her favorite soap without worrying that it got him excited. Sarcastically she replied, "I suppose if you say it, it must be true. After all, you're the expert, aren't you?"

"You know what they say—practice makes perfect." She caught a flash of white teeth in the darkness. "It starts with a look—the kind that makes her feel as if no one else exists."

His soft, slightly accented words made Annie's breath catch in her throat.

"Then sound—a whisper of her name in the darkness."

She could almost hear it; the whisper of her name. . . .

"Scent comes next. Sometimes soft and alluring, other times musky and potent. And touch. The heat of a hand on flesh. Lips against lips. The heart starts beating, fast and furious—" He turned his head, looked pointedly at her breast. "Just like yours is now."

Her gaping mouth shut with a snap. He was right, damn him; her heart rate had tripled. She crossed her arms over her front and flopped onto her side, not trusting the darkness to hide the perking of her nipples from his view. Damn him. He'd done it on purpose, tried seducing her with words. "You think you know so much about women."

"I know what they want, and I know how to give it."

It wasn't a boast, just a simple statement of fact that had the power to kindle a fire in the pit of her stomach. "And what does she get out of it?"

"She gets to feel needed. Cherished. Desired."

Each word fell in tempo with her heartbeat. "Think about it, Annie.

She did. In excruciating detail. Worse, she had the picture of him wading in the creek to help her. All that muscle. All that power. All that . . . utter and absolute *maleness*. And it could be hers with a crook of her finger. She could hardly remember the last time the blood in her veins felt so hot. "Is bedding women all you think of?" she demanded.

"Bedding you is all I can think of."

Even if she could think of a reply, Annie wasn't sure she could utter it. The timbre of his words made her feel as if she were the most desirable woman on earth. Her tongue stuck to the roof of her mouth, and her heart galloped in her chest. For despite the lightness of his remark, she detected a seriousness that both disturbed and aroused her.

"You don't believe me?"

This is not a conversation she wanted to have with him. It made her remember all the things she'd lost, all the things she missed. The touch of a man, the warmth of his embrace, the sensual connection of two people sharing a mutual need. "I think you'll do or say anything to get what you want from any woman handy."

"Your opinion of me grows more flattering by the day. Tell me, who gave you such a low opinion of men?"

"Who gave *you* such a low opinion of them?"

"What's that supposed to mean?" he asked, sounding confused.

Annie realized that she wasn't quite brave enough to answer. So he was strict with the men who worked for him. So he wasn't as patient and tolerant a teacher as Sekoda had been. Who was she to judge him? "Never mind. Let's just get some sleep."

She rolled onto her side and crunched the blanket beneath her head. What kind of fool was she, anyway? Seduction could just be part of Corrigan's plot to deceive her, and here she lay with him nearby, letting him stir up forgotten memories, letting him weaken her with his words, letting him rouse longings inside her that she'd buried four years ago. . . .

Damn him for making her want to feel like a woman again.

As always, Brett awoke long before the rest of his men. Whistling an aimless tune, he dropped sourdough batter into a dutch oven they'd found in the wagon. He replaced the lid, then crouched near the fire with his hands clasped around a cup of Arbuckle's and waited for the biscuits to bake.

He couldn't say what had put him in such fine spirits. A dismal gray sky hovered over the plains, yet the bright glow of success warmed his insides. Annie would deny it to her last, but he knew damn good and well that she'd been sexually aware of him last night.

Just as he'd been aware of her. Hell, visions of

her racing that mustang had haunted him the entire day. She'd looked glorious—her color high, her blues eyes glittering, her hair tousled from the wind. He'd never wanted to be a horse so bad in his life. If she looked half as glorious in the throes of passion as she had racing the wind, he wasn't sure he'd survive it.

It amazed him that he'd been able to resist rolling across that wagon bed and pulling Annie into his arms. Though it had taken every ounce of control he could muster, he'd managed to keep his distance, even at the cost of another night of misery.

Woo them. Win their trust.

Brett knew better than anyone that the two went hand in hand. And if he kept playing his cards right, he'd have her in his bedroll by the time they found the herd.

"Aw, dadburn it—Dogie!"

Brett glanced behind him and saw Flap Jack sitting on his bedroll, pouring what looked suspiciously like last night's leftovers out of his boot.

"Damned young pup," the tracker grumbled. Catching sight of Dogie, he dashed into the rain in his stockinged feet, stood in the lean-to's entryway, and shook his boot in the air. "When I get my hands on you I'll take a switch to your tail end!"

Brett shook his head and sighed. Sometimes that boy could test the patience of a monk. Then he found himself grinning. He sure kept things interesting, though.

"¿*Qué es ese olor?*" Emilio asked, his nose curling.

Brett's attention shot toward the Dutch oven. "Aw, damn it, my biscuits!" He grabbed the lid, then wrenched his hand back with another curse when his fingers met the hot cast-iron handle. The lid clattered into the fire. Sparks and bits of prairie coal sprayed up, then filtered back down into the kettle.

Emilio and Flap Jack joined him in staring down into the oven at the mounds of dough, scorched around the bottom edges, doughy and sunken on the top.

Flap Jack looked at him. "Canned peaches and hardtack again, Ace?"

Brett grimaced. Five men and one woman in this outfit, and not a damned one of them knew how to cook. "Come on—let's get these supplies gathered up and covered with the tarp before we head out. Someone will be coming back for them sooner or later." He'd make inquiries in Sage Flat over who the wagon belonged to, so he could pay for what they'd used. In the meantime, the least they can do was see that the rest didn't spoil.

He bent over and, wrapping his shirt around his hands, lifted the Dutch oven off the fire.

Wade Henry chose that moment to appear in the opening of the lean-to, mud up to his knees, his eyes wild. "Ace, somethin's wrong with Annie."

Brett dropped the kettle. Pushing past Wade Henry, he raced across the sodden ground, slipping and sliding all the way to the wagon. He yanked Dogie out of the way, gripped the tail gate, and peered inside. In the dim interior, he saw Annie's slight figure curled up in the corner, whimpering like a wounded animal. "Annie? What happened to her?" he demanded of Wade Henry.

"I don't know—I heard noises, and when I came to check on her, I found her like this."

Brett clambered over the end board to her side. His hands hovered above her helplessly. Was she ill? Had he been pushing her too hard? She'd been fine just a few hours ago. . . . "Annie, are you awake?"

A skein of pale hair shielded her face. Needing to see her face, he brought his hand over her shoulder. The instant his fingers grazed her cheek, she wrenched herself around.

Brett fell backward on his heels. His heart dropped to his stomach as he stared down the barrel of a Smith and Wesson six-shooter. "Jesus Christ . . . Annie, put that thing away!"

The order was met with an ominous click.

"Get away from me," she said, her voice as cold and deadly as the weapon in her hand.

"Annie . . ." he croaked, lifting his hands palm-out on either side of his head. The last time she'd pulled a weapon on him, he'd been more surprised by her nerve than afraid she'd shoot him. This time he knew without a doubt she'd pull the trigger. "What are you doing?"

She held the small revolver steady and firm, her mouth tight, her cheeks white, her blue eyes almost black.

Only then did Brett realize that she didn't see him, but something—or someone—else. Lowering his hands with agonizing slowness, Brett kept his gaze locked with hers, willing her to snap out of whatever spell had her in its grip.

"Annie, it's Brett." He cautiously stretched his hand toward her. "Give me the gun, sweetheart."

She tightened her grip on the trigger.

Brett paused. Sweat broke out on his brow. "I'm not going to hurt you, darlin'. Just give me the gun."

A thousands heartbeats passed before the glaze slowly receded from her eyes. Her arms went limp; her shoulders drooped.

He slowly pried the gun from her loose fingers and set it behind him, out of her reach. "Christ. You scared the liver out of me."

She bowed her head. Shaking hands lifted to her brow. "The biscuits were burning," she whispered. "Oh, God, I'm going to be sick . . ."

Brett grabbed the first container within reach—which, unfortunately, was Wade Henry's hat. He sat helplessly by as Annie purged the contents of her stomach, wanting to stroke her hair, rub her back . . . something. Yet he was afraid he'd make things worse if he touched her.

What could have happened? Had she eaten something bad? But none of the others felt poorly. Had the heat gotten to her?

Questions, questions, and no answers.

Her shoulders finally went limp, and the retching stopped.

Brett gently took her arm. "Come on, let's get you some fresh air."

"Don't . . . touch me." She flung off his hand and scrambled toward the front of the wagon, out of his reach. "Don't *ever* touch me."

The venom in her voice made Brett's blood run cold. He lifted his palms in supplication. "Annie, I'm just trying to help."

She turned on him with fire in her eyes. "God dammit, Corrigan—can't you get it through your thick head? I don't want your help! I've survived this long without it and unfortunately, I'll go on surviving. So stop treating me like some fragile flower, and start treating me like you would any other member of this outfit."

Brett felt the color leave his face. Was that what she thought he was doing? Treating her like a fragile flower? And here he thought he was being a friend.

Obviously Annie didn't need one of those.

He gave her a brittle smile. "As you wish."

When he climbed outside, he found the men waiting with their hats in their hands and worry in their eyes.

"She okay, Ace?" Dogie asked.

At that moment, Annie dropped out of the

wagon, paused to glare at Brett, then raced through the mud toward the horses.

"What did you say to her?" Henry demanded, accusation thick in his raspy voice.

Brett watched Annie flee, wanting to go after her so bad his teeth ached. He replayed the incident in his mind, and still couldn't see anything he'd done to make her react so wildly. "Nothing."

"You musta said something—she tore outta this wagon like a bat out of the church belfry."

"I didn't say anything!" The volume and force of his denial echoed across the prairie and bounced back, slamming into Brett's chest with such force it nearly knocked him backward. "Get the men rounded up. We've got horses to find. And for crying out loud, do something with those damned biscuits."

Rain fell throughout the day in a steady drizzle that matched everyone's mood. Annie led the search party, keenly aware that Corrigan and the others traveled some distance behind her. Nausea continued to sit in her belly like liquid lead, the stench of burning biscuits as fresh in her nostrils now as it had been this morning—as fresh as it had been that morning four years ago. . . .

"Annie, me and Bandit are going to round up the horses," Koda said, setting two sets of saddlebags near the front door.

"Don't take too long," she said, sliding a pan of

biscuit dough into the oven. "Breakfast is almost ready."

Strong arms wrapped around her waist. Moist lips pressed against her neck. "I can think of something I'd rather be eating."

Smiling, Annie let her head fall back. "If you keep this up, we'll never find that herd."

He nibbled her earlobe and sent need careening through her nerve endings. "The herd can wait thirty minutes. I can't."

She turned into his arms and covered his mouth with hers. Half their clothes were already unfastened when a sudden riot of screaming shattered the mood.

Sekoda's entire body went alert. Releasing her, he moved on silent moccasined feet toward the window and drew the curtain aside.

"What is it?"

"Something's in the corral scaring the horses."

Annie peered over his shoulder through the window. The mustangs they'd brought in just last month were milling in a tight circle, as wild as the day they'd found them.

Sekoda grabbed the shotgun from above the mantle. Annie grabbed the only other weapon in the house, an iron skillet, and followed him to the door.

"Stay here, Annie."

"I'm going with you. Those are my horses, too."

He paused a moment to brush his finger down her cheek. "Sweet Annie. If I'm worried about you, I won't be able to concentrate on what's out there."

He didn't make it halfway to the corral before a blood-chilling battle cry rent the air. The horses burst *through the fencing; a painted-faced warrior charged toward him, a rifle raised high above his feathered head. Sekoda took aim and fired. No sooner did the Indian tumble off his horse than another rider bore down on her husband. With a mighty swing of his rifle, he clubbed Sekoda across the head.*

"Nooo!"

She could think of nothing beyond reaching Sekoda, and getting him out of the path of the stampeding horses. She raced into the yard, slid her arms under his and dragged him into the house.

Annie sat on the floor of their cabin, Sekoda's head in her lap, blood gushing from the back of his skull. The smell of biscuits burning in the oven twisted with the taste of fear and confusion in her mouth as she pressed a wad of her dress against her husband's wound. Why would Comanche raid the property of one of their own? They'd been living in peace for over a year, with Annie and Sekoda extending them count-less gestures of hospitality and friendship.

None of it made sense to Annie—until the door opened.

A hulking figure blocked the sun. She couldn't see his face, but his voice came at her from the deepest bowels of hell.

"Why, howdy, Annie." A match flared, casting a hellish glow on his smooth, rounded features.

"What do you want?" she whispered, fear choking the breath from her lungs.

He smiled. "Everything you've got."

*   *   *

Jerking her head up, Annie found herself not in the flaming cabin of her nightmares, but on one continuous mesquite flat, dotted here and there with patches of open prairie. She swallowed the lump in her throat and blinked away the blurry film from her eyes. He'd taken it, too. Everything she'd had—her hopes, her dreams, her reason for living. Gone.

The worst thing had been Corrigan's compassion. She'd never wanted to be held so badly by anyone in her entire life as she'd wanted to be held by him. Yet if it hadn't been for him awakening her emotions, the nightmares wouldn't have returned in the first place.

The time had come to get this job done, she decided with a firm set of her jaw and a flick of the reins. If she didn't find any signs of the horses by the time they reached the Palo Duro, she'd leave and take her chances on her own.

Chapter 9

The tension between Annie and Brett grew thick enough to carve with a cleaver. Brett kept his distance as they rode, but it didn't stop him from watching her, from worrying about her. Again and again he tried to make sense of her outburst. It had something to do with burning biscuits, he'd gathered that much. And it had something to do with whatever she was running from. If she would only talk to him, trust him with her secrets. . . .

But Annie didn't talk, and she didn't trust. That grated the most; had he ever given her reason to *mis*trust him? Hadn't he been straight with her from the start?

By the time they reached the South Fork of the Red River, his mood hadn't improved. Swollen from the recent downpour, brackish water churned its way downstream and licked at the clay banks with rapid force, as if warning trespassers away.

It reminded him of Annie; calm and clear until a storm hit, when it lashed out at anything in its path.

"Ace, you want us to pitch camp till the water level drops?" Wade Henry asked.

Brett stared grimly at the water. "No, we're running out of time. We don't even know if we're on the right trail."

"One more day won't make much of a difference," Annie said.

"If I don't catch those fillies before that stallion ruins them, I'll lose my contract."

"What is so damned important about this contract? You obviously aren't hurting for money. Buy yourself more horses."

"Not everything is about money. Sometimes it's about trying to make an honest living. But then, you wouldn't understand that, would you, Annie?"

Brett regretted throwing her own words up in her face the instant they were out. He'd been very careful not to mention what he knew of Annie's nefarious past, partly because he was in no position to cast stones, and partly because he didn't want her bolting on him.

But damn it, she had a way of making him do or say things he wouldn't normally do or say.

Her stricken expression remained in place as he turned to his men. "Flap Jack, start scouting upstream for a place to cross. I'll head downstream. The rest of you stay with Annie."

"Can I go with you, Ace?"

He looked at Dogie, at the hope in his green eyes. Had he ever been that young? That eager?

Once maybe. Until the day life had crushed both under its merciless heel.

With a nod, he agreed to Dogie's company. They rode in silence along the banks, studying the churning waters for a safe place to cross. After a while, the quiet became too quiet.

Brett looked back, just to be sure Dogie was still with him. Sure enough, the kid rode his pinto a horse-length behind, sitting as tall in the saddle as his four-and-a-half foot frame would allow.

He couldn't ever remember being alone with the boy before; from the time Dogie had showed up on his ranch, he'd been under Henry's direction. Now that it was just the two of them, Brett felt vaguely unsettled. He didn't know how to act around kids. His brothers had been much older than him—hell, he'd been an uncle before his fourth birthday.

"You ever drive horses across a creek before?" he asked, just for something to say.

"No, sir. Didn't know anything about horses till I started working for you. What are we watching for?"

"A place where the water doesn't swirl. There are undercurrents that can unbalance a horse. You don't want anything too smooth, though, or you'll find yourself either in water too deep to swim or sinking in quicksand."

They continued on, the horses picking their way through the weeds that grew along the banks. The rushing current camouflaged the sounds of the winds whistling through the cottonwoods. His brow wrinkled. He hoped Annie was all right. Not that he didn't think Emilio or Henry capable of watching out for her . . .

Why was he worrying about her, anyway? She'd made it clear that she didn't want his worry—or anything else. And that, he finally admitted, was what really stuck in his craw. There was nothing more loathsome than failure, yet everywhere he turned with her, he wound up with a mouthful. Three days he'd spent, making a fool out of himself trying to catch her notice. He'd used every approach in the book and he was no closer to having Annie in his bedroll than the day they met. For every forward stride he made with her, she shoved him a mile back.

He hadn't felt this . . . insignificant since he'd been a young boy following his brothers around the farm, wanting nothing more than to be a part of their adventures, only to have them swat him away like a pesky bug.

Hell, his hired hands got more attention from Annie than he did.

Why was he going through so much trouble to please a woman who could hardly abide his presence, much less his touch? A woman who, once this job was completed, would leave him without a backward glance?

Maybe she was right; maybe he should start treating her like any other member of his outfit. Thinking of her as one of his men would certainly douse this flame she kindled inside him.

But thinking of Annie as a man was a hell of a lot easier said than done, especially at night, when he'd lie watching the even rise and fall of her back, or when the snores of his men couldn't drown out the soft sounds she made in sleep, or when her sweet fragrance rose above those of horse and sweat and earth.

Hell, the only thing manly about Annie Harper was her grit.

"Hey, Ace, hear that?"

Diverted, Brett glanced back and noticed Dogie dawdling under the branches of a tree. The sound of buzzing reached him.

"I wonder if they've got any honey," he said, guiding the pinto closer.

"Those aren't honey bees, those are hornets. Get away from there before you get stung."

No sooner were the words out of his mouth than Dogie jumped back and slapped his neck. A second later, the buzzing escalated to an angry hum.

Hornets swarmed from the tree like Comanche on the warpath. The pinto screamed; Dogie screamed.

"Damn it!" Brett spurred Fortune toward Dogie, who danced in a circle, batting frantically at himself.

"Ace! They're gettin' me, they're gettin' me!"

Action ruled over thought as Brett rode into the stinging attack, swung his arm around Dogie's waist, and swept him out of his saddle and into his own. A swift jab of his heels to Fortune's flanks sent the horse barreling into the water. Brett leaned over the side and released the reins, dumping himself and the boy into the murky depths.

Only after his head broke surface did Brett begin to worry that he'd jumped straight from the frying pan into the fire. With Dogie sputtering and coughing over his arm, Brett fought the current and dragged both of them toward the bank.

"What happened?" Annie cried, bringing her mustang to a skidding halt.

"We heard screamin'," Henry said as he and Emilio reached to pull Dogie up the slick bank.

Brett was beyond listening or explaining. All he could hear was the sound of his own heart kicking inside his chest and Dogie's screams as he battled the hornet attack.

Once he and Dogie were on dry land again, he grabbed the boy by the shoulders and gave him a stern shake. "You goddamn fool! What the hell did you think you were doing? I told you to stay away from there!"

"I didn't think—"

"That's right—you didn't think. You did as you damn well pleased and look what happened." He paused and dragged in a deep breath. "Just . . . get the hell out of my sight."

For a moment the kid stared at him, his eyes moist, his lower lip quivering. Then he tore away from the creek.

Brett almost went after him. The urge hit him hard and fast, like a maverick's kick to the gut. Yet his feet seemed rooted to the spot, and before he could command them to move, Henry followed in the kid's wake.

Brett shook off the lingering urge and took stock of his surroundings. A hornet or two still cut through the air but most of the others were gone.

He felt Annie's gaze on him, hard and burning, and when he finally dared to look at her, her expression was pure condemnation.

With a curse, he spun away. What else had he expected? Her understanding? Her empathy?

He flopped down at the edge of the creek and whisked his shirt over his head. His back stung in a dozen places where the hornets had speared him. Filling his hand with a glob of wet earth, he then slapped it on several welts on his chest.

He should have known bringing Dogie along would be a mistake. The boy was too impulsive. Always getting into mischief, always pulling pranks on people. Always thinking danger was a toy to be played with.

Brett scooped up another handful of mud and slapped it on his upper arm. Why hadn't the kid just *listened*?

"Didn't your mama ever teach you that it isn't smart to stir up a hornet's nest?"

Brett's hand froze in the process of reaching for a sting on his shoulder blade. A surprised glance over his shoulder brought Annie into view. He'd have figured she'd be tending to Dogie.

It surprised him more when she lowered herself to her knees behind him. A second later he felt the cooling relief of mud coat one of the welts at the center of his back.

Her touch was so tender as she smeared more than a dozen stings that he couldn't speak. Of all the ways he'd imagined Annie laying her hands on him, not one fantasy had involved the dredges of South Fork. It aroused him nonetheless, and he wanted to take her right there.

With his emotions strung as tightly as they were, though, he wouldn't be gentle, and Annie deserved more than a rough tumble in the muck.

So he kept his fists tightly clenched, and suffered the torture of her touch in silence.

After a while, a voice of soft steel broke through the hush. "You didn't have to be so hard on him, you know."

Brett stiffened. She always took up for the boy. "Give him an inch, he'll take a mile. My men will always know who ramrods this outfit."

"How can any of them forget, with you shoving it down their throats every time they turn around?"

Brett swung to face her. Her eyes glittered like

wildfire and a vein in her neck throbbed. "Who the hell made you their champion?"

"Who the hell made you their keeper?"

"They did," he spat. "Each and every one of them—from the moment they showed up on my ranch looking for a way to put food in their bellies and a roof over their head. There isn't a man in my outfit that doesn't know what's expected of him."

"And if they don't meet your expectations, there will be hell to pay. Dogie's human, he made a mistake. Not everyone can be as perfect as you."

Her sarcasm didn't escape Brett—nor any of the men standing nearby, listening to the exchange.

Brett sharply averted his gaze toward the horizon. His jaw clenched; his breaths came hot and heavy. No one talked to him the way Annie did and got away with it. No one. And if he started making allowances for her, he'd have every man in his outfit believing him a push-over. "I'll make a deal with you—I won't tell you how to handle your horses, and you don't tell me how to handle my men."

"Fine," she snarled. "But you'll never catch me kowtowing to you the way they do."

No, he didn't expect he would, Brett thought, watching her spin away. Annie had a will of iron that couldn't be bent or shaped, no matter how hot he stoked the fire.

And therein lay the problem.

Her smart-assed attitude and the rebellious glitter in her eyes drove Brett passed reason.

Christ. He couldn't take this anymore. He grabbed his hat and strode toward Fortune. He had to get out of here, for a little while at least, because he had a feeling that if he didn't get his emotions under control soon, he'd wind up hurting somebody.

Her throat tight and burning, Annie examined the mud-smeared stings covering Dogie's scrawny back. Emilio and Henry had urged her to tend to Corrigan while they saw to Dogie, and as far as she could tell, he hadn't fared nearly as badly as Corrigan. God, the man's back had been all but covered with stings. Even now she felt pain to her own flesh at the thought of the insects attacking him.

Why his pain would affect her so strongly she couldn't say, nor did she want to examine it. It was so much better—and so much easier—to deal with him when they were going head to head. At least then, she didn't feel this compelling need to hold him. To touch him. To curl herself around him and protect him from the world's evils, the way he'd protected Dogie from the swarm.

"Miss Annie?"

"Hmm?" She lifted her gaze and found Dogie watching her through serious eyes.

"I owe you."

Her brows furrowed. "What for?" she asked, her voice unusually raspy.

"I heard you standin' up for me back there. I ain't had anyone do that in a long time."

She swallowed the lump in her throat and pulled Dogie's shirt down over his back. "One of these days you're gonna have to learn to stand up for yourself."

"He'll fire me," Dogie replied softly. "I ain't got no place left to go."

Annie grimaced in sudden irritation at the power Corrigan seemed to hold over his men. "There's always someplace else to go."

Dogie lifted soulful green eyes to her. "For you, maybe. Everyone wants you, Annie. Even Ace." He ducked to fasten the buttons of his plaid shirt. "Especially Ace."

She stared at Dogie's bent head with a frown. Sensations came crashing down upon her—of the warmth she felt each time Corrigan looked at her, of the tingles down her spine when she heard his voice. Of more intimate reactions when he came too near. . . .

If Corrigan's desires were so obvious that a thirteen-year-old could recognize them . . . were hers?

Sage Flat was like a dozen other range towns thrown up to cater to the needs of local cowboys: four brothels, two watering holes, and a livery lined the disreputable side of the dusty dirt road;

a hotel, barbershop, and general merchandisery constituted the respectable side.

Brett had chosen this particular town to rendezvous because there was no law to speak of, yet the few stares in Annie's direction reminded him that the law wasn't her only threat. Best just to get her settled out of sight before she attracted too much notice.

Recognizing a pack of Triple Ace mounts stationed at the hitching rail in front of the Silver Spur Saloon and Casino, Brett told Annie, "I need to meet up with the rest of my men and see if they've had any luck spotting the horses. There's a hotel across the street. Get a room as my missus."

"The hell I will."

Brett turned on her so fast he nearly threw his neck out of joint. "The hell you *won't*! For once, don't give me any guff. It's for your own safety."

She leveled a glare on him that would have flattened the Rocky Mountains, but Brett couldn't decide which she objected to more: being told what to do, or using the protection of his name. It nettled him that she'd not even accept that much from him.

Well, too damn bad. He had enough on his mind without worrying about the kind of attention she'd bring to herself if word got out that she was in town, and he refused to let her make him feel guilty for trying to keep her safe.

He dismounted, flipped the reins around the hitching rail and stepped up onto the boardwalk, only to discover he'd acquired himself a shadow.

Brett grabbed Dogie back by the scruff of his collar. "Where do you think you're going?"

He puffed out his scrawny chest. "A man's got a powerful thirst."

"So slake it in the horse trough. You're staying with Annie."

"Come on, Dogie," came Annie's tight response. "We'll find something to keep us busy."

Brett waited until they'd crossed the street and disappeared through the doorway of the two-story excuse for a hotel before he pushed his way into the Silver Spur. The familiar sounds of a lazy weekday afternoon greeted him as he walked through the door: the clink of a glass against glass, the intermittent plunk of piano keys from an undeveloped tune, the monotone snoring from a sot in the corner with more time on his hands than ambition in his heart.

"Ace, over here!"

He spotted Tex and his crew waving him over to a table in the back corner. A week's worth of trail dust and whiskers made them almost unrecognizable, and made Brett acutely aware of his own unsavory state. First a report, then a bath. His priorities in line, Brett meandered around a table piled with chips, pocket watches, and folds of paper—some triple digit bank notes; others, deeds to land from those who believed they would triple their holdings by a turn of a card. The sight was as familiar to Brett as his own name; he'd lived it from the time he'd turned fourteen and left his father's house with nothing more than the clothes on his back, a deck of cards in his pocket, and a vow in his heart to prove the old bastard wrong.

"When did you ride in?" he asked Tex when he reached the table.

"Hell, the dust ain't settled yet."

One of the ropers vacated a chair. Brett dragged his hat off his head, lowered himself into the chair, and crossed his forearms on the table top. "We haven't seen so much as a hoof-print of those horses. I hope you've had better luck."

"They might as well have been wearin' a sign on their asses that read 'follow me.' We tracked 'em all the way from Clarenden into the north end of the canyon."

Brett would have been relieved if he didn't sense more was to follow. "And?"

"You ain't gonna like it, Ace. We gave chase. Woulda caught up to him, too, if that devil hadn't started zig-zagging through a prairie dog town north of Palo Duro Creek."

Brett knew what was coming the instant Tex paused to take a healthy swallow of whiskey.

"Two mares went down in holes," he said. "We had no choice but to shoot 'em."

He sank against the back of the chair and rubbed his brow. Sonofabitch. Not only had that devil stolen his fillies, but now he'd caused the destruction of two fine mares.

"We figured you'd be hitting town soon and

would want to know, so we came here to wet our whistle before headin' out again."

"You figured right." He could use a good sousing about now, himself.

As if in answer to a prayer, a bottle of bourbon appeared on the table in front of him. He glanced up and found himself the object of undisguised appreciation.

"Howdy, stranger." Two fresh glasses joined the bottle. "Buy a girl a drink?"

Sloe-Eyed Chloe, as they called her, was as sultry a doxy as they came, with cat-like eyes, a milky complexion, and a bosom that should have been outlawed.

Tex cleared his throat. "Uh, boys, looks like the boss's got better things to do than swig whiskey with us saddle tramps." He stood. "We'll meet up with ya in the mornin', Ace."

After the men moved their drinks and cards to other tables, Chloe slid into Brett's lap and twined her arms around his neck. "It's about time you ambled into town." She leaned forward, the motion pushing the rounded curve of one breast perilously close to escaping its scanty confines. "I put fresh sheets on the bed."

Women had a delightful way of distracting a man from his woes, and Chloe, he'd discovered, was one of the most talented in the business. She'd helped him pass many a troubled night, and after Annie's cold shoulder, her interest should have been a balm to his bruised ego.

Instead, it only made him feel more inadequate. How was it that Annie could take the one arena in which he felt totally confident, the one manner that made him feel worthy of being a man, and shoot it down like a tin can on a fence? He could gain the favors of other women just by walking into a room, yet not Annie. Was he so repulsive to her?

"What do you know of a woman named Annie Harper?" he found himself asking Chloe.

"Who?"

The blank answer reminded Brett that few knew her by any other name than the notorious one she'd earned for herself. "Mustang Annie."

"Oh, her." Chloe tucked her chin and looked up at him from beneath lashes thickened with kohl paste. "About as much as anyone, I suppose. She used to live on a spread south of here with her grandfather. They'd come into town now again to pick up supplies but otherwise pretty much kept to themselves. One day, they stopped coming. Some say Clovis caught the gold fever, others think vigilantes got him."

"Why would vigilantes want him?"

"Rustling. One of the best—or worst, depending on the way you look at it."

"And the girl?"

With a lift of her eyebrows, Chloe drew back. "Aren't you the curious cat? You aren't thinking on trading me in, are you, darlin'?"

The note of jealousy in her tone caused Brett to draw her closer to him. "Now, why would I want sour milk when I've got sweet cream right here in my hands?" A satisfied purr against his neck told Brett that his sweet talk had soothed the scrape to her vanity. "It's business, sweetheart. Just business."

Chloe nibbled on his earlobe. "What kind of business could a lusty fella like you have with a scrawny thing like her?"

Had it been a man asking, Brett would've deflected the question with nothing more than a steely-eyed warning. But he knew Chloe only wanted an assurance of her own prowess. "Why, horses, darlin'." He smiled. "Mustang Annie has a reputation for capturing wild horses. I've got one that needs catching."

"Is that all you men ever think about? Horses?" Chloe straddled Brett and pushed herself against him. "Maybe if I grow myself a mane and a tail you'd think about *me* a little." She helped herself to a drink from Brett's glass, and even that seemed a design in seduction. Her tongue traced the rim of the glass as she gazed up at him through her lashes.

Weeks of celibacy, the press of her womanhood against him, and the erotic play of her mouth on his glass had Brett hardening immediately.

Feeling inexplicably shamed over his body's reaction to Chloe, he gripped her hips to still her. "The girl. What happened to her?"

Chloe shrugged carelessly. "Last I heard, she married up with some half-breed drifter. Nobody's seen hide nor hair of her since."

Brett froze, and his arousal shrank as quickly as it had risen. His heart plunged to the pit of his stomach. Married? His Annie? To an Indian?

Where was he now? Dead? Alive? In prison?

Again, the questions. But this time, by God, he'd get some answers—one way or another.

Chapter 10

Sitting on the balcony in a chair tilted back on its rear legs, her boots propped on the railing, Annie watched the saloon across the street. A humid breeze carried to her the faint plunking of a piano and the nicker of horses at the hitching rails. Dogie sat cross-legged in another chair beside her, his head bent over the strips of leather she'd produced from her own saddlebags. The idea of teaching Dogie how to make halters had been stirring at the back of her mind ever since that first showdown with Corrigan, and with nothing to do but wait, now seemed as good a time as any.

"You don't talk much, do ya, Annie?"

She continued staring at the street below, remaining tense and alert. Towns made her edgy, especially this one. It had been a long time since she'd been in Sage Flat, but people had long memories. "You talk enough for the both of us."

"I reckon I do." He turned and looked at her over his shoulder. Several angry welts still remained on his angular face as souvenirs from his battle with the hornets. "You don't have to stay with me," he said. "I can take care of myself."

She couldn't resist ruffling his cap of wheat-gold hair. He might resemble Corrigan a bit but he reminded her so much of herself sometimes it was frightening. "I thought *you* were supposed to be protecting *me*."

"You don't think they'll come after ya here, do ya?"

Annie considered playing dimwit, yet it seemed pointless to deny what the kid had known from the moment he'd seen her back at the ranch. He might be young, but he wasn't stupid.

"They might." No sense in sugar coating the truth either. A horse thief was a horse thief. Even if they couldn't prove her crimes in Texas, she'd clinched the bounty on her head the day she'd fled Nevada. U.S. Marshals were probably on her trail as they spoke, and it wouldn't take long before they started making comparisons between Annie Harper and Mustang Annie. She could only hope others didn't discover the truth as easily as Dogie.

"Keep practicing on that hackamore," she told him. "Before you know it, folks will be buying them from you faster than you can make them."

"Your granddaddy teach you to make halters like this?"

A memory of Sekoda sitting behind her, his long, deft fingers helping her fashion soft leather strips into head gear for the wild ponies, evoked a bittersweet smile. He'd been so patient with her clumsiness, so persistent in her tutoring. She'd decided to teach Dogie not because she had a soft heart, like Corrigan had accused, but because she saw the same promise in him that Sekoda had once seen in her—and it seemed a shame to let that go to waste. "No, someone else very dear to me taught me how."

She pushed the image to the back of her mind and returned her attention to the saloon, only to have her heart freeze in her chest at the sight of the man stepping onto the boardwalk.

With his back turned to her she couldn't see his face, but something about the way he stood, feet splayed, his hands resting on the butts of a pair of holstered pistols, sent a chill up her spine.

A saloon girl from the drinking establishment next door paused to chat. Whatever she said inflamed the man; he grabbed her by the arms, hauled her against his chest, and covered her mouth with his. Annie's breath stuck in her throat. Horror crept into the fringes of her mind. A knot of revulsion uncoiled in her belly. Annie remained fixated on the scene, even as the nightmare once again began to unfold.

He swaggered with cocky confidence into her cabin. She stared up at him, her arms tightening around Sekoda's shoulders. The brim of his hat shadowed his face but she would know him anywhere, despite the twelve months that had passed since she'd last seen him.

"I warned you what would happen if you left me, Annie."

She couldn't speak over the tight knot of fear in her windpipe.

Another man appeared behind him, and Annie recognized him as the one who had struck Sekoda with his rifle. "Get out of my house," she ordered in a high-pitched voice hardly identifiable as her own.

He laughed. Then with the swiftness of a serpent, he seized her by the arm and wrenched her away from her husband. Annie stifled a scream.

"What's the matter, Annie?" She shied away from the hot, fetid breath scorching her cheek. He pinched her jaw between his thumb and forefinger and forced her to look at him. Cold, angry eyes drilled into her. "We're not good enough for you anymore?"

With a shove to her jaw he sent her flying across the room. She landed on the table beside the bed she shared with Sekoda; a kerosene lamp crashed to the floor. Annie crawled backward across the broken glass, oblivious to the shards boring into her elbows. He advanced toward her like a mountain lion intent on its prey. Fingers like talons clutched the front of her dress and rent it from neck to navel. Annie's breath came in panicked gasps. She reached behind her, searching blindly for a weapon. Her fingers grazed the base of the lantern. Just as she brought her arm up and swung, he caught her wrist. Annie cried out, feeling as if he were snapping her wrist in half.

"You filthy whore," he sneered. *"Wake that breed up,"* he ordered the second man. *"I want him to see what happens to those who betray me."*

The very real sound of laughter snapped Annie to the present activity. The woman beat against the man's shoulder with a futile fist. His comrades, still on horseback, cheered and whistled and howled their approval.

Dogie laughed along with them. "Looks like that doxy's gettin' a taste of a real man."

Without thinking, Annie cracked him across the face, surprising herself as much as Dogie.

He looked up at her through wide green eyes. A red imprint of her hand stood out against his pale cheek. "What did you do that for?"

"I don't ever want to hear you talk like that again. I don't care what a woman chooses to do with her life; that doesn't give any man the right to treat her rough."

"But they like it when a man takes charge."

"Who the hell told you that?"

"No one. I've been around—"

"Have you ever seen Corrigan mistreat a woman?"

"No."

"Have you ever seen him have trouble getting a woman?"

"No."

"Then if you want to know what women like, ask him."

She could hardly believe she was defending

the man, much less turning this impressionable kid to him for "training."

Dogie visibly wilted. "He won't tell me nothin'—he barely knows I'm alive unless I'm doing something wrong."

Wasn't that the truth? The whole camp noticed Dogie then, too.

They fell quiet for a long while. Annie's nerves continued to sit on edge and she opened her pouch of makings, needing the comfort of a cigarette. Even after the man on the boardwalk disappeared into the saloon, she couldn't make herself relax.

"Think Ace is giving Chloe what women like?" Dogie asked quietly, distracting her.

"Chloe?"

"His favorite. He always visits her when he goes to the Silver Spur."

Annie felt as if she'd been turned inside-out. Was that why he'd given in so easily when she'd demanded he treat her like his men? Because he'd known he'd be paying a call on his harlot?

What the hell did it matter, anyway? She didn't want him. She didn't want any man. Yet the thought of Corrigan looking at another woman the way he looked at her, of his strong hands stroking her body, his mouth caressing her flesh. . . .

"Which room is hers?"

"The one on the corner, I think. Why?"

"You ever made a stink bomb before?"

* * *

Annie slipped back into her room a half an hour later. Still grinning over her and Dogie's antics, she stripped out of her shirt. She'd give her eye teeth to have seen the look on Corrigan's face when the sulfuric bottle flew through the open window. No doubt he and his painted piece of fluff had just taken up again in another room, but it gave Annie some satisfaction to spoil at least part of his enjoyment.

A knock on the door startled her from her thoughts. Reflexively she clutched her shirt to her breast, then reached for the pistol in her boot just as the door opened.

The broad-shouldered frame that filled the entrance almost made her wilt in relief. Annie closed her eyes and released her grip on the revolver.

She didn't bother asking how he'd gotten in. Though it had galled her to the core, she'd taken the room as his missus, figuring it would make it more difficult to trace her. Unfortunately, it also meant no one would question his request for a key.

"I don't recall inviting you in here, Corrigan."

"I don't recall asking for an invitation."

"What's the matter, didn't your little doxy give you what you came for?" she taunted.

His lips curved into a smile that didn't come close to reaching his eyes. "Oh, she gave me more than I expected."

He strolled to the window overlooking the street below. Moonlight pouring in through the glass silhouetted his head and torso. The sight reminded Annie of the night she'd seen him on the prairie, practicing with the lasso. Bare backed, muscles rippling.

Tension uncoiled in her stomach and a forgotten and wholly unwelcome desire began to tingle through her breasts.

"Where's your man, Annie?"

The question hit her like a maverick's kick, ripping the ground out from beneath her, knocking the breath out of her. "What?"

"Your man." He pinned her with a ruthless stare. "I was told you'd married and I want to know where he is."

Annie's mind reeled. How had he found out? What did he know? Obviously, not enough, or he wouldn't have barged into her room in the middle of the night to interrogate her.

Who could have told him? Other than an occasional trip to trade horses, she and Sekoda had lived in almost total isolation, partly for her protection and by choice. They'd never missed the company of other people; they'd had each other.

Even now, what they'd shared remained her most treasured memories . . . and her greatest sorrow.

She pushed shaking fingers through her hair and lifted her chin. "It's none of your damned business."

"I'm making it my business."

"You're still sore because I won't sleep with you."

He laughed. "Don't flatter yourself. Contrary to what you might think, I do have other things on my mind besides getting between your legs— I have my men to worry about. I'm responsible for them, and the last worry I need is having some enraged husband storming into my camp one night after you, and putting them in danger."

Annie might have laughed at the ludicrousness of the statement if it weren't so sad. "That's one worry you'll never have. And if you ever pry into my personal affairs again, you'll be lookin' for another mustanger. Now, get out."

The room all but hummed as she matched him glare for glare.

Just when she thought she'd have to shove him out herself, he gave her a mocking bow and strode out of the room.

After the door slammed behind him, Annie sank to the bed, trembling with incredulity and cold rage. Damn Corrigan. He had no right digging onto her past with Sekoda. And why would he want to? What threat could a dead man possibly pose? Sekoda was no danger to him.

She was.

Outside in the hallway, Brett pressed his back against Annie's door, struggling with the gamut of emotions roiling inside him. Frustration. Rage. Jealousy.

The last was foreign to Brett. He'd never before cared whose boots had been under the beds of women he'd taken a fancy to, but the idea of someone else getting from Annie what he'd spent the last week coveting filled him with a sense of possession. Invasion. Much like the stallion stealing his fillies.

He tried telling himself that it was none of his business, that what Annie did with her life outside this job was her own affair, yet a sense of betrayal gripped him like barbed wire, and he knew he'd not rest until he discovered what happened to the man she'd pledged herself to. If Annie wouldn't give him the answers, he'd have to get them elsewhere.

And he knew just who to start with.

It didn't take long to track Henry down, for wherever the horses went, Henry could be found.

Brett strode into the livery, his rapid pace stirring up dust and kicking up hay stems as he sought out noises in the last stall.

Henry looked up at him over Fortune's back; the brush halted in his hand. "Ace—somethin' wrong?"

"I want to know what happened to Annie's husband," Brett stated. "Tell me everything you know about him—his name, where he's from, where he is now."

Taken off guard, Henry's mouth opened, then closed. Then he shook his head. "I'm afraid I can't he'p ya there." He went back to sliding the brush down the stallion's neck. "Annie was just a young'un last time I saw her. I never knew she'd gotten hitched, much less met the feller she hitched up with."

"Then find out."

"With all due respect, those are questions you should be askin' Annie."

"I did. She'd just as soon put a bullet between my eyes as tell me anything about herself. She'll tell you, though. She trusts you."

"At one time, maybe, but Annie's different now. Keeps to herself more."

The careful choosing of words had Brett's eyes narrowing. "Are you refusing an order?"

Henry stared at Fortune's mane for a moment before lifting troubled eyes to Brett. "I reckon I am. I've always done everything you ever asked of me, Ace, but this time you're askin' somethin' of me that I just cain't give."

"Can't? Or won't?"

Standing taller and straighter than Brett had ever seen him stand before, Henry answered. "Both."

His emotions pooled together into one vat of fury. What was this, some sort of conspiracy? But short of threatening the old man with his life, Brett couldn't see any way of forcing his foreman to talk.

He left the livery feeling out of control and out of sorts, only to come up short at the sight of Ike Savage descending the steps of the Silver Spur. Oddly enough, the man didn't appear half as surprised to see Brett as Brett was to see him.

He smiled cordially. "Well, Corrigan, fancy seeing you here."

"Savage. You're straying a bit farther south than usual."

"Enjoying the finer comforts of life." He indicated the Silver Spur, then rocked back on his heels. "I hear you're missing a couple of horses."

"Where'd you hear that?" Brett asked, sliding his thumb into his front pocket and cocking his hip in a casual pose.

"Same place I heard you hired a woman to find them."

"Word spreads fast." No use denying such a indisputable fact.

"That it does. Word also has it that the woman bears a striking resemblance to a rustler known as Mustang Annie. Some even say she *is* Mustang Annie."

Brett went on instant alert. Only a handful of people were even aware that Annie had joined his outfit. "Maybe you shouldn't believe everything you hear."

"Never said I believed it, but I do find it puzzling."

"Why's that?"

He leveled on Brett a stony-eyed stare. "Because I killed Mustang Annie four years ago."

Chapter 11

His grip loose around the neck of a bourbon bottle, Brett spent the rest of the night seeking oblivion in drink. He hadn't thought anything could shock him more than learning Annie had married.

He'd been wrong.

He tipped the bottle against his mouth, letting the bourbon's sweet fire burn its way into his belly.

Mustang Annie was becoming more mysterious by the minute. Savage claimed that he'd caught her with a herd of stolen horses, and when he'd tried to take her into custody, he'd been jumped from behind by a vicious savage intent on killing him. In the struggle, a lantern fell and caught the house on fire.

When asked why this fact wasn't made public, Savage told him that he'd been running for sheriff at the time. How would it have looked if he'd gone public with killing a woman—even if by accident, and even if that woman had been a known criminal?

The more Brett struggled to separate fact from fiction, the more confused it made him. Jesse claimed Annie was a celebrated mustanger before turning con artist and horse thief; Wade Henry claimed she'd been a spirited child with an affinity for horses; Chloe claimed she was the wife of an Indian and Savage claimed she was dead.

Were Mustang Annie and Annie Harper the same woman?

If they were, and Mustang Annie was dead, then who was his Annie?

And what about this husband? Who was he? *Where* was he? Did he have anything to do with the "unfinished business" she claimed had compelled her to join his outfit in the first place?

And how did Wade Henry fit into the picture?

Nothing made sense. And the only one who could give him the answers he sought was Annie. Brett knew without a shred of doubt that if he confronted her, demanding answers, he'd scare her off or wind up with a bullet between his eyes. And if by some stroke of fate she did give him answers, how could he be sure they'd be the truth? She wouldn't even be honest about her husband.

The only thing Brett knew with any degree of certainty was that Annie was running from something—or someone—and until he could unravel the tangled threads of this puzzle, he wasn't going to let her out of his sight.

The resolve only strengthened itself as they left Sage Flat the next morning. When they reached the north end of the Palo Duro where Tex said he'd last seen the horses, Brett split the crew up again, sending one party led by Tex along the rim of the canyon, and another led by Flap Jack to scout ahead through the one-hundred twenty mile ravine known for its hardwood trees, rock formations and renegade hideouts.

Wade Henry, Dogie, Emilio and Annie made up Brett's crew. They picked their way down an old Indian trail that wound into the canyon. Stratum walls of red clay and sparkling gray limestone banked them on either side for a mile or so before they hit level ground littered with sage, mesquite, and ocotillo cactus. Trees abounded in the sandy soil: hickory, huckleberry, and cottonwood.

They drew the horses to a halt beside the Prairie Dog Fork of the Red River that ran the length of the canyon.

"Mustangs have been here," Annie said, studying the ground. "The way this grass has been eaten to nubs, it looks like they were here for a while."

"How long ago?" Brett asked.

"Hard to say. A few days. A week, maybe. They don't seem to be in any hurry."

"At least we know we're on the right track."

She looked up at him with such surprise that Brett couldn't resist asking, "What, did you think this was all some sort of game, Annie? That I invented the horses just to get close to you?"

The flash of guilt in her eyes told him that the thought—or a similar one—had occurred to her at least once. The depths of her distrust ground into him like crushed glass. "Let's get something straight—I'm too old for games. When I want something, I prefer honesty over subterfuge. I'd think that you'd have learned that by now."

Annie held his stare as resentful tension built between them. He'd been silent and withdrawn since leaving Sage Flat that morning, and she could tell by the simmering anger in his tone that their last conversation remained as fresh in his mind as it did in hers.

Was he now simply stating a fact, or was it a warning? Annie couldn't be sure, but he was right about one thing—if she'd learned anything about him, it was that he had little tolerance for secrets or deception, and his bitterness made her feel almost guilty for not telling him about Koda. Almost guilty for ever being married at all.

Why did she feel as if she'd somehow betrayed him?

No. She'd not let some misplaced emotion taint the one good thing she'd done with her life, the brief year of happiness she'd experienced with someone else.

One thing she could not deny, though: she might not completely trust Brett Corrigan, but she no longer believed he was planning on leading her to the authorities.

They made camp that evening near the mouth of a cave Annie remembered from her raiding days. As usual, Corrigan started barking orders: "Emilio, secure the horses; Henry unload the supplies; Annie, fetch the firewood—"

"I'll get it, Ace," Dogie jumped in.

"You've got horses to curry."

Annie glared at him. "I told you in the beginning that I don't take orders, Corrigan."

"You also said you wanted me treating you like any member of this outfit, and the first rule is you never argue with the boss."

He'd cornered her there.

Pressing her lips tightly together, Annie slid out of the saddle. After stripping Chance and giving her a good brushing, she scoured the area for dead branches. Mr. Henry joined her a few minutes later to help.

"Keep your eyes peeled for a nice sturdy one that I can use to clout your boss over the head," she said.

"He is bein' a bit ornerier than usual."

"He's being a complete ass, Mr. Henry." Annie picked up an arm-sized limb that would suit her purposes.

"Just Henry, Annie. I ain't been a mister in a long time." After a moment, he quietly added, "He's asking about you."

She knew he was talking about Corrigan. "Let him ask."

"He wants me digging up information about your marriage."

She whipped around. "That yellow-bellied—why did ask you to do his dirty work?"

"He thinks you trust me more."

"What did you tell him?"

"You ought to know better than that."

Annie sighed. "You're right." A lot of years and a lot of secrets had passed between the two of them, and she'd never been given reason to believe he'd betray her, nor would she dream of betraying him. However, she'd also seen the way all the men jumped to Corrigan's bidding. "There are things in my life that are only my business, and I resent him for trying to force you into making me talk about them."

"I've never seen him so curious about a woman before."

Annie looked across the campsite and found Brett staring at her with that heavy-lidded intensity she found so unnerving. "He just wants to poke me."

"I think it's more than that. I think he's taking a shine to you."

That shine had dulled real quick the minute a brassy bit of fluff stepped into the picture. Surprised that the harlot still bothered her, Annie finished loading her arms with branches and carried them up to the cave where Emilio sat with his legs hanging over the edge.

She dumped the firewood near the mouth, brushed her hands off, then moved to stand near

Emilio. Following the direction of his wistful gaze, she realized he was looking at a red formation veined with white gypsum that resembled the ruffles on a skirt. "They call them the Spanish Skirts," she said, not sure if he understood.

He seemed to, because he nodded. "*Me recuerdan de mi esposa.*"

"Sorry, Emilio, I don't understand a word of what you're saying."

"He says the cliffs remind him of his wife."

Annie looked over at Corrigan, who leaned against the wall behind Emilio, smoking a cheroot. "I didn't realize he was married."

"There's a lot of that going around."

She averted her face and gritted her teeth. Damn it, he would *not* make her feel guilty for not telling him about Sekoda. "What's your wife's name?" she asked Emilio.

Corrigan repeated the question in Spanish.

"Rosalina," Emilio answered with a smile that left no question as to the woman's place in his heart. "*Ella es embarazada. Voy a vender los caballos, como Señor Ace. Llamaré a ellos cuando ho criado una manada grande y cuando ho comprado un rancho pequeño para degarle a mi hijo.*"

Again, Corrigan interpreted. "He says he plans on catching a few from the herd and selling them to buy a small ranch where he can raise his children. He hopes for a son."

"I suppose every man does."

"Not every man. Some would rather have daughters."

Somehow it didn't surprise her that he'd prefer daughters.

"¿Y usted, Aña? ¿Quiere usted un baron o una embra?"

"Emilio's asking if you preferred a boy or a girl."

For a moment, Annie couldn't speak. Another dream gone, another promise ripped away. "Neither. I won't be having any children."

"Why not? You're still young."

"Because there's nothing inside me anymore."

Horrified that she'd bared such a private and painful testimony, she hastened to the woodpile and began arranging the branches in a circle. All the while, she felt his stare drill into her back.

When Annie could take it no longer, she rounded on him. "Will that be all, *master*?"

"Actually, now that you mention it, nobody has fetched water or unloaded supplies."

Annie clenched and unclenched her fists. He was perfectly capable of doing both those chores yet he seemed to take great delight in pushing them off on her. "If you think to break me, you're in for a surprise, Corrigan."

She stormed outside to the packhorses for buckets to fetch water, only to burst into laughter at the sight that met her eyes.

Every mane and tail of every horse in the remuda had been meticulously braided and tied with bright pink ribbons.

Dogie had struck again.

Chapter 12

〰️◯◯〰️

"**D**ogie," Annie whispered, shaking the boy awake before dawn the next morning. "Let's go for a swim."

He lifted his head and squinted at her. "Huh?"

"Come on, I know a great place."

"A swim?" He sat up fully. "Now?"

"It's not far. If I don't get out of here, I'll go mad."

He looked around, then nodded. Annie waited outside the cave while Dogie grabbed his boots. He joined her a couple of minutes later, hopping on one foot while he shoved the other in a boot. His cheek bore creases from where the sleeve of his shirt had been scrunched against his face all night.

"What about Ace?" he whispered so as not to wake the others.

"He can find his own swimming hole."

Dogie kept up with her swift pace as she led him to one of her favorite places in the world. He stared at the canyon wall, a smooth, steep incline of rock that just tempted one to slide down it into the pooling water below. "Wow!"

"I know—isn't it wonderful?" Annie grinned. She stopped at the sandy bank of the pool and stripped herself of her boots, trousers and shirt. Dogie did likewise. "I used to come here when I was your age."

Clad in a pair of long-handled underwear with the legs cut up to her knees and the sleeves shorn just above the elbow, Annie drew out her lasso. Moments later, a rope hung from the branches of a sturdy cottonwood tree.

"You want to try?"

"What do I do?"

"Stick your foot in that loop just like you would a stirrup, grab hold of the rope, then swing yourself over the water and let go. Here, I'll give you a push to get you started."

Annie clasped her hands together to make a foothold.

Dogie quickly caught on, and soon the two of them were taking turns dropping into the bracing depths of the creek. The rising sun seemed to smile on their enjoyment, and the cottonwood branches around them embraced their laughter.

They spent another hour frolicking in the water until, finally free of the tension she'd been carrying for two days, Annie climbed onto the banks and dropped with pleasurable exhaustion upon a bed of reeds. "God, I needed this," she gasped.

"Ace is gonna kill us if he finds out what we've been doing."

"He won't find out." After a second's pause, she asked, "Dogie . . . is Corrigan your father?" The question had been niggling at her ever since the day of the hornet's attack. She'd noticed a vague resemblance between the two from the first time she'd seen them together, but until that day, until Corrigan had stared into eyes an identical shade of green as Dogie's, she hadn't made the connection.

Laying beside her, Dogie's head snapped around to her. "How did you find out?"

"Call it a hunch. He doesn't know, does he?"

The stricken, almost fearful look on his face told her that her guess had been on the mark. Looking closer, she wondered that no one had realized their kinship before. If they had, they certainly hadn't said anything.

"Yes. No. I don't know." He shook his head. Curls a shade lighter than Corrigan's hair flopped against his collar. "What does it matter? He wouldn't care if he did know."

He had a point. Men fathered illegitimate children all the time and gave them no more regard than a slice of moldy bread.

Annie had a hard time believing Corrigan would turn the boy away if he did know; the man was fiercely possessive about what belonged to him. But neither could she guarantee his feelings toward Dogie would soften—especially after his remark about preferring daughters.

"Besides, I don't even know for sure if he is," Dogie added. "I only know what my mother told me."

"What did she tell you?"

"That he came along when she needed him most. That he was big and strong and brave, and that someday I was gonna grow up to be just like him."

A twinge of regret struck Annie at the thought of Dogie growing as tall and broad as Corrigan. She'd like to see that—the two of them standing eye to eye and will to will would be quite a sight. Unfortunately, she wouldn't be around to see him reach manhood. As soon as she caught Corrigan's horses and collected her fee, she'd be losing herself in Mexico. What she'd do after that, she hadn't yet figured out. She'd learned a long time ago just to get through one day at a time.

"You ain't gonna tell him, are you?" Dogie asked apprehensively.

"That isn't my place." Suddenly aware of how high the sun sat above the horizon, Annie snapped to a sit. "We best get back before we're missed."

Just as they finished dressing, Dogie called out to her again. "Annie?"

"Hmm?"

"Would you wait for me?"

"Wait for you?" Hell, he'd better hurry up!

"To grow up—so I can marry you."

Annie's heart squeezed, and her eyes went misty. "That's the nicest thing anyone's ever said to me." She clasped Dogie's hand in her own. "Someday, a girl's going to give her heart to you, and when she does, you take extra special care of it—because they're real fragile."

As they headed back, both tried coming up with good excuses to feed Corrigan for their absence. It was too late in the season for berry picking and too early for nut gathering, but the ideas grew more outrageous, and by the time they reached the cave, their stomachs hurt from laughing so hard.

Their laughter died abruptly at the sound of Corrigan on the rampage.

"Wade Henry! Where'd you pack the shells for the rifle?"

"Uh, I reckon I musta forgot to bring 'em."

"You forgot? How in the devil do you expect me to use a shotgun without any shot?"

Annie and Dogie shared an apprehensive look. Maybe she should have taken Dogie more seriously when he said Corrigan would kill them.

At that moment, he emerged from the cave and spotted them. The tightness of his jaw and the cold glitter in his eyes left no doubt that he was mad as thunder. "Where the hell have you been?" he asked in a deceptively quiet voice.

Dogie's backward step took him behind Annie. "N-n-no place."

She tilted her chin with phony bravado. "We went for a swim."

"You went for a swim," Brett repeated. A red fog of rage crept inside him, infusing his bloodstream, clouding his vision. When he'd returned from watch and found them gone, the only thing he could think of was that someone—bounty hunters, renegades, Annie's husband—had stolen into the cave during the night and taken off with them.

Fear unlike anything he'd ever felt before consumed him. He'd torn the area apart, had sent Emilio out searching, had driven Fortune almost into the ground in his own attempt to find them . . . and they'd gone for a goddamn *swim*.

He didn't know what had him more furious—that he'd been so worried for nothing or that Annie looked happier, healthier, and more beautiful than he'd ever seen her before. Her damp hair lay thick and unraveled down her back, her eyes glistened, her cheeks bloomed.

In a voice that belied the strength of his rage, he told Dogie, "Pack up your gear. You're going back to Sage Flat until I can find someone to take you back to the ranch."

Dogie's mouth fell. "What?"

"I warned you what would happen if you pulled another stunt. You've got ten minutes to collect your things or they'll be left behind."

"Corrigan, don't be ridic—"

He jabbed his finger in Annie's direction. "*You* keep out of this."

"The hell I will! What did he do that was so criminal this time?"

"He disobeyed a direct order."

"What, he didn't kiss your ass long enough?"

The red haze before his eyes distorted her unyielding expression. "You . . . are treading into dangerous territory here, Annie."

"So are you, Corrigan," she retorted, her eyes going as flat as her tone. "For the last two days you've done nothing but bark and bite at anyone who comes within ten feet of you, and frankly, I'm surprised the whole lot hasn't committed mutiny."

She was right, damn it. He'd been in a foul mood even before they'd left Sage Flat and his men were bearing the brunt of it. They weren't to blame for his building frustration over Annie and his irrational obsession of her.

At the same time, he couldn't let Dogie get away with thinking he could leave the protection of camp whenever the mood struck, nor could he let Annie think she had the power to counter his authority. "Dogie knows better than to leave the outfit and he did so anyway—*and* he took you with him. Now he can pay the consequences."

"I dragged *him* along! If you want to be angry at someone, be angry at me."

"Believe me, anger doesn't come close to how I feel toward you right now." More like enraged. Infuriated. And so goddamned relieved it was a wonder his knees didn't buckle.

"And you and I both know it has nothing to do with Dogie." Her chest heaved, her eyes sparked. "Cuss ten ways to Sunday if you want, but the boy isn't going anywhere."

Brett didn't know whether to kill her or keep her. One thing was certain—Annie had more pluck than any woman he'd ever met in his life. "Give me one good reason I should let him stay."

"If he goes, I go."

Somehow, he knew she'd hand him that ultimatum.

Brett swung away, only to discover the rest of his men watching the scene. Hell. Breathing deeply through his nostrils, he sifted through his choices: he could send the boy home and fire Annie for her insolence; or he could send the boy home and watch Annie leave with him. Either way, he'd keep his pride and his men's respect, but he'd lose both Annie and his only hope of getting his horses back on time.

There was a third option, but it meant swallowing his pride and risking his authority: let the boy stay, keep Annie, and hope like hell one of them didn't end up dead.

As much as it galled him to admit it, Annie and the horses were worth more to him than his pride or his men's respect. "Are you going to take responsibility for him?"

"If I must. But he's a big boy; he can take responsibility for himself."

"Fine. He can stay. But if he pulls one more stunt, it's back to the ranch he goes."

*   *   *

"Why do y'all put up with him?" Annie asked Henry as she watched Corrigan storm toward the remuda. "I can see why Dogie might, in a twisted way, but why do you?"

"Ace? He ain't such a bad sort."

"He treats you like dung. Surely there are other men you could work for who would appreciate your experience."

"And leave my horses?" Henry shook his head. "Been with 'em too long to walk out on 'em now. 'Sides, Ace pays better wages than any feller in the territory, and he don't 'spect nothin' from his men that he don't do himself. Cain't ask for more'n that."

"A bit of respect."

"When a feller respects himself, he don't need it from anyone else."

"So you're just gonna stick it out with him and let him order you around like some lackey?"

"He needs me, Annie. I know it don't always seem like it, but you don't know him like I do. Not many folks got much use for a crippled old cowpoke, but he keeps me busy, even when there ain't nothing to keep busy with."

"Why are you making excuses for him?"

Henry set a branch atop the pile he'd accumulated. "I reckon you'd see it that way, but underneath all the bluster, he's a decent man. You'll learn that for yourself if you give him a chance."

"He doesn't deserve your loyalty, Wade Henry."

"Maybe not, Annie Harper, but he's got it anyway."

Annie watched the old man hobble away. He could barely walk, much less ride anymore, yet Corrigan *did* keep him busy: cooking, wrangling, directing . . . she had thought his men resented the tasks he imposed on them; it hadn't occurred to her that they might appreciate them.

Her gaze veered toward the string of horses where Corrigan stood beside his gray, jamming a rifle into the saddle scabbard. Could she be judging him too harshly? Was it possible that she simply searched for things to hate about him, because she couldn't bear the alternative?

He needs me.

And she realized then, that all the Triple Ace men were misfits, each in their own way, not fitting into the everyday world. Flap Jack with his giant body and tender heart, Dogie with his reckless and sometimes dangerous energy, Emilio's seclusion into a world and language only Corrigan could understand, and Henry with a gnarled body unable to keep up with his quick mind.

The Triple Ace was a gathering place of lost hopes and last chances, and Corrigan a gambler willing to take a risk on them.

Annie couldn't decide what alarmed her more: the urge to run—or the ache to belong.

Chapter 13

∿ᴑᴑᴑ

Corrigan didn't return to camp for several hours, and when he did, Annie almost wished he'd stayed away. His mellow disposition might fool the rest of his men, but it didn't fool her. Beneath the calm a storm still raged, compelling her to keep her peace and her distance. Corrigan might not rattle Henry and Emilio, but he rattled her. He seemed to bring out emotions in her that she'd forgotten even existed: an almost reckless defiance, a compulsion to prove herself indestructible, a need to belong . . .

That realization shook her the most, for she'd been on her own for a long time now, by her own choice.

They headed out after a meal of roasted rabbit and spent the rest of the day following one of the many narrow trails carved into the canyon walls. Since Henry had spent as much—if not more—time as she in the canyon of the hard wood, he'd been elected to lead their party down the slanting path. Dogie followed, then Emilio, with Annie and Brett bringing up the rear. She much preferred that Emilio follow her, for then she wouldn't have to endure the searing gaze burning holes into the back of her head.

Annie grit her teeth and squirmed in the saddle and hoped they found the horses soon. She didn't know how much longer she could tolerate living in this state of raw nerves.

A sudden shift of gravel and slide of hooves yanked her attention back to the trail. "Easy, girl," she soothed, bringing Chance onto firmer footing.

A few minutes later, she noticed a hitch in the mare's gait. Annie pulled her to a stop and swung out of the saddle, heeding the drop-off to her left.

"Damn it," Annie cursed under her breath at the stone lodged in Chance's hoof. After flicking away the nugget with the blade of her pocket-knife, Annie released the hoof, brushed her hands off and scanned their surroundings grimly. Heat shimmered off the glittering sandstone sheets imbedded between layers of clay and limestone. The men had probably reached the bottom of the trail by now, and with them, Dogie with the extra horses. Heck of a place to wind up on foot. Her only other option—

"Care for a ride?"

—didn't bear consideration. "No, thanks." She

wound the reins around her wrist and tugged. Chance balked for a second before obediently following Annie along the narrow path, favoring her tender front leg.

"Don't be stubborn, Annie. Fortune is perfectly capable of carrying two."

"In this heat, he doesn't need the extra weight."

"Fine. If you walk, I walk."

She watched him dismount and gather the gray's reins in one gloved hand. "Don't humor me, Corrigan."

"Humor you? If I ride and you walk, I'm being callous. If I ride with you, I'm a lecher. If I walk beside you, I'm humoring you. Hell, I can't win."

"It took you long enough to figure it out. Now that you have, you might as well just throw your cards on the table."

Annie regretted the flippant remark as soon as she saw the uncompromising glitter in Corrigan's eyes.

"As you wish."

Two solid strides brought him around Chance's front. A single swift motion had Annie caught up against him. His mouth swooped down, capturing her surprised gasp.

Annie went stiff in his arms, too stunned to react. Her mind shut down, her nerves strung tight. A voice at the back of her mind chided her for gambling with a gambler.

Then, sensations awakened. His lips warm as wine on hers; his arms solid and secure around her back; his scent, hot and potent in her nostrils.

Giddy pleasure made her head swim and her limbs turn to liquid. She felt herself weaken. She parted her lips, and her knees folded when his tongue swept across hers. Her arms slid up his sides to clutch the muscles of his back. He groaned against her mouth.

The kiss was demanding yet gentle, ravenous yet savoring.

This was what she'd been aching for since she'd begun this journey: his strength, his heat, his passion. She'd been weak and cold and lifeless for so long. . . .

She couldn't hold back a cry of regret when his mouth left hers. Regret turned to bliss when he dropped kisses on her cheek, her chin, on the sensitive flesh beneath her jaw. She arched her neck, giving him clearer access.

Long-denied need rose, overwhelming her with its power. Wanting him closer, she tangled her fingers in his soft hair, lifted his head, and sought his mouth. Hungry lips closed over hers in a torrid kiss that drove away all but an awareness of the man pressing tight against her, chest against breasts, midriff to belly, loins against womb.

Brett drew back and set her on her feet, his breaths rapid and heavy against her cheek. "There. My cards are on the table—now there's no guessing my hand."

For long moments she could only stare dumbly at him, her lips burning, her body aching. A hawk screeched over the treetops; the rushing waters of the nearby creek lapped against sunbeams playing on its surface; a squirrel spiraled up the trunk of a hickory tree. Though Annie was dimly cognizant of her surroundings, the moment seemed to narrow down to her and Corrigan and a powerful desire that kept her trapped to the spot.

As they stared at one another, the air took a subtle shift, becoming charged with an invisible promise that penetrated clear to the bone.

"I could ride you like you've never been ridden before."

"You don't know what you're missing."

"I know what they want and I know how to give it."

Images tangled themselves in her mind, a confusing swirl of resentment and desire, of strength and weakness, of pain and pleasure. And above it all, a fearful realization.

If he hadn't set her away, she'd have demanded he take her right there in the dirt as if she were a two-bit whore.

She doubled up her fist and let it fly, giving him a full-knuckled whollop to the jaw that would have knocked a lesser man out of his britches.

Brett only winced, and pressed two fingers to the corner of his mouth. "What's the matter, Annie—stakes too high?"

Annie spun on her heel, grabbed Chance's

reins, and marched the rest of the way down the trail. She hoped he never realized just how high.

The night's campsite was set beneath a flat-topped plateau, surrounded by huckleberry trees and grape vines.

Annie was as tightly silent now as she'd been since he'd kissed her and Brett wondered if he'd taken this game too far.

Yes, Annie had a way of provoking him beyond control. Yes, he'd wanted to see her feel something besides that damned indifference. But not that way.

Just thinking about the way he'd behaved caused him shame. Annie was married. No matter how many times he told himself that if her husband wanted her, he'd be with her now, it didn't change the fact that she was off limits.

Long after everyone else had fallen asleep, Brett lay awake, watching the gentle rise and fall of her shoulders. Even the snores of his men couldn't drown out the soft sound of her breathing, and her sweet fragrance rose above those of horse and sweat and earth to taunt him.

"You awake, Annie?"

"No."

He flinched at the sharp reply. "I don't suppose it would do any good if I told you I was sorry."

"Not as sorry as you will be if you ever do something like that again."

"I give you my word. I won't ever touch you unless I'm invited."

"That'll be a cold day in hell."

All right, so maybe the kiss hadn't been his usual passionate, provocative effort. When he'd kissed Annie, he'd . . . well, he'd just . . . *felt*. She'd felt something, too—he knew she had.

Hadn't she?

Suddenly, he felt twenty again. Unsure, inexperienced, too damn eager. The question slipped out before he could stop it. "Was it so loathsome, Annie?"

Before he could coax an answer from her, the pounding of hooves and a jubilant cry shattered the night.

"Horses!"

Brett sprang up from the bedroll, his pistol ready, just as Flap Jack charged into camp. He pulled on the reins, bringing his lathered horse to a skidding halt.

Gasping for breath he announced, "Herd spotted . . . six miles south . . . small stream off the Prairie Dog Town Fork."

The rest of the men scrambled to their feet and crowded around Flap Jack.

"Are my fillies with them?" Brett asked.

He nodded vigorously. "Lookin' a bit ragged and lean, but healthy enough."

Brett bounded into immediate action, shoving his feet into his boots and buckling on his gun belt. "Flap Jack, change horses. The rest of you boys mount up—we're gonna catch us some fillies."

They spotted the herd just before sundown the next day, right where Flap Jack said they would be. Horses—two hundred or more in every color combination possible—grazed languidly on grasses and wild rye. Duns, sorrels, greys, pintos, paints, bays, buckskins, blacks. . . .

Annie gazed in awe, reminded of the first time the sight had filled her eyes. She'd been ten when her mother died, and Granddaddy began leaving the farm shortly after that for work. She hadn't understood at the time why she couldn't go with him, but he remained firm that she stay at the farm. Annie hadn't ever disobeyed her granddad before, yet, weeks would sometimes pass before he returned, and the days got so lonely. . . .

So she went searching. For what, she couldn't say. A purpose. Maybe adventure. Quite possibly just someone to talk to.

She'd found the mustangs.

She'd also found Sekoda.

Even at her tender age, she'd been drawn to him. Not a boy, not yet a man, he walked among the herd as if he were one of them, his lean, bronzed body created by sun and grace, his long black hair flowing in the wind. She remembered envying his ability to communicate with the animals, more than fearing his heathen lineage.

She returned often to the canyon over the years. The bond of their friendship became stronger with each visit, until her sixteenth summer, when Sekoda stopped looking at her as a friend and playmate, and started looking at her like a woman.

"See that speckled filly grazing on mesquite bark north of the river fork?" Corrigan asked, breaking into the memory.

He lay beside her on his stomach, close enough that Annie could feel the heat from his body. He was much longer and broader than Koda had been, his hair streaked golden brown instead of solid black, his eyes a silvery green instead of sienna. Yet oddly enough, it felt ... right ... sharing this view with him. Almost as if the mustangs were forging her destiny once again.

Annie pushed the disturbing thought to the back of her mind and took the scope he handed her. She sighted down the metal tube. "I see her."

"That's Liberty Loo. The bay with the blaze down her nose is Sophie's Star."

Sliding the lens to the left, she focused on the second horse. "What did you do, name them after lovers?"

The remark earned her a sharp glance.

"I don't see the stallion," Dogie said from his spot on the ridge.

"He's probably circling the herd, defending it from marauders."

Corrigan reclaimed the scope and searched the outer edges of the canyon. A slow grin told her he'd gotten the stallion in his sights. "Ah, there's my thief."

Annie lifted her hand to the brim of her hat, extending the shade. Sure enough, on the fringes of the herd paced the patriarch, his hide so black it appeared blue in the sunlight.

Collapsing the magnifier, Corrigan started to rise. "Let's get into position so we can get this show over with."

Annie raised her hand to halt him. "Not here— it's too wide open. Once the horses catch our scent they'll start running, and we'll be eating their dust three miles behind. Best just to follow them for a bit and find someplace to head them off."

"There's a split gorge a couple miles north," Henry suggested. "We could drive them there."

Annie knew the place well. The canyon walls reached several hundred feet in the air, forming a natural blockade on all but one side.

Corrigan made no secret of his disagreement. "I don't want the whole herd, just my fillies and the stallion."

"And you'll get them," she said. "But we do it my way. Horses are flight animals. If we charge down there and start swinging our ropes they'll scatter, and it'll take us days to track them down again. Is that what you want?"

He clenched his jaw and peered back down into the canyon. "All right, we do it your way."

Annie couldn't contain a smug smile at the disgruntled reply. The man could use a bit of humbling, and if she were the one to make it happen, all the better.

After waving the men together, Annie crouched on the ground with a stick in her hand and drew the plans for capture. "The canyon walls are here and here." She scratched a V in the dirt. "First thing we need to do is build a gate and get it in place. Once we get the herd close to the pen, Emilio and Flap Jack will drive the horses straight into the pen. Dogie and Henry will take position at the open ends and shut the gates as soon as the last horse is in."

"What will you and I be doing?"

Annie glanced at the man beside her. Corrigan looked at her from beneath the brim of his hat, his face at an angle. The sun cast his face in shadow, leaving nothing visible but firm lips surrounded by a week's growth of whiskers. For a moment, she could only stare at him with her breath lodged in her throat. The words were so simple, the question so innocent. Yet they took her back to a time when there had been a "you and I," instead of just her. She licked her dry, dusty lips, then swallowed the lump in her windpipe. "We'll be making sure your thief doesn't escape."

The ground shuddered with the force of pounding hooves against earth. Brett's pulses throbbed with the tempo as they propelled the horses toward the fork. Clouds of dust stung their eyes and clogged their throats.

They'd spent the last two days moving camp just close enough for the herd to catch wind of them, then backing off, effectively driving the band toward the natural pen without scaring them into stampeding.

Annie had taken complete control of the operation: the construction of the fence; supervision of the men; even the examination of each man's mount and tack.

There didn't seem to be an aspect she couldn't handle and Brett found himself impressed by her competency.

Now, as they performed the last aspect of Annie's strategy, organization reigned. Flap Jack and Emilio drove the whinnying herd straight toward the pen. Annie moved into flank position; Brett closed in on the other side. Hooves thundered, pulses hammered, blood pumped hot and heavy.

Fortune stretched to his full length, spurred on more by his own adrenaline and love of speed than by Brett's commands. Around him, clipped shouts filled the air.

The herd drew closer to where Dogie and Wade Henry waited, and like a river with only one path, they began to stream into the quarter-mile enclosure.

Brett couldn't contain a triumphant shout. "We got them! Annie, we did it! Your plan worked!"

Silence met his praise.

A sudden gut-twisting sensation had Brett

searching over the heads of the herd. "Where's Annie?" he called out to Emilio.

"*Yo no sé.*"

"What do you mean you don't know? She was right next to you!"

Frantically he scanned his surroundings, and noticed that the herd had begun to split: half streamed into the pen while the other half veered west, running toward the open fork. The slow thunder of his heart picked up speed. He pictured Annie caught in the crush, her tender flesh beaten, her beautiful hair trampled. . . .

And then, he saw her. In the midst of slick hides and flying manes rode Annie at full gallop, her bottom high off the saddle, her legs bent to hold her weight, her body bowed, her fingers buried in Chance's mane. The wind had torn off her hat and it slapped against her spine, leaving her long, silky hair to stream behind her like a rippling sunbeam.

"*Mi Dios, ella es asombrosa,*" Emilio breathed.

"Yeah, she is amazing." As he watched her take control of the mustangs, pride rose inside him, along with a powerful desire, and a possessive need to capture her as she captured the horses.

And it hit him then with the force of a fist that with the horses caught, she'd no longer have any reason to stay.

The sudden tightening in his chest took Brett by surprise. The thought of a woman leaving had never bothered him before. Maybe because it had never happened before.

But the thought of never seeing Annie again, of never seeing that spark in her eyes, never smelling the wind in her hair or the sun on her skin, of never again waking up next to her, left a hollowness inside him that he couldn't explain or understand. He couldn't trust her. He couldn't tame her. He couldn't seduce her. She added nothing to his life but aggravation—

And he wanted her more than he'd ever wanted a woman in his life.

A motion at the corner of his vision captured Brett's notice. Blue Fire, as though understanding the threat to his freedom, reared up on powerful hind legs and pawed the air. A shrill whinny cut through the dust hovering above the pen, just before he plunged forward through his harem.

"The stallion! Annie, he's getting away!"

While Henry and Dogie hastened to stem the flow of escaping horses, Brett spurred Fortune toward the rogue. Annie, also catching sight of the stallion, wheeled Chance around. The realization that Chance could never catch the swift steed must have occurred to Annie at the same time as Brett, for she urged the mare toward Sophie. Once the mare was pressed tight to the filly's side, Annie reached over and, clutching tight to the filly's mane, swung onto her bare back. With a few practiced twists, she had a string of rope fashioned into a halter around the filly's head and nose.

Seconds later, she was racing after the stallion.

Brett caught up to the stallion. Wild hysteria glittered in his black eyes and foam speckled his muzzle. Brett pulled Fortune ahead, then cut in front of Blue Fire. Annie's lasso created a whirlwind above her head, then it fell around the stallion's neck. Brett followed suit, his own noose settling neatly atop hers. The stallion reared, ears pinned back, front hooves slashing the air.

"We got him!" Brett shouted.

"Reel him in—keep that line tight!"

"Keep clear of his front, Annie, he's a nipper."

While Annie kept the rope gripped in both hands despite the stallion's lunging and bucking, Brett twisted the end of his lasso around the saddle horn. Then Emilio and Flap Jack joined them, and between the four of them, they managed to drag the stud into the pen with the rest of the mustangs.

Brett's chest heaved from the exertion, sweat poured from his brow like rain, and his whole system felt as though it glittered. Behind him, the men cheered and whistled and slapped each other on the back.

"We did it, Annie," Brett laughed.

Slowly, she lifted her face and their gazes locked.

Brett's victory died at the raw emotion in Annie's eyes. She sat upon Sophie, untouchable, alone. And so damned vulnerable that it nearly brought him to his knees. For endless moments they stared at each other, neither moving, neither blinking, barely even breathing.

There was something frightening about her sorrow, almost as if in capturing the horses, she'd sacrificed something much more precious. Brett couldn't begin to guess what she might have lost.

It chilled him all the same.

And in that moment, he realized that Mustang Annie Harper wasn't nearly as tough as she wanted everyone to believe. She was probably more fragile than any of them ever knew.

Chapter 14

The men were in high spirits that night. Emilio's guitar seemed to have caught the fever, for the songs that came from his fingers hopped and whirred with an energy that had the temperature rising several degrees. Henry's spoons kept up with the blurred tempo, and Dogie and Flap Jack do-si-doed all over the campsite.

They had every reason to celebrate. They'd gotten the horses, a band of sixty or so head including the stallion, rounded up and penned into a makeshift paddock. Tomorrow they'd cull the herd of lactating mares, old horses and unhealthy nags, choosing those best suited to begin building their own herds. The yearlings, late yearlings and two-year-olds were top choice.

For the first time in years, Annie wished she could join in their sense of victory. She didn't think it possible to want that again, but anything was better than this dull ache that now seemed to reach clear to the marrow of her bones.

From the instant she'd thrown the rope over the stallion's neck, she felt as if she'd been sucked back in time, then spit out into the present. No thrill. No victory. Only an unbearable emptiness that had nowhere to run and nowhere to hide. It sat in her, a lead weight dragging her down and making her wish the world would just close over her head.

Every motion a brittle effort, Annie crushed out her cigarette, then unfolded herself from the ground and wandered to the edge of the paddock, where the horses bunched together tighter than a bushel of apples.

Memories twisted in her heart: the very first time she'd seen the horses as a young girl, the surprise of seeing Sekoda for the first time, the anticipation of taking that last journey into the canyon for the stallion. . . .

It should have been him riding with her.

The flare of a match caught her by surprise. She glanced toward it and found Corrigan standing a short distance away, his arms crossed over the top of the crude fencing, a cheroot clasped between his fingers.

Annie wasn't sure if she should leave or stay. If she left, he'd think she was afraid of him; if she didn't, he'd think she sought him out.

"Why aren't you celebrating?" she asked, tucking a loose strand of hair behind her ear.

"Why aren't you?"

Leave it to him to answer a question with a question. He took a deep pull of his cheroot. The comforting aroma of tobacco mingled with the scent of sage and heat and horses. "He's a magnificent animal," Corrigan remarked.

Annie folded her arms atop the makeshift corral and watched the stallion pace. He hadn't changed much in the last four years. He was ten, maybe twelve winters old and at least sixteen hands high, with a massive build that denoted his command. He'd make a valuable stud; his blood ran through half the herd, proof of his virility.

But Corrigan couldn't have any idea what he was letting himself in for. The devil was in that boy's eyes.

"He's too proud for his own good."

Silence tightened between them, broken only by the nicker of a frightened filly in the next pen.

"Tell me something, Corrigan—you've got over a hundred head on your spread. Why go through all this trouble for a wild stallion?"

"Because he took something that belonged to me. I don't begrudge him taking my ladies; that just shows that he has good taste. But I'm not about to let him have them for nothing. If he wants my horses he's got to give me a return on my investment."

"His freedom for your profit."

"Nothing comes without a price."

Sometimes the price was higher than a person could bear, though.

"You were amazing out there today," he said after another quiet moment.

"You weren't half bad yourself."

His brows lifted. "A compliment? We're making progress."

She forced herself to take a mental step back. No sense in giving him any encouragement. "I just didn't expect you'd ride so well."

"Guess it's in the blood. My father had me in a saddle before I took my first steps."

Was that bitterness in his voice? "Was he a cowboy?"

"A trader down in Baton Rouge—till the Yankees confiscated all his stock."

Baton Rouge. So that's where the bayou accent hailed from. "And here you are, taking up where he left off. You must be his pride and joy."

"On the contrary—I'm his greatest disappointment."

There was no missing the pain in his tone. How could this ambitious, enterprising man be a disappointment to anyone?

As if he'd revealed more than he'd intended, Brett straightened his spine. "We'll start herding the horses back to the ranch tomorrow."

Her attention snapped to his face. "You aren't serious! You saw how wild they are when we brought them in."

"Once we get them back to the Triple Ace, Tex

and his boys will have them broke in a couple of days."

"And you'll spend the next couple of months undoing the damage—if they aren't completely ruined. Breaking a horse kills its spirit."

"Annie, you've done the job I hired you to do. How I handle my horses is no longer your concern."

Strangely, the words stung. Until this moment she'd forgotten that the tie binding them together had been broken the instant the gates shut, leaving her free to go on with her own life. Not that she had much of a life to go on with, but still. . . . "Fine. Take the horses back now. And when that stallion breaks for freedom first chance he gets, and takes the herd with him—including your precious fillies—don't say I didn't warn you."

"So what do you suggest?"

"Settle them down here first, in the environment they're familiar with. Let them get used to being around humans. Let them learn to trust you—especially that stallion. Then take them back to the ranch and let *him* lead the herd."

"That will take months, Annie, and I don't have that kind of time."

"It won't take months—I've had mavericks eating out of my hand in a matter of hours."

The instant Corrigan gave her that slow, sensuous smile, Annie knew she'd regret her boasting.

"Why, Annie Harper, that sounds almost like a challenge."

"What are you talking about?"

"If you can have that stallion tamed and this herd ready to travel in a few days, I'll double your fee."

"Another wager?"

He inclined his head. "In a matter of speaking."

Warning bells went off in her head. Taming them wasn't part of the deal. "And if you win?"

His eyes went dark as sin. "Anything I want."

Annie's first impulse was to tell him what he could do with his wager. She'd recovered his fillies and the stallion, and then some. Best just to collect her fee and make for the border while she was ahead.

Yet four thousand dollars was a mighty powerful temptation. Not only could she lose herself in Mexico, but she could live quite comfortably without ever having to rustle another horse.

Which was another point—staying in the canyon with Corrigan was a whole lot safer than backtracking with him to the ranch; at least the canyon offered her places to hide should the need arise.

"It's a deal Corrigan—under one condition: I want cash payment in my hand at the end of three days."

"You're so sure you'll win this one?"

"I'm sure."

This was one wager she couldn't lose.

*   *   *

The men gathered around the paddock at the crack of dawn the next morning, their anticipation as tangible as the dew clinging to the wild rye. Under Annie's direction they'd erected more fencing, creating a circular arena some distance from the main pen.

Resting his forearms on the fence, Brett stared across the paddock at the patchwork collection milling in the distance.

He was the first to admit that he was a greedy bastard. He wanted what he wanted, and he did whatever he had to do get it—including take advantage of any situation that presented itself.

For the first time, though, he felt almost ashamed.

What could he have been thinking, making that wager with Annie? How had he let her provoke him into sinking so low? Was he so desperate to keep her a little while longer that he'd let her risk her life?

He'd seen for himself what she could do with a bucker. Hell, the image of the first time he'd seen her haunted his every waking and sleeping moment. But they weren't talking any old buckers here; they were talking twenty-five bred-in-the-badlands mavericks.

Then again, wasn't that Annie's style? And wasn't her grit one of the things he found so appealing about her?

Even now, just looking at her made him throb clear down to the pit of his stomach. She entered the paddock, worn chaps snug around her jean-wrapped legs, a loose cream-colored shirt billowing in the breeze.

Judging from the wonder on the men's faces, he wasn't the only one affected by Annie. What was it about her that enthralled them all so? What was it that set her apart, and made all other women pale in comparison? Her mystique? Her untouchable aura? That rare hint of vulnerability that reminded them all that beneath the tough exterior beat the heart of a woman?

Her hips swayed in a blood sizzling manner as she approached the center of the paddock, while a late yearling hugged the outer circle, eyeing her. She'd said she needed to single out the older bachelors and mares before working with the colts and fillies. Brett knew from experience that the younger the horse, the easier the training. The older ones had already begun to form habits that they would pass down to their brothers and sisters. Adjusting those habits, Annie claimed, would make the rest of the herd follow the precedent set by the leaders.

"She'll hire herself onto some outfit, tame the wildest mavericks, and collect her fee. A couple weeks later the horses would turn up missing."

The sudden recollection of Jesse's report caused Brett's stomach to tighten with apprehension. Was she even now planning on taming the mounts, then coming back and stealing them?

"You fellers are in for the treat of your life," Dogie declared, interrupting Brett's thoughts.

"Nobody can bust a bronc like Annie."

"How would you know?" Flap Jack asked.

"I saw her once."

Brett's attention went to the kid's face. "When would you have seen her?"

"Few years ago down at the Tongue River, when she was with—" Dogie's face suddenly paled.

"*Who* was she with?" Brett demanded.

"Maybe it wasn't her. Maybe it was someone else."

"And maybe you better start talking." The tone of his voice brooked no argument.

Still, several seconds passed. "An Injun," Dogie finally blurted. "She was with an Injun. They brought some horses in to trade, and she had to ride one cayuse just to prove he could be ridden. I don't know who the feller was, but he seemed to like her well enough."

. . . married up with some breed. . . .

. . . savage came out of nowhere. . . .

Was that who Annie was hiding from? Was her husband even now hiding somewhere in the canyon, stalking her? Brett scanned the outlying plateaus, some stretching a good mile high. The faces of the canyon walls were riddled with caves and niches where a person could conceal themselves and bide time for an unguarded moment.

Brett gripped Dogie's shoulders. "If you know anything else that could mean trouble for Annie, anything that might be a danger to her, you had better tell me now."

Dogie looked over at Annie, then back at Brett with an expression of misgiving. "Well, she seemed real nervous back in Sage Flat. Especially when that feller showed up at the saloon and started gettin' rough with one of the girls. Annie told me women don't like that."

"Was it the same man she was with at the Tongue River?"

"I don't know. I don't think so but I only saw 'em both for minute."

Brett stared into the boy's fearful green eyes long enough to convey the warning that he'd not hesitate to thrash the boy within an inch of his life if he was holding back.

When the fear faded to the dull light of resignation, Brett released Dogie's shoulders with a curse. Why hadn't he thought to use Dogie before? As much time as he and Annie spent together, Brett could have had the boy wrangling information from her. Yes, it was underhanded. But damn, he had no other way of getting the answers he sought.

"What is she doin'?" Flap Jack asked, drawing Brett's attention back to Annie. "Why ain't she getting on his back?"

His voice full of pride, Henry informed them, "She's wooin' him. Gettin' him to trust her first."

Brett stared into the paddock. He didn't understand how standing there staring at the horse could be considered wooing, but like his men, he could do little more than watch, captivated by his own curiosity.

The horse ran a full circle, then stopped and looked at Annie. Annie turned her body and the horse stopped to study her. She turned again, and the horse bolted. Countless minutes slipped by as Annie repeated the process. Simple gestures, like the angle of her head, the movement of her hand, either sent him running around the pen again or made him stand in a tight stance, tossing his head.

Just when Brett began to wonder if Annie was trying to pull some sort of con on them, she turned her back on the horse and waited.

No one moved, no one breathed, mesmerized that such a slight woman would turn her back on a wild mustang.

Then the horse ducked his head, as if asking forgiveness, and took one step toward Annie. Another step followed, and still another, until he stood directly behind her and nuzzled her shoulder with his nose.

Brett found himself grinning from ear to ear. What she was doing didn't make a lick of sense, but he knew he'd just seen something so unreal, so fantastic, that nobody would believe him if he repeated it.

His grin faded with a startling realization: this was what Annie had meant by wooing, by winning trust. It wasn't about smothering a person with attention, or going to extreme lengths to catch their notice.

Sometimes it meant turning your back and letting them come to you.

Chapter 15

After thirty minutes of "talking" to the horse, Annie spent another thirty minutes acquainting him with her scent—walking around him, stroking his hide, blowing into his nostrils, then laying a blanket over his eyes and dragging it across his back. The process had worked for the Comanche for countless years, and Sekoda had spent hour after hour teaching her the ways of his mother's people.

When the mustang finally allowed her to place a blanket and saddle on his back, she knew it was now or never.

She approached the sorrel, feeling as if she were preparing for battle. This is what she did—it's what she *was*. A bronc rider. A mustanger. She'd tamed mounts unrulier than this one, so where did this sudden nervousness come from?

Maybe because she'd never had so much at

stake before. She knew good and well that if Corrigan won this wager, she'd lose more than her dignity. She'd lose a piece of herself.

She took a deep breath, let it out, then did another slow intake and release. "Easy boy." She nudged his underbelly with her knee. He ducked his head, but didn't bolt. She slipped her foot in the stirrup and hoisted herself against the horse's side. Again she paused, laying over the saddle, allowing the horse time to reject her weight. When he did nothing more than swing his head around to see what she was doing, she eased her leg over his back and positioned herself above, then into, the saddle.

Forcing her body to relax so it would flow with the horse's motion rather than against it, she whispered to herself, "Buck up, Annie, it's time to ride."

At her nod, Emilio loosed his hold on the bridle. No sooner did he scramble out of the way than the cayuse beneath her tasted his freedom.

Annie's head snapped back with the first slam of forehooves against packed earth.

Let him think he's in control. Let him dance around a bit, feel his oats. Keep his head up, though; he has to lower his head to buck. Annie gripped the halter and pulled with all the strength of one arm while she kept the other extended to the right to maintain her balance. One slip of concentration, one violent lunge of the beast beneath, would mean the difference between maintaining her seat or crashing to the ground.

"Ride, Annie, Ride!"

"Bust that bucker! Show him who's in charge!"

The shouts of encouragement reached deep into the recesses of Annie's mind, yet she heard them not in the voices of Corrigan's men, rather Sekoda's deeply timbered tone.

Then another voice rose above them all—softer, huskier, almost unhearable in the din, yet so clear it could have been murmured in her ear. "You can do it, Annie."

Annie mentally latched onto the words, unaware until that moment how badly she'd needed the boost to her confidence. As the mustang twisted and plunged and kicked beneath her, she held her position with focused poise.

By the time the horse finally settled down, both he and Annie were drenched in sweat. Their bones and muscles quivered from exertion and exhilaration. Annie spent the next ten minutes caressing the animal, patting him, stroking his damp hide, telling him without words how very proud of him she was. She took him a couple turns around the pen and he kept his head high, proclaiming to one and all that the only reason she remained on his back was because he allowed it.

Undefinable and unexpected emotion roiled just below the surface as Annie dismounted to the cheers and whistles of Brett's men. For the first time in years, she felt almost proud of herself.

"Amazing!"

"Never saw the like!"

She met Brett's gaze. Saw the pride. The praise. The desire. And something a little more disturbing—a knowledge, as if he'd just discovered a deeply rooted secret.

Annie's breath caught. He suddenly seemed very, very dangerous.

She whirled away from him and called out, "Bring on the next one."

By the end of the second day, Annie fully regretted the impulsiveness of accepting Corrigan's wager. She dismounted an especially irascible mare, unable to do anything more than lean weakly against the horse's side. Every bone and muscle in her body hurt beyond belief.

"Annie, you've got to stop this."

At Flap Jack's gentle chiding, she stiffly pushed herself away from the sweaty hide. "No, I've only got six more to go counting the stallion, and one day left." Then this damned wager would be done and over with.

"He'll kill you Annie, if you don't kill yourself first."

Only if she got lucky. "I'm fine, Flap Jack. I'll get a good night's sleep. Come morning, me and that ole cayuse will come to an understanding."

Pain ripped up her spine and down her legs as she made her way toward her bedroll. Though her stomach grumbled and her pores felt clogged with dirt, she was too weary even to eat or wash up.

Before she made it halfway to the campfire, Dogie waylaid her.

"Ace wants to see you, Miss Annie."

"Now?"

Dogie gave her a beaming grin that set her on instant wariness. This best not be one of the boy's pranks. She was in no humor to tolerate it today. "I don't suppose he told you why."

"Nope. Just said soon as you were finished he wanted to see ya."

Whatever it was, it had better be important. She didn't have the energy for any of his tomfoolery. "Where is he?"

"Just yonder of those rocks."

She looked toward the outcropping of red clay where he'd jerked his thumb, but saw nothing save the saddle-shaped formation.

Every step toward the rocks was torture to her aching body. She limped past the rough impression of a cantle and rounded the rear side. "This better be import—"

The rest of the sentence escaped Annie at the sight that met her eyes. Candles. Dozens upon dozens of fat, flaming candles were scattered about the clearing, their flickering wicks dancing upon the ground, chasing away the encroaching shadows. And in the center sat a tub—a real tin tub filled to the brim with steaming water, an invitation to her weary, beaten body.

Her mind reeling with awe, Annie wandered past the outer ring of light to trace the rim lightly with her fingertips. The trouble, the time this must have taken to set up. . . . Nobody, not even Koda, had ever been so considerate.

She turned her head to one side, then the other. "Corrigan?"

No answer.

"Did you do this?"

Again, silence.

"Of course he did," she told herself. The whole scenario—the candles, the bath, the intimate setting—bore the brand of his hand all over it.

But . . . why? Was this part of a new plan to seduce her? To knock her off balance? Was he even now watching her from some hidden spot?

She looked at the tub again with longing. The steam rising into the air beckoned, called out to her like an answer to a plea. No cold scrub in the creek late at night while the men slept, or early in the morning while they were otherwise occupied, but an honest to God, muscle-soaking, brain-numbing *bath*.

Her best intentions crumbled, and suddenly she didn't care whether he watched or not. Her body hurt like it had never hurt before, and if she had to suffer his spying, it was a small price to pay for relief.

Even as it occurred to her to fetch clean clothes from her saddlebags, a pile of folded fabric next to the tub caught her eye. Annie reached out slowly, removed the top garment, and shook out an ankle length divided riding skirt made of the softest kid skin she'd ever touched. She stroked the fringe decorating the outer seam in wonder.

She couldn't remember the last time she'd worn women's clothes.

"Do you like them?" came a sensuous drawl from behind her.

Annie swung around, clutching the skirt to her front. He stood in the shadows, one shoulder against the rock separating them from the rest of the men. His hat was tipped low over his eyes, his arms crossed over his chest. Annie couldn't be sure if it was the heat of the candles or Corrigan's presence that warmed her skin.

She swallowed the lump in her throat and splayed her hand over her breast, as if to hide the sudden quickening of her heartbeat. "You shouldn't have done all this."

"Me? You honestly didn't think I would provide a bath and new clothes for any of my crew, did you? No, you have the men to thank for this. I'm just the decoy."

Her half smile told him she wasn't buying his story for an instant. But then, could he really expect to con a con artist?

"All right," he sighed. "Guilty as charged. But it really wasn't that much trouble. A friend of mine let me raid his dugout."

"And you just happened to find a spanking new riding skirt in the stash."

"Consider that a bonus for recovering my horses." He tipped his hat. "Enjoy your bath. If you need anything, I'm just a holler away."

He was leaving? He wasn't going to post himself someplace and watch? Annie couldn't decide which act she was more grateful to him for: the bath . . . or his granting her the privacy to enjoy it in peace.

"Thank you . . . Brett."

"You're more than welcome . . . Annie."

And then Brett did the hardest thing he'd ever done in his life. He spun on his heel and walked away.

Back at the campsite, he discovered that Tex and his men had finally rejoined the outfit. They stood at the paddock fence, staring at the dark shadow pacing by the far wall. Brett debated for a moment whether to meet up with them, but a distraction was exactly what he needed. If he allowed his mind to linger on the woman he'd just left, he feared he'd not have enough strength to resist the schoolboy impulse to peek.

Unfortunately, his thoughts strayed there anyway. Right about now she'd have her boots off, and was probably unbuckling her chaps. Untying the thongs. One, two, three . . . then the other side. The weight of the leather would make them drop to the ground while she unbuttoned her britches.

Brett paused and groaned. He shook his head, trying to shake the picture out of his head. But like a flame to dry tinder, the fantasy raged on.

She'd be peeling her britches off her hips, then down her firm legs, finally down to her ankles and kicking them free. Her shirt tails would reach to mid-thigh, giving him an incredible view of pale, bare skin below the hem; above it he'd have to guess. For damn sure her skin would be just as soft, just as smooth, but the wondering, the anticipation, could drive a man just as wild as the actual beholding.

He'd look at her face, and she'd be looking back at him, drowsy-lidded invitation in her eyes, a come-hither smile on her lush lips, her index finger curling inward as she coaxed him closer.

He pictured his legs carrying him to her, steam all around them, candlelight turning the rugged cove into paradise. . . .

The kiss, oh damn, the kiss came from memory rather than fantasy, and that made it worse. He knew exactly how sweet her lips would taste, how slick and supple her tongue would feel sliding across his. . . .

Brett almost doubled over from the pressure in his loins. What the hell was he doing? He was thirty-four years old, for crying out loud, not a lad on the verge of his first season. His imagination was fast becoming his own worst enemy.

With excruciating effort, he managed to douse the images, and once his erection relaxed, he joined the men at the paddock.

"Henry tells me your little mustanger plans on taming this beast tomorrow," Tex said.

"That's right." Brett lit a cheroot with trembling fingers.

"You really think she can do it?"

"No question of whether she can, it's how long it will take her."

The remark instigated a round of wagering between those who had yet to see Annie's amazing technique and those who had. Brett listened to the good-natured bantering as his thought shifted to his own wager with Annie. Anything he wanted covered a lot of ground. His first choice would be Annie, no question, but he'd settle for answers.

Assuming, of course, that he won the wager.

The way Annie was going, those odds were looking mighty slim.

A frown dug into his brow. By the end of the first day, she'd had eight horses eating out of her hand; today, another eleven were following her around like pups. The remaining six seemed nothing more than foreplay to the taming of the stud.

In his heart he already knew who'd won, and the knowledge left a gaping hole in his chest. By sundown tomorrow, Annie would have the herd settled and ready to drive back to the ranch. He'd turn the fillies over to Albert Moore and get his endorsement, while Annie would take her money and bolt like an unbroken filly given her freedom.

And Brett knew he'd never be able to look at the mustangs without thinking of Annie.

Chapter 16

By the time Annie dragged herself out of the tub, dressed in the clothes Corrigan had provided, and returned to camp, the rest of the outfit had already turned in for the night. Closest to her bedroll lay Corrigan, his hat drawn low over his eyes, arms folded over his broad chest, legs crossed at the ankles. Even if she weren't familiar with the shape of his body she'd have recognized him by smell. No other man had his sensually distinctive scent.

Annie closed her eyes. Damn this awareness of him—of the way he slept, the way he walked, the way he smelled . . .

She forced herself to step over him to her own bedroll, rolled out and waiting a short distance away. She didn't understand herself anymore. She'd been the one to demand that he keep his distance. Yet when he did, she only wanted him nearer.

Night after night she found herself blocking the memory of his lips on hers, the press of his body, the command of his touch.

She brought her fingers to her mouth; traced the dry cracked flesh. *Was it so loathsome?*

Oh, if only it had been.

Annie flopped onto her side. "Stop it." She wasn't sure if she were berating herself or him.

"Did you say somethin', Annie?"

She swung her head around and noticed Henry struggling to sit up. "Nothing important. What are you doing awake?"

"I've got the midnight-to-three shift."

"How about if I take it?"

"You need your rest tonight."

"I'm too restless to sleep." Unfortunately, the bath seemed to have revitalized her rather than relaxed her. And she could use an excuse to get away, to put her tumultuous thoughts in order. "Look, I'm just as capable of pulling watch as the rest of you, and I need . . . I need to be alone for a while."

Henry looked as if he'd argue with her further but must have decided it wouldn't do any good, because he dropped back onto his bedroll with a sigh.

A vigorous breeze tousled her hair as she headed for the pile of rocks where one of Tex's men watched for intruders. He looked startled at the sight of her, but didn't argue when Annie told him it was her shift.

She settled on the rock with her back against a tree and her revolver across her lap. Her gaze veered toward the paddock. They'd separated Blue Fire from the rest of the herd, yet he still stood sentinel over his treasures.

"Tomorrow's the big day, Fire," she told the stallion. "If you don't let me on your back, he'll have won the wager. I think we both know what 'anything I want' means."

Could she do it? Could she give herself to him? There was no doubt in her mind that bedding her would be his request. He hadn't made a secret of his desire since the day they'd met.

She supposed she'd simply turn off her feelings. It had worked before.

Then she remembered the candlelit bath, the polished saddles, and the bedrolls laid out at night, and she remembered the remark he made about knowing how to make a woman feel protected, cherished, and desired. And Annie feared that she might not be capable of *not* feeling. That's what made him so dangerous—his ability to awaken these sensations.

Even if she wanted a . . . relationship . . . with a man again, no one could be more wrong for her. Never had she met a more demanding, possessive, volatile man than Brett Corrigan.

But he could also be so . . . passionate. And kind. And safe.

How could he be so harsh and relentless one minute, so gentle and considerate the next?

Annie forced herself to empty her mind of everything except how to approach the stallion come morning, until a crunch of loose rocks alerted her to company. Moments later, Corrigan's broad-shouldered figure appeared on the ledge. "What are you doing here? Where's Henry?"

"I took over his watch."

"Damn it, Annie—"

"Don't start with me, Corrigan. I couldn't sleep so I figured I might as well put the energy to good use."

"I liked it better when you called me Brett."

That was the last thing she expected to hear him say, and it stumped her for a reply.

"I figured you'd be sawing logs after the last couple of days," he said, settling into the spot beside her.

"I don't snore."

"Yes, you do. Okay, maybe it isn't exactly snoring, more of a . . . purr."

That he would notice such a personal detail about her made Annie's stomach flutter.

"Why can't you sleep?" he asked.

"My mind won't shut down. I keep thinking about tomorrow."

"The stallion?"

She nodded.

"Me, too."

Yeah, she'd bet he was jumping up and down

with glee at the prospect of winning "anything he wanted."

"I don't think he's ready to let me ride him," she confessed. "He doesn't trust me yet."

"If anybody can do it, you can."

Annie let out a short laugh of disbelief. "What makes you so sure?"

"I've watched you. You have a gift with horses." He leaned back on his elbows and crossed his ankles. "In fact, I've been thinking . . . once we get these animals to the ranch, I might come back here and round up some of the horses that got away. They don't belong to anyone— and men are rounding up cattle and selling them, so why not horses?"

"I'm thinking you don't know what kind of trouble you'd be borrowing," she answered. "Mustangs are the most temperamental, unpredictable, rilesome breed you'll ever run across. You've seen them. They kick, they bite, they bolt. . . . They'd just as soon throw you as look at you."

"Not if you helped train them."

A long, stunned silence followed. Annie stared at his profile, at the flat, high brow, the straight blade of his nose, the flare of his lips. "Are you offering me a job?"

"For as long as you want it."

An honest living. It had been so long since she'd even contemplated staying in one place and doing what she loved that the notion felt foreign—yet oh, so tempting. If not for the constant threat of being discovered, she might have given it more consideration. "I'm not up to that commitment again," she whispered, looking away.

"Then you have done it before."

Before Annie could respond, a wild, animal scream shattered the night. Both Annie and Brett twisted around in the direction of camp. Another scream, then a human shout made them scramble to their feet.

Brett skated down the rocky face, sending a spray of shale down the slope. Annie slid into him, lost her balance, and landed on her bottom. Brett grabbed her hand and hauled her to her feet and they took off running.

Chaos met them back at camp. Horses milling, men shouting and racing, the air thick with confusion.

The stallion crow hopped and kicked in a violent attempt to dislodge the rider on his back.

Annie gasped. "Oh, Jesus—Dogie!"

"That damned fool!" Brett growled

Annie threw herself onto the back of the closest horse, while Brett searched for a Triple Ace mount. He heard a shout from behind, then spotted Fortune, freshly saddled by one of Tex's men.

By the time Brett closed in on the stallion, Emilio, wearing only his long underwear, already had his rope in motion. Annie, too, was readying hers into a coil while Flap Jack and Henry tried to distract the stallion by waving their arms, which also served to keep the frenzied herd away from Dogie, who was being whipped back and forth like a sheet in a wild wind.

Brett unsnapped the band holding his lariat to the saddle, then set the rope swinging above his head. Annie tossed, but missed. Emilio's noose hit the mark, landing around the stallion's neck just as he reared up.

Brett let his rope fly. Instead of soaring overhead, it got caught beneath his heel, pinning his boot to the saddle.

He struggled to untangle himself while around him, commotion reigned. The mustangs all but crawled over one another in disoriented terror. Dust surged up from the ground, blinding animals and riders alike.

Old fear crept passed Brett's control, rising inside him, threatening to smother the breath from his lungs. He pushed it down and focused on freeing himself, knowing if he let the fear get its grip on him again, it would control him for the rest of his life.

When the bind around his boot refused to give way, Brett leaned back and dug into his pockets for the jackknife. As he sawed at the hemp, he kept his eyes on Annie and the activity surrounding her.

Annie again swung her lasso, and even as it hit its mark, Brett knew she'd never have enough strength to hold the horse down. She must have known it too, for she used it to pull herself closer. He knew the maneuver—within seconds, she'd be shifting herself onto the stallion's back.

Horses pressed around him—thousands of pounds of solid muscle and unleashed power. They kicked. They screamed. They milled in terror.

Brett felt himself thrown back into the paddock of his childhood. Panic surged up again, closing around his lungs so tight he could hardly breathe. His heart slammed in his chest hard enough to crack a rib. His mind grew so numb it froze his reflexes.

Be a man.

He saw himself frantically carving at the latigo, but couldn't feel it; heard the hysteria around him as if through a tunnel; tasted the suffocating frenzy clear to the back of his throat.

Can't you do anything right?

Then the rope snapped. With an enraged cry, Brett raced into the melee like a warrior, his face contorted with determination, his blood hot with purpose. Just as he reached the stallion, the animal reared. It lifted Emilio off the ground, ripped the rope from Annie's hand, and nearly broke Dogie's spine as he bowed backward. The boy's grip went slack on the thick black mane just as Brett scooped him onto his own horse.

He searched for Annie in the thick haze of dust. He suddenly saw her standing in her stirrups, and gasped. His heart shot to his throat; her name tore from his mouth as she lunged onto the stallion's back.

Everything happened in a split second. The horse fish-tailed, plunged, then bucked. Annie lost her grip on his mane; the next thing Brett knew, she was flying over the stallion's side.

"Annie! Jesus, Annie!"

Brett unloaded Dogie at the edge of the action, then tore back to where Annie had fallen.

She'd already begun to pick herself off the ground when Brett reached her. He leaped off his mount. Wrapping his arms protectively around her back, he half-pushed, half-dragged her to safety.

The stallion reared again and yanked Emilio off his feet. Wicked, pawing hooves struck Emilio on the head and shoulders, driving him into the ground. And still Emilio held on.

Brett screamed to his men, but their own shouts coupled with the hysterical horses and the quaking of the ground drowned out his orders. The stallion dodged left, then leaped into a gallop, crashing through the fencing, dragging Emilio a hundred feet across cactus, gravel and brush before freeing himself of the human anchor and disappearing around a bend.

While Flap Jack and Henry raced for Emilio, Brett brushed Annie's tangled tresses out of her eyes. He had to make sure she was unharmed before joining them. "Annie?"

"I'm fine," she said, trying to stand. "Just got the breath knocked out of me." Too shaken to object when his hands slipped under her arms, she allowed him to help her get her footing. "I'll have it back in a minute." She folded over at the waist, her hands braced on her knees, and willed her head to stop whirling. She'd taken worse spills, but this one had done a number on her. "What about the others?"

"I'm not sure yet."

Before she could tell him that he should go find out, a third presence crept out of the shadows. They both looked up to find Dogie standing before them, his head bowed, his hat a twisted lump of felt in his hands.

Brett went deathly still, and Annie felt his rage climb through his system as if they were connected from front to back. She dared a glance at him, then wished she hadn't. His eyes had gone nearly black, his face absolutely tight. She'd seen rage run that cold and deep only once, and she had to force herself not to take a step away from it.

"I'm going to check on Emilio." His voice trembled as he told Annie, "Tell the boy he's got fifteen minutes to pack his things. I'll allow him a horse and saddle, nothing more."

Only after Brett spun on his heel and strode toward his men did Annie address Dogie. "Help me get these horses rounded up."

Tex and his boys had already begun the process, and a couple more hirelings were working to repair the broken fence.

Once the last of the herd was secured in the pen, Dogie let the latch click shut, then stood with his head bowed. "Annie . . . I'm really sorry."

"You should be. That was a very stupid thing you did."

Her looked at her with sad eyes. "I only wanted to ride like you."

"Why? To get Corrigan's attention? Did it ever occur to you that putting every man in this outfit—not to mention yourself—in danger is not the best way to go about it?"

"I never meant for anyone to get hurt!"

"But someone *did*. That stallion was nowhere near ready to be ridden, and all the apologies in the world aren't going to help Emilio right now."

"Is he going to be all right?"

"I don't know," she told him frankly.

His thin shoulders fell; his big green eyes went moist. "I don't expect I'll be seein' you again after this."

Her attention swerved to Brett, who was bent over Emilio. They'd gotten him to sit up, but from this distance she couldn't see much else. No matter how far away she stood, though, there was no mistaking the compassion and comradery between Brett and his men. They were the Triple Ace, and she . . . was just the wild card. A part of them, yet not truly belonging.

Funny how that hurt.

"No, I don't expect you will." Annie grabbed her saddle off the fence and strode toward Chance, who waited in the middle of the clearing. "In the meantime, you best do as he says, and steer clear of him." Even she couldn't ignore that he'd crossed the line this time. She doubted Dogie had meant any harm, but neither could she protect him. Not only had he caused injury to a talented roper, but he'd caused the loss of the stallion.

Out of the corner of her eye she saw Brett get up and lope toward her. "How is Emilio?" she asked when he arrived.

"His arm is mangled. We need to get him to a doctor to see if they can save it."

Annie closed her eyes. It would devastate Emilio if he lost the use of his arm. He was so counting on building a home for his wife and unborn child . . .

Annie turned back to Chance and threw a blanket over her back.

"Where are you going?"

She covered the blanket with the saddle. "After the stallion."

He gaped at her in astonishment. "Annie, don't be foolish."

"We made a deal, and I intend to see it through. I've got just as much at stake as you do."

"I'll give you the damn money—you've more than earned it."

"It isn't just about the money. You want the stallion; I want his colt."

"Take your pick! Over half this herd came from his seed."

"I want his and Chance's colt."

They stared at each other, eye to eye, will to

will, until Corrigan finally broke the contact. His gaze turned to the bend where the stallion had disappeared, then toward Emilio, then back to Annie, indecision plain on his face. Annie almost felt sorry for him. She knew he was torn between sticking with his men and going after the stallion.

"Go with them, Corrigan. They need you more than I do."

"I won't leave you out there unprotected."

She laid her six-shooter across her lap. "I won't be. You forget, I've been on my own before."

"Not on my payroll, you haven't."

He didn't trust her. He didn't say it—had never said it—but she saw it in his face. The knowledge stung, despite the fact that he had every reason not to trust her.

Then, in typical Ace Corrigan fashion, he started barking orders. "Henry, take Emilio into Sage Flat and see if you can scare up someone to doctor his arm. Flap Jack and Tex, get these horses rounded up. You're taking them back to the ranch."

Chapter 17

A t dawn, the only signs left of the last few days were the remains of fence sections, large patches of trampled dirt, and a cloud of rolling red dust in the distance.

Brett and Annie's gazes met, then darted away, both acutely aware that this was their first time alone since that day on the trail. Ordinarily Brett wasn't at a loss as to what to do in the company of a beautiful woman. He'd charm her with a smile; whet her appetite with a look, a gesture; serenade her with his touch.

But this was no ordinary situation, and Annie no ordinary woman. She still didn't trust him—was probably wise not to. Brett didn't entirely trust himself around her. Despite every attempt to forget that kiss on the ledge, it remained etched in his memory, as clear as the day it had happened. If he'd known today would not be the end of their working relationship, but rather the beginning, he wouldn't have surprised her with the bath and added agony to torment.

Yet he'd given his word. He'd keep his hands to himself even if it killed him.

"Annie. . . ." Brett paused and searched for the right words. "I just want you to know that I appreciate you not giving me any guff about Dogie."

"Believe me, if I hadn't agreed that sending him back to the ranch with the men wasn't in everyone's best interest, you'd have heard about it."

His chuckle seemed to break the spell of awareness. "I'm sure I would have."

"He'll settle down. Just give him time."

Brett was glad *she* had so much confidence in the boy.

Annie clapped her hands together. "Well, boss man, how do you want to do this? Ride the ridge or follow the floor?"

Brett squinted up the canyon walls. "Seems to me we'd have a better vantage point from up top."

"Then let's hit the trail."

"Keep your eyes peeled for renegades," Brett advised, swinging into the saddle. "Tex said he found a cold camp about twenty miles south."

"How does he know it's Comanche? It could just as easily have been outlaws or buffalo hunters."

"It could, but apparently Quanah Parker has

been on the rampage. Rumor also has it Santana has joined up with him."

"The Kiowa are joining up with the Comanche?"

"Frightening thought. The Army is ready to pull their hair out. Someone is supplying guns and they can't trace the source."

Annie fell quiet, and a troubled frown wrinkled her brow. Brett couldn't help wondering if her Indian husband were somehow involved in the conflict between red man and white. It would explain why she refused to talk about him. It would also explain why he'd left her to fend for herself. Women with no means of support often turned to avenues they wouldn't have dreamed of before. He'd seen it happen during the War Between the States: genteel women reduced to becoming laundresses, harlots . . . thieves.

By midday they still hadn't spotted a traversable path to take them to the crown. The sun beat hard upon their backs. Hooves sank into rich, rolling earth thick with clumps of yellow amaryllis and vibrant orange Indian paintbrush. Tall shade trees clustered together beneath an overhang of clay. As they drew closer, Brett noticed a curious mound between the trunks. The mound took clearer shape, becoming a pile of timber banked by abutting . . . walls?

An abandoned homestead? It sure looked like it.

He studied the ground. Here and there, verdant grasses grew up and over chunks of blackened wood, and he thought he saw the remains of a stone border around various cacti and thorny bushes, almost as if someone had been cultivating a flower garden.

"There's a creek about a quarter mile from here," Annie said. "Beyond that is a decent trail. We can rest the horses before making the climb."

Brett barely heard her, fascinated by the signs of neglect. A few hundreds yards further, away from the grove, hewn slats cracked by the weather hung perilously to leaning posts by rusted nails. Beyond the grove a full-structured building came into view. It was obviously a stable, and still in moderately good repair. A new roof, definitely. Possibly some erosion at the foundation, but nothing a bit of local wood and a few nails wouldn't fix.

"Who would leave this place to go to ruin?" he asked, envisioning the possibilities of the land.

"Someone who didn't want to be here anymore."

He found it hard to believe anyone wouldn't want to be here. The land was enviably fertile, with a grove of cottonwoods to the west, and a score of acres to the north rich in grasses. Perfect pasture land. He imagined paddocks much like the one Annie had built for the herd replacing the broken-down fencing, a comfortable home of stone harvested from right here in the canyon sitting atop the site of the rubble.

The more he thought about it, the stronger the

temptation gripped him to locate the owner and persuade him into selling. Not that he needed another enterprise to worry about, but it seemed a pity to let the land go unused.

As they left the homestead behind, though, he discovered that initiating talks with the owner might not be possible. From amidst the flowered stalks, a worn cross jutted up from the ground. Brett craned his neck to read the inscription: "Beloved."

Someone very special lay there, he realized. From the size of the grave and the epitaph, he assumed an adult. A wife, maybe. Or a husband.

Flashes of conversations suddenly seized his mind.

"They used to live south of here. . . ."

"When she wasn't getting into mischief she was runnin' with the herds."

"Heard she married up with some breed."

"Found her with a herd of stolen horses . . ."

Brett felt as if a stake had just been driven through his gut. It couldn't be—Annie's land? What were the odds?

He shot a glance at her, riding beside him. The tight posture, up-tilted chin and ghostly pale complexion told him that he'd guessed correctly.

Who was in the grave? Whoever lay there had meant something to Annie, that was certain. Her grandfather? Her husband? He'd heard somewhere that many tribes feared being buried, though. Was it just wishful thinking on his part?

They reached the creek, the banks as stony as

the silence between them. While the horses drank, Brett and Annie crouched at the water's edge to quench their own thirst and fill their canteens. Annie's movements seemed as mechanical as the clock on his mantle back at the Triple Ace.

Brett wet his kerchief and swiped it across his damp brow, then his jaw. "That's your land back there, isn't it?"

She didn't have to answer. He knew he'd guessed right when her hands stilled.

"You should have told me."

"It's none of your business."

"I would have gone around the land."

She face him, her eyes blazing. "Did I ask you to?"

"You wouldn't ask. You'd rather torture yourself."

She gathered her canteen and started to rise.

Brett grabbed her gently by the arm, preventing her from escaping yet again. "Don't run from this, Annie. Whatever you're holding inside, let it go. Share it with me."

The compassion in his husky voice pinned Annie to the spot more firmly than if he'd just clapped shackles around her ankles.

She *wanted* to let it go; it amazed Annie how much. She hadn't talked to anyone in so long. There was always the danger of being discovered, of being betrayed, of winding up like her granddad. Even now the two threats existed, closer than they'd ever been before.

"Does it have anything to do with the bounty on your head?"

She closed her eyes. "So you do know."

"That you're Mustang Annie, horse thief extraordinaire? Since the beginning."

Her eyes snapped open in surprise.

"It didn't matter then; it doesn't matter now."

"It should."

"I don't see why—unless you're planning on stealing my horses. I'd have to take that personally."

His attempt at humor brought a wry grin to her face. "I'd be lying if I told you the thought hadn't occurred to me once or twice."

"Yet you haven't," he pointed out. "Look, Annie—I'm not the law, I'm not a bounty hunter; I'm just a horse trader willing to do whatever it takes to save his ranch."

"Why? You could buy a hundred ranches."

He leaned back against the tree, stared up at the clouds scudding across the sky, and sighed. "Haven't you ever wanted to prove someone wrong? Haven't you ever wanted a second chance to make things right?"

Her lips parted, then pressed tightly together again, trapping whatever words she'd been about to speak.

Brett sighed. "I spent over half my life cheating and conning and lying to get ahead. The Triple Ace is the first thing I ever won fair and square. No palmed cards. No weighted dice. No marked decks. A fair and square triple ace deal. I've sunk over half of everything it took me years to amass into that ranch, and I'm not about to let it go without a fight."

"Not everyone is in your position."

"No, they aren't. Talk to me, Annie. I can't help you if you won't be straight with me."

"Why would you even want to?" she cried.

"Besides the fact that I don't want to see that pretty neck of yours in a noose? Because you never fail to amaze me. You can't bring yourself to laugh, yet you'll fight to shelter an old man. You take on extra chores to lighten the load of a kid. You run from the law, yet you stand up to me. Someone with that mix of gumption and mercy doesn't become a fugitive without cause. And they don't leave a paradise like this without a reason."

Before Annie could stop the words, they spilled out. "It was my granddad's land." She sat down beside him, brought her knees up to her chest and wrapped her arms around her shins. "He'd settled on it years ago, and when my father died, my mother and I went to live with him. But when I was ten, my mother died. Granddad refused to leave me. He tried raising sheep, but what disease didn't kill, the drought did. Then he started leaving home a lot. Sometimes he'd be gone for weeks at a time. He was so busy tending to business that I think he forgot I even existed."

"Did you know he was stealing horses?"

"I suspected, but I didn't know for sure until I was thirteen. He came home one day to find a half a dozen Comanche sitting in our kitchen." Annie couldn't quite bring herself to reveal Sekoda's part in her life at that time, how he had brought them into her home. "They were harmless, but from then on he refused to go anywhere without taking me with him.

"One day we'd gone to the Tongue River to do some trading. A couple of his 'friends' weren't too happy with him for dragging a kid along, and told him that if I could rope and ride a particular horse, that they'd not give him any trouble."

"And you did?"

"I had no reason not to. I didn't know at the time what kind of people they were."

"If you had?"

Annie shrugged. "I probably would have done it anyway." She plucked a blade of grass and scored it up the center with her fingernail. "They devised a scheme. I'd hire myself on to a ranch and break the boss's horses. If I didn't, I wouldn't get paid. Ranchers must have figured they didn't have anything to lose, so they'd let me join their outfit. A couple weeks after the horse was settled, I'd go back in and steal it. Once we had a good-sized herd, we'd take them down to the Tongue River and sell them."

She glanced at Brett to gauge his reaction. He simply stared at the rocks across the creek, seeming not to be surprised.

"And Mustang Annie was born," he said.

"Not exactly. That's just when she became so

well known." Annie turned her attention to the water. Her reflection stared back at her, yet it wasn't a twenty-four-year-old fugitive she saw, but a wide-eyed young girl who would have walked on water for the man who had raised her.

"Granddad and I lived well enough on our share, but he was getting on in years and started worrying about what would happen to me if anything happened to him. He started pulling side jobs." She swallowed hard. "He got caught with an iron. He hanged. They let it happen—they *made* it happen."

"What do you mean? How could his friends have made it happen?"

The betrayal felt as fresh now as it had the day she'd seen him strung up from the branches of an old oak tree. "They set him up. Ike said he knew of a place—"

Brett's head swung around, his mouth agape, his eyes stunned. "Ike?"

"Ike Savage. Do you know him?"

"Are you kidding me? Ike Savage was part of your gang?"

Annie laughed. "He wasn't part of the gang, he *was* the gang. He called all the shots, arranged for the trading, divided the money . . . hell, you name it, he did it."

"Why didn't the law go after him?"

"Ike *was* the law—an elected official of Seymour, Texas. Crooked as a bucket of horseshoes, but he had more ranchers and businessmen in his pocket than you could shake a stick at. No one could ever prove he was involved in any of the rustling."

"They could if you testified."

"It would be my word against his. You've got to remember I was little more than a kid. Even if I could convince someone to believe me, it wasn't worth seeing other members hang."

"Like Henry?"

"You know about Henry?"

"I've had my suspicions that he was involved in some shady dealings, but to my knowledge, he hasn't ever committed anything illegal while he's been on my payroll."

"That's because he's been out of it for years. He'd already been getting slow by the time I got mixed up in the whole mess. He wound up taking a bullet in the leg when they went after some horses up in Oklahoma Territory."

"So that's why he walks with a limp."

"He was lucky he survived at all. Shortly after that, he hired on with Levi Durham."

"And Savage let him go? Just like that?"

"I think they had an arrangement. Henry would never snitch and Savage wouldn't kill him."

"Your grandfather didn't get off that easy, though."

"No, he didn't. Ike was furious when he found out Granddad was rustling on his own. So he gave him a tip on some unmarked quarter horses, then waited for him to show up."

Annie didn't think it was necessary to reveal

the details. Corrigan was smart enough to figure
them out on his own.

"Afterward, I had no choice but to stay with
the gang. I pulled a few jobs for them, tried to
figure out how to get off the paddlewheel. Then,
they started . . . *looking* . . . at me." Bile rose in
Annie's throat, and she rubbed her arms to ward
off the chill of those slimy brown eyes following
her every move. "That's when I knew I had to
get out."

"But you didn't, did you?"

"Actually, I did." Her gaze was drawn to the
land behind them, to the forlorn cross invisible
at this distance, but manifested in her heart. "For
a while."

"Who's buried in the grave, Annie?"

It was along time before Annie could speak
over the lump in her throat. Then she looked him
directly in the eye and gave him the only answer
she could. "Me."

Chapter 18

~~~~~

Dumbly, Brett watched her emotions suddenly close up and her vivid blue eyes lose their luster.

"I don't want to talk about this any more," she stated, gathering herself together as efficiently as she collected her gear. "If you want to help me so damn bad, then help me track down that stallion so I can get paid."

Brett remained crouched beside the water after Annie walked away. *I killed Mustang Annie four years ago.*

He could almost believe Savage's claim, and he couldn't say which impulse was stronger—the urge to shake Annie to life, or pull her into his arms. She'd trusted him with this much, why not the rest? Why did she continue feeding the riddles surrounding her?

But Brett knew if he prodded and poked, she'd

crawl so deep back inside herself she might never again come out.

Patience.

Patience.

In time, she'd tell him. Hopefully then he could figure a way to get her out of this mess.

Right now, it was all he could do to absorb the fact that Ike Savage lived a dual life, that his foreman once rustled horses for a living, and that the woman he was falling in love with lay in grave not five hundred yards away.

The realization slammed into Brett like a load of buckshot. "Oh, my God." He brushed his hand across his head and closed his eyes. How had his feelings for her changed so drastically in such a short span of time? Why hadn't he seen it coming?

Shaking hands slipped into his shirt pocket and withdrew a cheroot. After a moment, he drew out a second one, approached Annie, who was looping her canteen over Chance's pommel, and handed her the smoke.

She cast a startled look at his face, then slowly reached for the cheroot, her long, slender fingers shaking as badly as his. He watched her as if he'd never seen her before. The plait of her braid had loosened. There was smudge of red dirt on her cheek, and circles under her eyes. Sweat and dust stained her shirt. And still she was so damned beautiful she took his breath away.

Gratitude sped across her face with the first pull. "God, I needed that."

He closed his hand into a fist to keep from touching her cheek, her lips, her hair. "Annie. . . ."

Long, sweeping lashes lifted to reveal the question in her eyes.

Suddenly he didn't know what to say. *I love you? Stay with me? I won't let anything hurt you?*

Brett swallowed. Words he'd uttered a hundreds times before into feminine ears in the throes of passion now seemed somehow cheap. He managed a weak smile. "Let's get going."

The rest of the afternoon passed in somber silence as the horses picked their way up the trail and out of the canyon. The difference between below and above was so incredible that to Brett it felt as if they had stepped into another world. Blue skies and amber grasses stretched as far as the eye could see, with not a tree to relieve the banality, not a creek to gurgle in the distance. Just wind and grass and the two of them.

They paused near the ridge to rest the horses before beginning a search for the night's campsite. Brett could no more deny their effort at procrastination than Annie, though neither admitted to it.

While Annie dug oats out of their packs for the animals, Brett wandered to the edge of the canyon, pulled out his scope, and scanned the juniper shrouded floor. From here, he could see for miles in either direction. Peninsulas of rock jutted through the valley like dagger blades. The

Prairie Dog Fork wound around the western wall like a satin ribbon. Caves created black blotches on a stratum face.

Brett spotted several deer bounding beneath a rock formation that resembled a lighthouse, a pair of hawks circling the cottonwood grove, and a pack of dogs drinking from a stream. But not a single, solitary horse.

He slid the scope to the left to scan the plains, on the off chance the stallion had escaped the canyon. Annie had mentioned the possibility.

A magnified view of firewheels and feather-topped grasses came into focus, then the flicking withers of the buckskin, then the gentle swell of buttocks tightly wrapped in denim. . . .

Dynamite couldn't have torn him from the sight of Annie's figure. Of its own accord, the scope made a slow sweep down her legs. The creases behind her knees gave way to smooth, tanned leather around her calves, then silver spurs attached to tooled leather boots. Up the scope went again, Brett's mind stripping her down to bare skin, his mouth going dry at the thought of those legs wrapped around him, his hands spanning her waist, cupping her breasts—

"What are you doing, Corrigan?"

Brett flicked the scope to the left and cursed under his breath. "Looking for the stallion."

"All right. Let's get this over with."

The sharpness in her tone made Brett's attention shoot back to Annie.

His mouth dropped.

She sat in the grass, her vest off, her hands working loose the straps of her spurs, her expression rigid.

"What are you doing?"

"A deal's a deal," she said.

"Deal?"

"The wager. You won. I didn't tame the stallion in three days. I'm ready to pay off."

Understanding unfolded, spreading through him like a bad meal, making his stomach roll and his face heat. "You think a quick roll in the grass is what I meant by 'anything I want'?"

She froze in the process of pulling off her boot. "Isn't it?"

"Yes. No! Not like this. Not as some sort of . . . payment." He spat the last word out, feeling the bile rise in his throat. At one time he'd have taken Annie any way he could get her, and damn the repercussions. But now, the realization that she'd give herself to him like this filled him with disgust—partly at himself for his careless disregard, partly at her for regarding making love with him as some sacrificial act to be endured.

"I won't lie to you and say that bedding you hasn't been on my mind every hour of every day since I met you. But if and when we ever are intimate, it won't be because you feel you 'owe' me. It will be because you want it as badly as I do."

The sight of her sitting astounded and bewildered branded itself in the back of his mind as he swung the scope back up to his eye.

A sudden speck in the distance arrested his heartbeat, and for a second, as the speck grew closer, Brett's breath caught.

The object neared. A horse?

Brett's heart started again, a slow pound in his rib cage, picking up speed as the speck thickened, elongated, becoming a line across the horizon.

No . . . not one horse.

Hundreds of them.

Heading this way.

"Oh, shit—Annie!" Brett tore across the distance between them. "Annie, we've got to get out of here."

"What is it?"

"Stampede!"

"Let me see." She reached for the scope he'd forgotten was still gripped in his hand.

"There's no time—they're heading right for us!"

Instead of following his lead and mounting her horse, she spun around and shaded her eyes with her hands. "Give me the telescope."

"Damn it, Annie . . ."

"Give me the scope!"

He tossed it to her; she caught it in one hand and brought it to her eye. A second later, she gasped, "Oh, no, they're going to kill them."

Then she leaped into the saddle and slapped the end of one rein against Chance's flank. But she didn't head away from the thundering herd.

She ran straight for it.

"Annie!" Brett bellowed. "What the hell are you doing!"

"Saving the mustangs!"

Annie rode like she'd never ridden before. Prairie wind sliced into her face, ripped through her hair, stung her eyes. Yet her thoughts remained focused on the mustangs—and the group of men she'd seen driving them toward the canyon, toward certain death. It was hard to believe that people could be so cruel as to destroy the horses in order to destroy the Indians, but then, she never had been able to understand the human race.

As if realizing that the fate of her brothers and sisters rested on her shoulders, Chance put all her heart into the run. Her legs stretched into full spread; her hooves tore up the grasses and wild rye.

The distance between them and the herd closed quickly. Annie kept her sights on the lead horses.

A shot exploded through the air without warning. Chance stumbled in surprise; instinct had Annie snapping into a tight curl, her head falling onto Chance's mane, her knees jerking upward against the mare's flanks.

Who were they shooting at? The horses? Or her?

Soon another shot rang out, followed by more that came perilously close to her head. Around her, horses screamed. The earth quaked.

Tasting the fear and desperation of the mustangs, Annie gave little thought to the danger to herself. She curled into as small a target as she could manage while keeping one eye on the herd, the other on the squad gunning for her.

Ahead stretched nothing but flat land, yet she knew the canyon was less than a mile off. She urged Chance to go faster and the mare closed in on the herd. When she reached the edge of the band, she uncoiled her rope and let it whir above her head. "Ha!" she cried in a guttural command. "Ha!"

Despite the chaos, the horses began to respond to the motion. The outermost beasts veered inward, away from the sheer cliff wall, forcing the others to follow them.

Annie continued running with the curve of the herd until they'd been safely turned back into the wide open spaces of the panhandle.

She sat atop a heaving Chance, her own breaths coming fast and labored, and watched the dust roll toward the setting sun. She wiped her brow with her sleeve, then guided Chance around, only to come face to face with over a dozen men wearing dark blue uniforms and identical expressions of displeasure. Firearms ranging from pistols to Sharps rifles were trained on her; some still smoked from the shots already fired.

A strange mix of peace and regret stole through her. Annie closed her eyes, and Koda's last words passed over her lips as they had several times in the past. "It's a good day to die."

Just as she expected to feel the pierce of bullets, the ringing sound of spurs carried on the wind and wrapped around her heart.

She cracked open her eyes and saw Brett standing tall and proud between herself and the military. His eyes never wavered from them as he commanded, "Get on back now, Annie. Let me deal with this."

Chapter 19

The lieutenant was a slender, rigid-spined man of obvious breeding despite having more whiskers than face, and what Brett could see of that had gone florid.

"I demand an explanation."

Brett plugged his thumb into his belt band. "Funny, I was going to demand the same of you. I don't take kindly to having my wife shot at." The possessive claim on Annie was a last-minute inspiration in the hopes it would call less attention to her than she'd already earned for herself.

"Then perhaps you should keep a tighter rein on her," the lieutenant countered. "She had no business interfering in military matters."

"You call slaughtering horses a military matter?"

The man shot arrow straight in his saddle and the side of his mouth curled in a sneer. "Those beasts are tools of destruction. Savages use them to raid and pillage. If we are ever to control them, we must not make any concessions in the scorched-earth policy."

"Indians aren't the only ones who use them. Those were cavalry mounts, you fool!"

An angry buzz within the unit reminded him of the hornets Dogie had riled yet at this point, but Brett didn't much care if his lie caused the blue-coats to swarm. "If you want to wipe out the Comanche by killing mustangs, then fine, but it will be *you* explaining to your commander why he isn't receiving the mounts he commissioned us to catch and tame."

That seemed to give the soldier a moment's doubt. The rest of his unit looked suddenly uncomfortable at the thought of paying for the lieutenant's mistake. "You expect me to believe that the two of you could catch five hundred wild horses?"

Brett recognized the sarcasm as a ploy to save face in front of his men. "I would hope you aren't that gullible. We've been waiting for them to migrate into the canyon. I've got an outfit of men waiting below to round them up for marking and breaking. Thanks to you, it'll be weeks before that band returns. How happy do you think it's going to make your captain when he finds out what you've done?"

The jerky movement of the lieutenant's head and a sudden sour odor of anxiety told Brett that he'd hit pay dirt. He jabbed his index finger in the air. "I've got an idea—perhaps we should go back and find out." He turned to retrieve his horse, hoping like hell this gamble didn't blow up in his face.

"Halt!"

Masking a slow, satisfied smile, Brett pivoted on his soles, and lifted a brow.

"I see no need to further distress your wife by forcing her to journey to Fort Elliot."

So the Captain *hadn't* given this unit orders to destroy the mustangs. Brett had to repress a rush of elation that he'd read the lieutenant so accurately.

"Be forewarned, should either of you obstruct future campaigns, I will not be so lenient."

Yeah, Brett didn't expect he would. He couldn't say if this incident would be swept under the rug, or if the officers at Fort Elliot would even be made aware of it—but in any case, it had saved him and Annie from certain arrest, and the horses from slaughter.

The lieutenant finally motioned for his men to follow him, and Brett waited until they'd ridden completely out of sight before heading toward Annie. The two of them had some unfinished business to settle.

He expected to find her brushing Chance down after that frenetic ride. But the buckskin stood alone on the prairie, saddle still upon her back, reins dangling into the dirt.

"Corrigan."

He swung to the right and noticed Annie sitting bow-headed and cross-legged in the grass.

"I need help."

She lifted her face. The upbraiding he'd been about to deliver failed him at the sight of blood staining the front and left sleeve of Annie's shirt. "What the hell—"

"Don't fuss at me, just help me."

Her lips barely moved. Her eyes drooped, her cheeks were pale and drawn tight across her bones, her left arm lay limp in her lap.

Dazed, Brett moved to her side. His hands hovered above her arm. "Where are you hurt? Arm? Shoulder?"

"Arm. One of those idiots actually hit something."

Opening his pocket knife, Brett slit the sleeve from wrist to shoulder. Her choked whimper ripped through his heart. The pain in her blue eyes was nearly his undoing. Knowing the longer he took, the worse it would hurt, Brett peeled the fabric away from her skin. Fresh blood gushed from a small hole in the fleshy part of her upper arm. No exit hole, though. "It's still in there, Annie."

"Have you ever taken a bullet out before?"

"Only out of a box."

"Well, I reckon there's a first time for everything."

"Annie, I don't . . . I've never—"

"It's got to come out, and you're all I've got."

"I know, but . . ." Could he?

Then again, did he really have any choice? Sage Flat was at least thirty-five miles in the opposite direction. He couldn't leave the bullet in there and risk lead poisoning or infection.

Brett dragged his saddlebag close and dumped the contents on the ground. Socks, an extra pair of trousers and shirt, a box each of cheroots and ammunition, a silver flask and comb.

"I don't suppose you have any whiskey in that flask."

" 'Fraid not. I favor bourbon."

"I should have guessed."

He handed her the flask, then gave her another cheroot.

"If the boys could see me now," she joked as he lit the end. "All I need is a deck of cards."

"Sorry. Fresh out of those."

Maybe he shouldn't encourage a woman in drinking and smoking but Annie was big enough to make her own decisions, and he'd never been able to understand why certain things were acceptable for men and not women.

Like the horses.

The lieutenant's comment had rubbed him almost as badly as when Rafe had given him such a hard time about hiring Annie in the first place. He could understand an objection over allowing a woman to put herself in a dangerous situation—he didn't much cotton to the idea, either. At the same time, what gave him or any man the right to deny a woman of Annie's talents a chance to use them?

He grabbed his shirt, and just as he brought his blade to cut it into strips, he felt Annie's hand close over his.

"Use my shirt. I've got two extra, and this one's already ruined."

Instead of wasting time unfastening the two dozen tiny buttons down the front, Brett simply sliced the shoulder seams. "This is not how I pictured undressing you," he grumbled as the fabric fell around her waist. He must have sunk to really depraved depths, for even her injury didn't stop him from reacting to the sight of the smooth swells pushing above the thin cotton camisole.

"I'm sure. The blood does put a slight damper on things."

He shot a startled glance at her face. To his amazement, a teasing glint twinkled in her eyes. Trying to ignore her half-dressed state, Brett concentrated on tearing the shirt, while Annie made free with the liquor and smoke.

Once he had a pile of strips in his lap, he uncapped his canteen and poured a generous amount of water on her arm to flush the wound.

"This is pathetic," she said tucking her chin to look at the seeping wound. "I can't even get shot right. Hell, I could probably walk in front of a Gatling gun and still come out alive."

Brett stilled in horror. He didn't see a damn thing funny about the flippant remark. "Is that what you were trying to do? Kill yourself?"

She tipped the flask to her mouth. "It wouldn't be the first time."

Never had words caused his stomach to plummet as the ones just spoken by Annie. Brett had no idea how to respond to an admission that seemed to mean so little to her, yet shook him to the core. Though the bourbon was undoubtedly beginning to kick in, in his experience, a person under the effects of liquor tended to speak truths they wouldn't normally speak. "Don't talk like that, Annie."

"It's the truth. I should be dead a dozen times over but somehow I keep surviving. What's the point of living when you've got nothing to live for?"

With a calm that belied the tumult inside him, Brett said, "You don't really want your life to end, Annie. If you did, all you had to do was get caught stealing a horse or turn yourself in. You'd be hanged on the spot."

"I'm too much of a coward."

"Oh, Annie, you're the most courageous woman I've ever known."

"Courageous? I'm not courageous; I'm a death sentence to everyone but myself." She took another deep drink and laughed. "Maybe that's the punishment. To go on living when everyone else around you dies."

He focused on stemming the flow of blood with a damp swatch, even as he felt her glazed, intoxicated eyes watching him from beneath her lashes.

"You know what I miss?" she asked, her voice slurring. "The simple things. Shaving cream wet on the brush. Clothes over the back of the chair. The sound of footsteps early in the morning."

Brett swallowed roughly. She was talking of *him*—of her husband's presence in her life. He didn't want to hear it, yet he couldn't bring himself to tune her out.

The touch of her fingers on his cheek had him stilling. Brett had lost count of how many times a woman had touched him, yet not a one affected him as strongly as Annie did, making him feel as if he could move the world. The frightening truth of it was, he'd do it for her in an instant, if only she'd let him.

"And I miss the scent of man around me. On the sheets. On my pillow." The pads of her fingers lightly traveled across his face. Beneath his eyes, down his jaw. "On my skin."

His eyes shut. Oh, God. She was killing him.

"Most of all, I miss being loved." Her fingertips came to rest upon his lips. "Well and truly. Wildly and tenderly."

Brett's gut clenched. He could give that to her. *Wanted* to give that to her, more than he'd wanted anything in his life.

"God, I must be crazed to miss that after. . . ."

He knew the instant she became aware of her own words. Her fingers dropped from his mouth. The glaze left her eyes, to be replaced by that flat detachment he was coming to loathe.

"After what, Annie?"

She let her hand slowly fall to her lap, brought her shoulders back and her chin up, closing herself off from him as effectively as a door in the face. She gripped the liquor bottle tight and took a healthy swig. "Just get the damn bullet out."

Her head began to swim, her vision began to waver, but no amount of liquor had ever been able to dull the constant ache that lived in her heart whenever her thoughts turned to that night.

Brett's touch was gentle. His knuckles brushed the side of her breast, sending a spark of electricity shooting down her arm. She looked at the top of his head, bent close to her arm. A breeze ruffled through the strands of his hair, making them wave like grasses browned by the sun.

The tip of his blade slid into the bullet hole and Annie sucked in a hiss. He yanked the knife out. His ragged breathing carried a hint of panic. "Damn it, Annie, I don't want to hurt you."

The back of her throat felt raw. Her arm burned clear to the bone. "I won't feel a thing," she lied.

She sensed his internal struggle as he sat back on his heels, his head bowed, his hands fisted at his sides, his grip as tight on the hilt of the knife as on his emotions.

She wondered what his men would think if they could see him now, Master of Everything and Everyone, kneeling in the dirt at a woman's feet.

Then he raised his head. Their gazes locked. In a gesture so tender it brought a lump to her throat, he pressed his fingertips to her cheek in silent apology.

It was the last thing Annie saw before the blade entered her arm, and the day went black.

With the open prairie embracing them in her lonesome arms, Brett sat against his saddle, Annie between his upraised knees, her head against his belly. Her hair spread across his middle and spilled down his side, and as he dragged the strands of moonlight and sunbeams between his fingers he marveled at the strength and courage packed into her slender body.

He knew how much it had cost her to ask him for anything, much less for help. If she hadn't passed out, he didn't think he could have removed the bullet. Seeing those blue eyes of hers so filled with pain had affected him like nothing ever before, and if he thought it might have done any good, he'd have pulled her into his arms the minute she'd first touched him.

Not that Annie would have allowed it. She didn't let anyone get that close to her. In fact, she'd be throwing a fit to beat all right now if she weren't passed out.

He didn't know what to make of that, either—the mixed signals she seemed to send him. One minute she was looking at him as if he was the last drop of water on an arid desert, the next, beating the bushes to get away from him when he got too close.

He knew it wasn't his imagination, or the delusion of a sex-starved lunatic. Nor did he think Annie was purposely leading him on. He wondered if she was even aware of it.

She was like a wild filly, at once fearless and fearful, taunting one second, making a hasty retreat the next. He sighed and continued to savor the feel of her in his arms, committing the sight and feel of her to memory, knowing he'd never get this chance again.

Imagine, her thinking she was a death sentence. Nothing could be further from the truth. Annie brought more life into everyone around her than any woman he'd ever known.

When the sounds of the night gave way to the deep stillness of pre-dawn, Annie began to stir. First her head turned on his stomach, then her lashes lifted, then her left hand came up to touch her shoulder. Each movement captivated and filled him with regret, for he knew that as soon as she realized she lay upon him, she'd pull away.

She did.

Within moments, she stiffened against him, then pulled herself to a sit, and brushed her hair back. "How long have I been out?"

"All night."

When she made no comment, he asked, "How do you feel? Do you think you can ride?"

"I'm shaky as an hour-old foal," Annie admitted. It took all the strength she could muster just to sit up. Her head spun, her stomach pitched, and her arm hurt so bad from fingertip to collarbone that it was all she could do not to break down and cry.

It disgraced her to admit how weak she felt. One wouldn't think such a small hole could drain so much out of a body, yet she couldn't recall feeling so helpless in years, and it would do neither of them any good to deny it.

But he was right. Injured or not, they couldn't stay here. It was too open and there was no water.

"There's a cave not far from here." Gritting her teeth, holding her arm tight to her side, Annie scooted up to her knees. "We can . . . reach it . . . from the plateau," she added breathlessly. When Brett hastened to help her stand, she didn't shy away. "From there, we'll still have a good view of both ends of the canyon."

"What are you talking about?"

Annie hesitated at the confusion in his tone. "Holing up until we can go after the stallion. What are you talking about?"

"Getting you to Sage Flat to find a doctor to look at that arm."

"I'm not going to any doctor."

"Annie, you just took a bullet—"

"This?" She waved at the bandage. "It's little more than a scratch. A couple of days and I'll be good as new."

"You can't be sure of that. What if it gets infected?"

Annie sighed and sank back onto her heels. "Look, Corrigan, if you want to ride out of here,

I won't stop you. But I'm not about to make myself a sitting duck for every lawman and bounty hunter in the country."

He shut his eyes and raked his fingers through his mussed hair. "I can't believe I forgot."

"I suppose it's easy to do when you aren't the one living with it every day of your life."

"Are you sure, Annie?"

"I don't have a choice. But if you don't mind, I'll keep the bourbon handy—just to keep the edge off."

She didn't object when he helped her mount Fortune. As much as she hated to admit it, she didn't think she could sit alone for the next hour without falling off her horse.

After gathering Chance's reins, he climbed up behind Annie. Her heart started beating at double speed. She'd always been aware that Corrigan was no pint-sized cowpuncher, but as his arms closed around her to direct the reins, he seemed suddenly larger than life.

She held herself straight as they rode along the rim of the canyon, searching for the opening that would lead to the cave they'd stayed in before. Soon, though, the rocking motion of the horse and the strength of the man lulled her, and she sank against his chest.

Instant heat enveloped her. His arms buffered her from the wind. His heart seemed to beat against hers. Annie vaguely recalled a conversation with him. Had it been in her mind or had she really spoken her innermost thoughts aloud?

Spotting the tell-tale scattering of mesquite that marked the entrance to the cave, she pointed it out to Brett. He brought the horses to a stop, dismounted, then reached for Annie. She had to fight the impulse to lean into him once he set her on her feet. To her surprise, he was the one to take several steps back.

Weaving their way through the brush, Annie paused at the darkened cavity.

"This is it?" he asked, peering down into the chasm.

"It tunnels about forty feet down. We have to watch our footing, though, because it's a steep decline."

He stepped in, then reached for Annie, making sure his grip remained around the right side of her body so he wouldn't jostle her arm.

Despite bracing herself for the slope, her feet slipped several times. She and Brett worked as a team, his right hand on the right wall, her left hand on the left wall. It got dark as a tomb. The turns and twists seemed never ending. Musty granite assailed her as well as the scent of Brett's skin. Salt. Earth. Sweat. Man.

The combination made her senses reel. Just when Annie thought she might not last the rest of the way without swooning, a light appeared, growing brighter the closer they approached the main chamber.

Brett loosened his hold around her waist and guided her to the mouth of the cave. Annie lowered herself to the cool floor and rested with her back against the wall. From here she could see Lighthouse Rock to the right, and distantly, the Spanish Skirts just past the cottonwood grove. Below, the pool where she'd taken Dogie swimming shimmered like diamonds.

"I'm going to bring the horses down into the canyon and get them unsaddled. Will you be all right until I get back?"

Annie nodded, touched by his concern. It had been so long since anyone had worried about her.

She watched him head toward the back of the cave, his shoulders straight and broad, his stride loose yet determined.

"Brett?"

He stopped and looked over his shoulder.

"Henry was right. You really are a decent man."

Chapter 20

❧

Brett returned to the cave much later than he'd counted on and found Annie asleep.

He slung the blanket-load of wood to the floor. So as not to disturb her, he quietly arranged the wood, started a fire, and put a pot of coffee on to brew, then set about skinning a pair of the rabbits he'd bagged.

He loved watching her sleep. She had the prettiest face, soft and relaxed in a way that it wasn't when she was awake and on guard. Her mouth shaped itself into a little smile, her lashes fell in a soft fringe upon her cheekbones, and her chin sought a resting spot on her shoulder.

His chest swelled with the realization that whether she wanted to or not, she needed him. He hoped he didn't let her down.

Once the rabbits were cleaned, spitted and put

on the fire to roast, Brett brought out his telescope and searched the canyon.

"Still no sign of him?" Annie asked, rousing.

Brett lowered the scope with a grim set of his mouth. "Not yet."

"He'll be back."

"What makes you so sure?"

"He favors this place. Once he's sure the danger has passed, he'll be back. Probably with another harem."

And in the meantime, they were wasting time sitting around waiting for him. Only the thought that once they caught him, he'd lose Annie, helped curb Brett's impatience. The longer it took them to find Blue Fire, the longer he got to keep Annie with him. Though he hated that an injury had caused this delay, he also liked her dependence on him.

"You sure seem to know a lot about wild horses," he said.

"I should. When I was a little girl, this canyon used to be my playground. I think I spent more time here than my own home. When other girls were playing with dolls, I was racing the mustangs.

"One day . . . oh, I must have been twelve or thirteen . . . I found this little filly all tangled up in some grapevines. They were wrapped around her neck, her nose, her girth."

Annie's laughter had Brett's gut clenching.

"It was so pitiful it was funny. I cut her free and turned her loose, figuring she'd meet up with the rest of her family. Instead, she followed me. I spent all day trying to get her to stay but she insisted on trailing my footsteps. It started getting dark, and I knew I couldn't just leave her there for coyote bait, so I brought her home. Granddad was fit to be tied at first, but once he got used to her, he told me, 'You always said you wanted to work with the mustangs, so I reckon this here's your chance.' And the name stuck."

Brett found himself smiling along with her.

"It's too quiet out here," Annie said, bringing her blanket around her shoulders. "I keep expecting to hear Emilio play his guitar or Henry bang on those damn pots, or to see Dogie race through camp to escape the wrath of his latest victim."

Brett's jaw tightened. He didn't trust himself yet to think about—much less discuss—Dogie, not with the stunt that had cost him one of the best ropers he'd ever come across still fresh on his mind. He tucked his scope into his saddlebag, then sat down across the fire. With a stick, he poked the fire to bring it to life, then turned the spit. The delicious scent of roasting meat and drippings hitting the embers began to rise from the fire.

"Why do y'all call him Dogie, anyway?"

"A dogie is a little calf whose mama is dead and whose daddy has the wanderlust. He'll adopt himself into another family whether they want him or not. Most times, it's a scrawny little thing that has to be carried around in the chuck wagon till he grows into his legs. And that's exactly where we found him one day—sleeping in the bed of one of the wagons back at the ranch. He's been Dogie ever since."

"What will you do to him when you get back to your ranch?"

He stared grimly into the fire. "I haven't decided yet. I've tolerated his pranks for months. I didn't say anything when he put chili pepper in the coffee, or when he blew up my windmill, and I went easy on him when he almost drowned me. Dogie never means for anyone else to pay for his foolishness, but now he almost got a man killed—and that's not something a body easily forgets. Maybe . . . maybe his own guilty conscience will be enough punishment."

"You know, Corrigan," Annie drawled, "there might just be hope for you yet."

A glow started deep in his gut and spread outward, reaching to the deepest shadows of his being. There'd been a time in his life when he'd have sold his soul for compliments like that, yet Annie gave them to him without expecting anything in return. That they came so seldom made them even more valuable, since Annie didn't waste her breath on platitudes.

"Is that coffee I smell?" she asked.

"Fresh pot. Supper should be ready shortly, too." He wrapped a mug of scalding coffee in a towel and brought it to her. "Let me take a look at that arm."

Annie shrugged the blanket off her shoulders as he knelt at her side. He'd covered her with one of her shirts, but, afraid to jostle her arm, he'd just draped it over her shoulder and buttoned it below her breasts. Unfortunately it left her chemise exposed, and a teasing glimpse of cleavage above the scooped neckline.

Though he felt her watching him as he unwrapped the stained bandage, Brett avoided looking at her, lest her effect on him show in his eyes. She thought him decent. She couldn't be further from the mark. A decent man wouldn't be wondering what she looked like under that chemise. A decent man wouldn't imagine touching more than the wound on her arm.

A decent man didn't dream of making love to another man's wife.

"They killed him, you know."

The words came out in a low, raw tone, as if ripped from deep within her soul.

Brett lifted his head, somehow knowing by the sorrow in her eyes whom she spoke of. If he didn't know better, he would have sworn she'd heard his thoughts.

"He was my husband, my friend, my everything. His only crime was in loving me and they killed him for it."

Brett stared at her, saying nothing.

She looked away, her gaze landing blindly on the horizon where a setting sun painted the skyline in blood reds, rusty oranges and fiery pinks.

"That's what you've been wanting to hear, isn't it?"

Every egocentric thought, every callous word he'd said to her about the man came back to slap him in the face. After a long silence, he whispered, "I'm sorry."

"For what? The death of my husband or the guilt of being glad for it?"

He didn't know how to answer at first. He couldn't deny that his heart soared at the news that he had no rival for Annie, yet seeing her in such anguish cut him to the marrow.

"I'm not glad for anything that would cause you pain. I'd think you'd know that by now."

His reply made Annie wish she could take back the accusation. Maybe he was relieved that he no longer had the worry of an enraged husband coming after him. Could she hold that against him? Especially when he'd been nothing but patient and gentle the last few days?

He was still a man, after all. Just because talking of Sekoda's death aloud for the first time had shredded her heart in two didn't mean Brett had to share the emotion. He hadn't known Koda, hadn't built a life with him, hadn't dreamed with him and seen those dreams destroyed.

As with Molly, he'd simply come along when she'd needed him most.

Annie just hadn't realized it until now.

The days and nights passed in relative calm. Annie was almost grateful, for it gave her a chance to mend. Despite her claims to Brett, her arm hurt like fury, yet each day she worked it to rebuild its strength.

Though Brett said little to her, there was something comforting in his silence. He never pressed her to talk, but he made his presence known. He would look at her and smile. Cook their meals, tend to their horses and tack. It made her feel at once useless and cherished.

Annie tried steeling herself against softening toward him, but she found it much easier to resist Brett when she wasn't a target of his kindness.

"You never talk about yourself," she remarked one afternoon while they were washing their clothes in the creek. Everything Annie owned was filthy beyond recognition.

"There's nothing much to say. What you see is what you get."

His crooked grin made her stomach flutter. "What about your family?"

"I don't have any family."

"No brothers? No sisters?" She thought of Dogie. "Children?"

"Be careful, Annie. Any other man might mistake that as an offer."

Her cheeks warmed, and a tiny part of her delighted in the return of the rogue.

"Why the sudden curiosity?"

She shrugged with feigned nonchalance. "It just occurred to me that you know more about me than I do about you. That hardly seems fair."

"I see. All right, what do you want to know?"

"Well, you once said you didn't want a son."

"No, what I said was, most men want sons, but I'd prefer daughters."

"Why?"

"Girls are soft. Sweet. Innocent. Boys are rough. Loud. Domineering."

She tore her gaze away. "Boys just want to grow up to be like their daddies."

His tone tightened. "Not all boys. Some want to be as different from their fathers as they can be."

The stern set of his stubbled jaw, the tight grip on his shirt and the near violent scrubbing of it against the rock told her she'd hit a nerve.

"Was he that bad?" she asked softly.

His hands stilled. He turned and pinned her with a hard, unforgiving look that she sensed was directed more at the man who'd sired him than at her. "He was selfish and mean and over-bearing. He ruled over everything and everyone until he either killed them or drove them away."

Annie let her gaze drop and softly said, "Be careful, Corrigan, or you'll turn out more like the man you hate than you realize."

He flung his shirt into the water. "What the hell is that supposed to mean?"

She'd come too far to back down now. "The way you treat your men. For a man who wants to be so different from his father, you've grown up just like him."

Annie wished she could take back the words the instant they were out. Why hadn't she just kept her mouth shut? Now, the companionable peace between them was shattered, leaving behind nothing but regret and strained silence as they finished their wash. After draping her clothes over rocks to dry, Annie dreaded returning to the confines of the cave. She found a cushion of grass to rest upon where the late-day sun could warm her and a breeze could brush against her skin. Brett strode a short distance away to smoke.

Though barely a hundred feet divided them, it might as well have been miles. She realized then that she'd allowed herself to get too comfortable with him, and in a way, too dependent.

Maybe it was better this way. Surely the stallion would return soon. They'd catch the devil, get what they both wanted, and go their separate ways.

Oddly enough, the thought didn't appeal to her as much as it once had.

"You're right, Annie."

The remark drew her gaze to where Brett stood, close to the water's edge, his knee jutting out, his hip at an angle.

His gaze shifted to the diamond-tipped crinkles in the creek. "I'm turning out just like him."

That was the last thing she expected him to say. She lifted herself up onto one elbow.

"My family owned a horse farm in Louisiana." He ground his cheroot out beneath his heel and slipped his hands into his back pockets. "Father started out with nothing and built it with his own sweat and blood, and he never once let us forget it." He paused to shake his head. "Damn, but he was a hard man. Nothing we did was ever right or good enough. The horses weren't groomed to his satisfaction, the training didn't progress the way he demanded, our studies always came short of his expectations . . . but even my brothers would tell you that he was hardest on me.

"Corrigan men had always been big but I was small and skinny and clumsy—the runt of the litter. My body never quite worked the way I wanted it to. My mother kept telling me that I would grow into my skin but it's not an easy thing to believe when you're surrounded by four tall, strapping brothers."

"Didn't they ever stand up for you?"

"Not often. They were quite a bit older than me, and I guess they figured I could use some toughening up."

He came to sit near her, his legs stretched out before him and crossed at the ankles, his arms bracing his weight.

"I threatened to leave a lot. Father would say, 'Go ahead—you won't last a day on your own. You're nothing without me.' "

The accent she'd heard only traces of came out

strong and thick, and with a rancor she hadn't thought possible even for him.

"I swore one day I'd make him eat his words, but I couldn't bring myself to leave Mother. He was easy on us compared to how he treated her. Always accusing her of cuckolding him with the neighbors. Always making her feel as if she owed him for putting up with me, who he swore came from one of her affairs. If you knew my mother, you'd realize how ridiculous the charges were. She had been the Belle of the South, could have had any man with a crook of her finger, and she chose him because she loved him. She'd have died before dishonoring their vows."

"Why would she stay with him if she was so unhappy?"

Brett shrugged. "Love. Fear. Obligation. I don't know." He stared at the worn tip of his boots for a long while. "She must have finally reached her limit though, because when I was fourteen, she threw herself down the stairs and broke her neck."

Bitter sorrow clouded his eyes. "He didn't deserve a beauty like her and she didn't deserve a bastard like him. She only wanted to love him and he treated her like dirt. I swore I'd never make a woman suffer the way she did."

Annie had no idea what to say, and so she simply stared at the water. Oh, to be that loved again. To feel that much devotion. She finally understood the loyalty that kept his men around.

"The day we buried her was the day I knew I

couldn't stay any more. My brothers were all gone by then, either married or courting, and I couldn't stand the thought of living in that house with such a hateful man. So I packed a bag and left.

"By the time I was twenty, I had more money and property than I knew what to do with. I'm not proud to say that when boys were gambling with their lives during the war, I was gambling with everything they'd left behind."

"Did you ever go back?"

"Once, after the war. The place had been burned to the ground, the horses gone, my brothers dead. I found my father living in a sanitarium with tuberculosis. Even to the end, with nothing left to claim as his own, he refused to acknowledge me as his son."

For a long time, as the creek rushed through the canyon and songbirds serenaded the summer from their perches, neither spoke.

"So now you know," Brett finally said. "Even if I wanted to change anything, I couldn't, seeing as how I'm the only one left. The last of the Corrigans."

Annie grappled with the unspoken promise she'd made to the young boy who wanted her to wait for him to grow up so he could marry her. If she kept quiet, she'd be committing as great a sin as Brett's father.

"No, not the last. There's still Dogie."

"Dogie?"

"Your son."

He looked as if she'd pole-axed him. "Where in the hell did you get a crazy notion like that?"

"He told me."

"And you believed him?"

"Why wouldn't I?"

"Didn't it occur to you that he was probably pulling another shine on you?"

Quietly, Annie asserted, "His mother's name was Molly. You met her over fourteen years ago at a dockside brothel. The man she worked for had gotten angry because she refused to satisfy one of his more brutal customers. You stepped in and challenged the man to a hand of poker—if he won, she'd pleasure the man; if you won, she walked out with you."

With each sentence, he'd grown paler. "This is unbelievable." He raked his hands through his hair.

"Surely you didn't expect to be able to sow your seed all over the country without a few taking root?"

"I was always careful," he insisted.

"Apparently not always. And if you deny him now, you'll be no better than your own father. Don't make him live with the same mistake you had to live with."

She knew when the words registered. His expression nothing short of awestruck, he unfolded himself from the grass and wandered toward the creek. "My God, I have a son."

For a moment Annie wondered if she'd done the right thing, poking her nose where it didn't belong . . . betraying Dogie's trust. . . .

"Why did he tell you this and not me?" Brett asked. "In all the months he's been with the outfit, he never said a word."

"Maybe because like you, he expected a father would know his own child without being told." It wasn't a criticism, simply an observation. "Why do you think he pulls all those pranks? Why do you think he tried riding that horse? He only wants your attention."

Brett nodded. "I suppose it makes sense." He then squinted into the sun. "Did he . . . did he ever tell you what happened to his mother?"

"She and her husband were killed in a storm three years ago. That's when Dogie began his search for you."

He closed his eyes and a bittersweet smile tugged at his mouth. "At least she got what she wanted. All she ever talked about was making an honest woman of herself."

"You were fond of her."

The first genuine smile she'd seen on him in days transformed his face, giving her a glimpse of the charming rogue she'd met so many weeks ago.

"I met her after my father died. I guess I was feeling pretty reckless at the time, maybe a little arrogant when I made that wager. I helped her set up a bakery and she paid me back by—" He cut off the sentence and Annie swore she saw his cheeks grow red. "Well, let's just say that Molly was the first woman who treated me like a man."

Dreading the answer didn't stop her from asking the question. "Did you love her?"

"I've loved all the women I've been with. But I've never been *in* love. . . ." His smile faded, and he pinned her with a look that made Annie's heart speed up. "Until you."

Annie stared at him for several stunned moments before he averted his gaze, then crouched beside the creek. His denim jeans pulled taut against his thighs and the curve of his rear. He snatched his kerchief from around his neck, dunked it in the water, and pressed it to his face.

He couldn't mean what she thought he meant. Men like Corrigan didn't fall in love, they fell in lust, and pretended it was more to get what they wanted.

But . . . was that so bad? she wondered, envious of his ability to be so free with an emotion she'd felt only once. Despite herself, an ache built inside her to be one of those women. To feel free to touch and be touched. To need and be needed. To love and be loved.

It didn't matter that the love would be superficial. And it didn't matter that once this job was over, he'd move on to his next conquest.

In fact, maybe that was better. No strings, no emotional ties—just a convenient arrangement, a simple using of each other's talents. Her talent was with horses; his was with women.

Suddenly a need consumed her to be like the old Annie, the fearless one, the passionate one— if only for a little while. Long enough to ease the restlessness she'd been feeling since this journey began. A restlessness *he* had awakened.

Brett had once said he'd overcome his fear by taking control. If it had worked for him, maybe it would work for her, too.

She sat up, then rolled to her feet and walked toward him. Her hand to the back of his head made him drop the kerchief from his face.

"You once said you wouldn't touch me again without an invitation."

He stared up at her, puzzlement plain in his eyes.

Feeling strangely emboldened, Annie flicked the buttons of her shirt open. "I'm invitin'."

Chapter 21

Brett's jaw fell.

As many times as he'd pictured Annie wearing nothing but bare skin, his imagination came nowhere near the perfection before him. Her breasts were full and high, the nipples dark and erect.

In awe, he watched them tighten and her breath quicken. "You . . . are so incredibly beautiful."

"Well? You've been after me for weeks—what are you waitin' for now?"

Her fingertips grazed down her flat stomach. God have mercy. A cautious step brought him closer to her.

"I'm almost afraid to touch you."

"But I want you to."

Brett lifted his hands and, fitting her face in his palms, looked deeply into Annie's eyes. He

275

had no idea what had brought on such boldness, and didn't want to question his good fortune. Yet he had to know. "Are you sure? Because I'm not a saint, Annie. Once I start, I may not be able to stop."

"I'm sure."

Seeing only his own desire reflected in the flawless blue depths of her eyes, he lowered his head. The first brush of his lips against hers sent a sweet charge of need coursing through his veins. One taste became two, then a third, then his mouth settled on hers, and Brett moaned, savoring the taste of summer winds and sweet promises. His palms slid down her neck, his thumbs grazing her throat. At her collarbone, he splayed his fingers against her smooth skin. Her breath quickened, and her breasts swelled. Her reaction to his touch had the blood surging in his groin.

Brett drew back, swallowed heavily and touched his forehead to hers.

He couldn't believe how nervous he was. He, who had pleasured more women than he could count, in more ways than he could remember, felt as if he'd never touched, never kissed, never stroked a woman. He had to laugh at himself. "It feels like the first time."

"Me, too."

The glow of her smile caressed him like sunshine.

"I'll try to be careful and not put a baby in you, but we both know how far good intentions go."

"That's one worry you'll never have with me. I'm barren."

So that was what she'd meant when she said no children. What a shame. He wouldn't mind having a few blonde-haired, blue-eyed daughters to bounce on his knee.

The thought disappeared as Annie took a step closer and licked her lips.

Brett's mouth went dry. He tilted his head and kissed leisurely, tenderly. Her arms came around his neck. He groaned as the heat of her breasts burned through his shirt to his chest. She parted her lips beneath his and tightened her embrace.

His kiss turned hungry, searching, his tongue slipping inside the warmth of her mouth to glide across hers. She returned the play with equal greed as her fingers curled into the hair at his nape.

Brett reached behind her and wrapped one arm around her slender waist while the other hand searched for the thong holding her hair back. Silky strands spilled into his palm. He crushed the tresses in his fist and drew her so close to his body that it felt as if they were melded together, and still he couldn't get close enough.

Clothes, he thought hazily. In the way.

In a single motion, he swept Annie into his arms and carried her beneath the shade of a cottonwood tree a short distance away. He fell to his knees, his mouth never breaking contact with hers, and lowered her to the ground. Only when she lay in the grass did his mouth seek the taste of her jaw, her throat, the swell of her breasts. She arched her neck and tangled her fingers in his hair. Soft moans of delight floated on the breeze.

Brett yanked his shirt over his head and released the button on his trousers, then lay down beside Annie. Her pert breasts seemed to plead for his touch. Tracing one with his hand, he marveled at its shape, its eagerness; cupping it, molding it, becoming intimate with its texture before guiding one swollen nub to his mouth.

Annie cried out his name and bowed upward as his mouth closed over her. Her fingernails scored his scalp, his neck, his shoulders. . . .

Even as he repeatedly drew her breast in and out of his mouth, suckling it, circling it with his tongue, Brett straddled her leg and pushed himself against her. The supple flesh of her thigh against his erection fed his hunger.

His mouth left her breast and once again sought her lips. Eager fingers reached for the fastening of her trousers and tugged.

He knew the instant she withdrew from him. Not physically, for there wasn't an inch of skin from the waist up that wasn't touching. But emotionally, he felt her pulling away from him.

Brett stilled, one hand buried in her hair, the other at the opening of her pants. His labored breaths wafted against her cheek.

"Brett?" She gave him a quizzical look. "Why are you stopping?"

"I've never taken a woman against her will in my life—and I'm not about to start now."

The bloom in her cheeks faded. "Do you see me fighting?"

"No, I see you detaching yourself."

"I didn't realize—I'll try harder."

Releasing her, he sat up abruptly and turned away to stare at the clouds sliding across the sun. Even now he couldn't please her. While his body throbbed with desire more powerful than he'd ever felt before, she had to *try* to enjoy his touch. "Don't do me any favors."

Her hands came to rest on his shoulders; her bare breasts flattened against his back. "Brett . . . don't stop. I want this. I need this." She pressed desperate kisses to his shoulders. "I want to remember, I need to forget."

He released a dry laugh. "You aren't making any sense."

"*We* don't make any sense."

No truer words had ever been spoken. "You're driving me insane."

"I'm sorry."

"I don't want you to be sorry," he spat over his shoulder, anger beginning to replace the humiliation. "If you don't want me, just say so."

"I do." Her lips blazed a path from one shoulder to another. "I do."

Brett clenched his eyes shut and tried resisting the temptation. But he'd wanted her so damned long. He'd wanted her to want him for so long.

He turned and searched her face. She was

scared to death. He saw it in the paleness of her skin, the pinch of her lips, the flare of her nostrils.

Yet there was a strength of purpose about her too, in the set of her shoulders and courage in her eyes. How could he deny her? How could he deny himself?

Honored that she'd chosen him, he took Annie in his arms, vowing to please her as she'd never been pleased before. Because he wanted her to forget, and he wanted her to remember—this night, only him.

Filled with fierce determination, he licked and stroked and caressed and kissed her from ankle to brow, staking his claim, proving to her that every inch of her belonged to him.

Only when he had her writhing and begging did he remove his trousers. He entered her slick folds with a single thrust. Annie's head rocked from side to side. Her fingers ripped out the grasses on either side of her by the roots.

Clasping her buttocks, he plunged into her over and over, his seed amassing with such force he feared he'd explode before she did.

Higher they climbed. Harder he pumped.

Annie met his thrusts with wild lunges of her own until finally, an animalistic growl of sheer pleasure tore from her throat.

Only then did Brett allow himself to let go. His mind spiraled into uncontrollable bliss as he spilled himself into Annie's wet heat.

Annie's hold on him loosened and her arms

drifted limply to her sides, her fingertips resting lightly on his bare hips.

His arms shaky, his muscles quaking, Brett lowered himself atop her, feeling her damp skin against his, and drew her close. His mind whirled without thought. Star patterns created a confusion of numbness and bliss.

His throat was dry, his mouth parched, yet he'd never felt so content in all his years of bedding women. With Annie, it felt like the first time, only better. With Annie, it wasn't bedding, it was loving.

He used to think he was the one who held all the power. Not anymore. Annie owned it all.

"I love you, Annie."

She brushed her fingertips across his temple and whispered, "I know you do."

For a long time after Brett fell asleep, Annie lay beneath his solid weight, staring at the inky branches above her.

She'd wanted to remember—that incredible sensation of being touched, of heat climbing through her body, of nerves quivering with need.

And she'd wanted to forget—the horrid taste of helplessness. Of invasion. Of having choice and dignity stripped away at another's whim. . . .

Annie knew if she hadn't experienced the wonder and joy of intimacy before that night four years ago, she might not ever have wanted to share her body with a man again. Knowing that the last vision that had filled her husband's eyes were of his wife submitting to another man in a vain attempt to save his life had filled Annie with self-loathing so deep it had become a part of her. She hadn't thought herself capable of anything else.

But almost from the moment she'd set eyes on Brett Corrigan, desire had flared to life. And had grown. And built. Now that she'd allowed herself to give pleasure and receive it in return, a numbness took its place, uncurling in her belly, spreading outward, slowly invading her bloodstream until not one vein was left untouched by the hollow sensation.

She grappled for the bliss felt only moments ago; tried to seize it. When that failed her, she sought refuge in the numbness that had been her friend and companion since that night—only to find that it, too, had deserted her.

She'd lain with a man.

She wanted so badly to think it didn't mean anything, that she hadn't enjoyed being with Brett. That she'd simply used him to fight her demons. To prove. . . . something.

But she couldn't lie to herself. If there was ever a time Annie had felt so complete, she couldn't remember it. Her life had begun and ended with Sekoda. Everything before and everything after had remained a foggy sensation, a cloudy memory.

Yet in Brett's arms, life felt precious again. She could almost believe in second chances.

Almost.

Carefully, Annie slipped from beneath Brett so as not to disturb him. Chance and Fortune watched as she wandered toward the creek, wind whipping the shirttails about her legs.

She climbed onto a sheet of shale overlooking the ravine. She folded her legs, rested her cheek on her knees and watched the diamond-tipped current chase itself around a bend. Her throat felt swollen and raw, her eyes painfully dry.

She'd been with a man. For the first time since that night, she'd lain with a man willingly, giving of herself that which had before belonged to one and one alone.

And the worst thing was, she'd do it again.

Already she missed Brett's warmth, the scent of his skin, the touch of his hands on her body—and the knowledge filled her with such shame she could hardly bear it.

She shut her eyes and whispered, "Forgive me, Koda."

How could she not only have welcomed Brett into her arms, but boldly invited him? How could she have thought for one minute that being with one man would help her remember another, and forget still yet another?

When had Brett become his own entity, his own memory, his own . . . force?

Annie had no idea how long she sat struggling with her own confusion before an odd instinct compelled her to open her eyes. Her breath trapped itself in her lungs as, like specters of ancient old, a band of thirteen white stallions approached the water's edge several hundred feet away.

Slowly she lifted her head in amazement.

She'd heard once of the band of bachelor albinos up near the Canadian River . . . what would bring them to the Palo Duro?

Another, deeper, sense of foreboding drew her notice to the towering formation of Lighthouse Rock. On a narrow ledge bridging the canyon wall, a dark, shadowy phantom stood silhouetted in wan moonlight, watching the band below with a ferocity that touched Annie down to the soul.

Suddenly the band went on alert, ears high and perked forward, bodies chillingly still. In the next instant, they broke into a gallop away from the stallion.

Not a sound had broken the stillness, not a motion had stirred the calm. The only thing that remained of the vision was a settling of dust near the side of the creek.

Had it been an apparition?

Or a forewarning?

Dread stole through Annie's bloodstream as she realized that the number of white stallions equaled the number of months she'd spent with her husband before he was slain. But what—or who—did the black stallion represent?

Her past?

Or her present?

Chapter 22

⌒◯◯⌒

Brett stirred and reached for Annie with a contented smile, only to discover the space beside him empty. His eyes snapped open, and he rose up and propped his weight on his elbow.

Had he only dreamed that Annie had given herself to him? Dreamed he'd held her in his arms, felt her body melt into his, heard her cries of pleasure?

God, was he losing his mind?

When his eyes finally adjusted to the darkness, he released a breath of relief at the sight of her sitting beside the creek on a pile of rock, wearing nothing but his shirt. Her arms circled her up-drawn knees, and summer moonlight kissed her bare legs. Blonde hair cascaded down her back and one shoulder in silky fall.

"Annie?"

Slowly, she turned her head and met his gaze,

and the emptiness in her eyes nearly brought Brett to his knees. There was something frightening about her lack of emotion—as if behind it lay an anguish too heavy to bear.

A sudden chill chased across his skin.

He wrapped the blanket around his waist and strode across to her. "What is it?"

She didn't answer. She simply turned her face away to look out into the canyon.

Brett followed the direction her gaze had turned. "Oh, my God . . . it's him!"

"Forget him, Brett."

"What?" Her words surprised him as much as the flatness of her tone.

"*Forget* the stallion," she repeated harshly. "I got your fillies back; be satisfied with that."

"Wait a minute—that wasn't part of the deal."

"Sleeping together wasn't part of the deal either, but that didn't stop you."

Astounded, he watched her swing off the rock, grab her trousers and shove first one foot, then the other into the pant legs.

"This whole thing was a mistake."

"Going after the stallion?" he asked with a false calm. "Or making love with me?"

She shot up to arrow-straightness. "You are the most conceited, arrogant—I didn't make love with you. I let you poke me because I felt sorry for you."

Brett sucked in a hard breath. No words had ever pierced so deeply or stung so badly. Could the rapture she'd shown in his arms have been an act? Could she really feel nothing for him?

No, he wouldn't believe that. He couldn't believe that. What he and Annie had shared had gone beyond sexual gratification; he felt it down to his soul. There had been connection between them that surpassed mere physical needs, and he'd bet his fortune that she hadn't counted on it any more than he.

"That's it, isn't it?" he challenged with sudden understanding. "You're feeling guilty because you enjoyed being with me."

"You don't know what the hell you're talking about."

"Don't I? You're not the only one who lost someone, Annie. I lost my whole family."

"I lost my soul!" She smacked her fist against her chest. "I lost myself!"

"But you're finding her again, aren't you? And that scares the hell out of you—that you might just want to go on living, that you want to feel alive again."

Her eyes flaming, she began gathering her clothes from the rocks where they'd been laid out to dry earlier that day.

Brett clutched the blanket around his middle and followed her. "You learn to deal with it, Annie. Day by day, week by week. You go numb. You get angry. You hurt, you grieve, then you learn to let go."

"I *am* dealing with it."

"You're hiding from it—just like you hide from everything else that threatens to break through the shield you've built around yourself."

"You bastard." She raised her hand to slap him; he caught her wrist in a firm but gentle grip.

"How many men have you lain with since your husband died?"

The question—more of a challenge—hung in the air with the weight of a tombstone. He stared at her, daring her to answer, and she stared back, silently defying him with every breath left in her.

"There hasn't been anyone but me, isn't that right? Because I'm the only one who touched you here." He pressed three fingers against her heart. "He might have been the first Annie, but I'll be the last. Wherever you go, whatever you do, I'll be right there with you."

She slapped his hand away. "This is just another game to you, isn't it, Corrigan? Someday you're gonna learn that not everything is about winning and losing."

"No, sometimes it's about the difference between living and dying."

He looked at her with such profound sadness that it made her heart ache. Annie twisted away, wanting to deny the truth of his words, knowing she couldn't. Because he was so right.

She didn't want to die. She wanted to live.

She just didn't deserve to.

Warm hands closed around her shoulders, and she felt Brett's solid strength against her back.

"Grief is like the seasons, Annie." His voice was soothing as a campfire at night and sunshine at dawn. "In the autumn, winds rip the trees bare to the branches. Winter cold sets in, freezing everything it touches. Then in the spring, the earth thaws, and grass begins to grow, and in the summer, the sun warms you from the outside in. There are calm days and stormy days, but it takes both the sun and the rain to make a rainbow."

Annie's breath caught and her eyes went misty. "My husband used to say that."

"He sounds like a smart fellow."

"He was." She swallowed the knot forming in her throat. "When we were together I felt... saved. Forgiven. As if I had every right to love and be loved as any other decent woman."

"You do, Annie."

Her eyes shut. "You wouldn't say that if you knew what I've done."

"Why don't you let me decide that?"

Annie twisted around, and the compassion in Brett's eyes made her want to. After a moment's hesitation, she began to speak. "The first time I saw Sekoda, he was walking through a herd of mustangs right here in this canyon. I remember feeling both awed and envious that they trusted him enough to let him do that, but over the years, I also understood why. He and I became friends quickly. Over the next six years, that friendship deepened, and we became lovers. We met whenever we could, in spite of the fact that if anyone ever caught us together, one or both of us would die.

"After my grandfather hanged, I stayed with

the gang for a while—I told you that. It was a huge mistake, because the looks I'd been getting from the men escalated into touches. It got so bad I started sleeping with a pistol under my pillow. I told Ike if it didn't stop, I'd leave, and he could get his own horses. Ike told me if I left, he'd make me regret it.

"I didn't believe him. I went to Sekoda and told him what was happening. He promised me the moon on a silver platter; I promised him I'd never steal another horse. He offered me a new life, and I took it. I was afraid he'd wind up being forced onto a reservation, so I convinced him to marry me and move into my granddad's house, because the gang didn't know anything about it. That was my mistake. Thirteen months later, Ike, along with a couple of his men and a couple of Comanche, came after the horses Sekoda and I had spent the last year rounding up.

"Koda . . ." She stopped to draw in a deep breath. "Koda tried to stop them and they hit him over the head. I dragged him into the house so he wouldn't get trampled. That's when Ike and one of the men burst in." The whisper sent a chill climbing up Brett's spine.

Annie closed her eyes and folded her arms around her waist. "I tried to . . . get away from him. A lamp fell. I tried to hit him with it, but he was too strong, and too angry. Ike ripped my clothes, then forced my husband . . . to watch. I was afraid they'd kill Koda. I thought if I just let him do what he wanted to me, he'd get his revenge and leave us alone. But he didn't. When he finished with me, he slit Koda's throat, then set the house on fire."

"Jesus. Why didn't you tell me this before?"

"It's not something I want to think about, much less talk about. If you want the truth, it feels like it happened to someone else. All I can really remember is the sight of his blood on my dress, and the smell of burning biscuits, and pounding the marker into his grave. I can't tell you details even if I wanted to. I can't even tell you where I spent the next year, because I don't remember and I didn't care. I couldn't go forward. I couldn't go back. It was better to not exist."

Pieces of the puzzle started clicking into place: her reaction that night in the wagon, the titled cross on an abandoned plain, her constant rejection of his touch.

The thought of Ike Savage laying his filthy hands on Annie filled him with a cold, dangerous rage. Somehow, Brett vowed, he'd make the man pay. For he hadn't just taken Annie's body against her will and killed her man; he'd also stripped her of her self-worth.

Three cautious steps brought him to her. With one finger, he tilted her chin, and his heart bled for what she must have endured.

"We'll get through this, Annie. And there will come a time when you can think about it without wanting to cry, and talk about it without your heart ripping in half. It's just going to take time."

"It been four years!"

"And it might be four more, or forty more. But you're not alone anymore, Annie."

Her eyes brimmed with unshed tears; her chest heaved with the force of her silent sobs. "I . . . don't know . . . how to do this, Brett. My hu . . . husband was everything to me. The breath I took, the beat of my heart. He was patient and safe and gentle; you are daring and ambitious and wild—everything I used to be. If he'd lived, we'd still be together and be happy. But he's gone. And I'm older and alone . . . and if you hadn't come along with your . . . *damned* . . . proposition, I never would have known how alone. Or how afraid."

"Of what?"

"Living again. Loving again." She loosed a teary laugh. "Koda taught me everything I knew about horses, but he forgot to teach me how to live—or love—without him."

He held her face in the palm of his hands. "I'll show you again, if you just give us a chance."

She wanted to. It amazed her how badly.

In his eyes she saw a little boy who'd been forsaken by everyone he loved. She didn't know what she felt for him. Sometimes her emotions got so tangled up with what she'd felt for Sekoda that she couldn't tell where one man ended and the other began.

But she wanted Brett. And she wanted him to love her. When he looked at her like that, as if his every breath depended on her decision, her senses reeled and her defenses crumbled. And she wanted nothing more than to be his breath, his very heartbeat—and he hers.

God, how selfish of her. Her happiness cost people their lives. Her sadness incited their rage. Her fear drove them to reckless bravery.

Two wonderful men had already lost their lives on account of her. She'd not be responsible for a third.

Her heart broke as she removed his hands from her face. "Some chances aren't worth the cost to take."

And before he could stop her, she grabbed her belongings, leaped onto Chance's bare back, and fled.

Brett ran after her, tripping over the blanket around his waist, paying no heed as it dropped in the dirt. Brush ripped through his soles and a stitch formed in his side.

Finally, his lungs screaming for air, he brought himself to a stop and bowed over, hands on his knees, eyes trained on the buckskin speck in the distance as he gasped for breath.

Damn it. Damn it. When was he ever going to learn to stop pushing her? Learn that when he sat back and let her come to him, she didn't run away?

Obviously not soon enough.

"Okay, Annie," he panted. "You win. Go ahead and run away if you have to. I won't chase after you anymore."

Chapter 23

❦

Fortune picked his way down a slim and treacherous trail as Brett followed the stallion with cold determination. When he reached bottom, he brought out his telescope. A gauzy image of Annie filled the lens. Grimly Brett brought the scope away, rubbed his eyes, then refocused. Annie's image disappeared as he'd known it would, for the sun had been playing tricks like this on him for days now.

Instead, a glossy blue-black coat and wild mane nearly hidden behind a peninsula of rocks below filled his sights.

"There you are, you damned devil."

Brett tucked the scope into his saddlebag and unsnapped his lariat.

It's all in the wrist.

"Get out of my head, Annie."

Three days had passed since she'd left him.

Three days he'd spent searching for her, trying to track her down, knowing it was useless even as he did so. Annie had spent years eluding the law, and it had only been a fluke that he'd been able to track her down in the first place.

All he could hope was that when she was ready to pull herself out of the grave she'd buried herself in, she'd come back to him.

And if not, well, he still had a stallion to catch.

Lasso at the ready, he clucked his tongue, urging Fortune to a lope. He kept the stallion in his sights as he moved out of the tree line into open terrain. A flickering memory of wicked hooves pawing air, of Annie tumbling off his back, of Emilio being trampled and dragged in the dirt, flashed through Brett's mind.

Let him go, Brett.

Doubt slivered its way under his skin. Could he control the horse once he had him roped?

Brett rejected the advice now as he had then. If he couldn't catch the beast, it wouldn't be because he didn't try.

The stallion moved into a clear pathway and Brett let his lasso go slack for the final charge. Just as he started to circle the loop, the steed froze, ears point-high, nose extended, eyes trained straight ahead, sensing something amiss.

At first Brett thought he'd caught his scent. But then a flash of movement near the canyon wall captured Brett's attention. Two riders on barebacked ponies suddenly appeared and Brett's mouth dropped open.

Fortune shifted nervously beneath him as he dug for his scope and honed in on the figures. Black hair streaming like banners behind them, one wore a yellow bordered cavalry coat and fringed trousers, while on the other wore a chest plate over bare skin and a calf-length breech cloth.

Brett's blood surged with disbelief, then fury. After all this time. . . .

A quick assessment of distance between the stallion and himself and the stallion and the charging Indians assured Brett that Fortune could easily beat the Indian ponies, but the same instinct that told him when to draw and when to fold now urged him to wait out of sight.

His patience paid off when the riders caught up to the stallion in mid-bolt.

One man jumped on the stallion's back in the same way Brett had seen Annie do, then flipped a rope around his nose while the second man threw a rope around his neck. The horse whinnied and reared; the Indian on his back held on with a grace that Brett envied. Once the forelegs made contact with the ground, the Indian quickly slid a gunnysack over the stallion's head.

Though the horse alternately dug his rear hooves into the dirt and whipped his head back and forth in frenzied objection, neither Indian seemed daunted. They both dismounted and approached the horse.

Brett couldn't hear, but he figured they were soothing the stallion.

His guess proved correct when, after long, pulsing minutes, the animal calmed. They mounted their ponies and led him blindly through the canyon floor.

Brett followed at a distance, his curiosity growing when they seemed in no hurry.

Only when they stopped at the remains of a familiar homestead, at the end of the day, did his curiosity turn to foreboding.

The plains stretched as far as the eye could see, the only difference between earth and sky a thin dark line.

She used to follow that line, hoping she'd reach it one day and just drop off the face of the earth. It had never happened, and now Annie realized she had nowhere to go anymore. Mexico no longer sounded appealing. Going west was certain death. East was a possibility, but she'd stick out like a sore thumb.

Maybe north. Granddad had talked about the beauty of the land, and she'd heard of men driving cattle and horses up to Montana Territory. Where there were ranches, there were horses needing to be tamed and ranchers to be conned. Since she'd never collected her fee from Brett, she'd have to make up the loss. . . .

She lowered herself against Chance's neck and closed her eyes. Who was she fooling? She didn't want to go to Montana. She didn't want to steal or lie or cheat.

She wanted to go home. Not just someplace to

hang her hat, but a place to belong, and someone to belong to.

Heaven help her, she wanted to be back in Brett's arms.

She missed hearing his voice asking her in the middle of the night, "Annie, you awake?" And she missed the scent of his skin on a hot summer night, and his strength when she felt alone or scared.

Strange how new memories formed, replacing old ones. At one time it had been black hair and brown eyes that made her heart swell, now the colors had lightened to wheat brown and green.

"Stop it, Annie. You'll forget him soon enough." She had to—for his own sake.

Yet as the days dragged on, the words lost their force. The sky seemed too vast, the nights too long, the days too lonely. The temptation to turn around grew harder to resist.

I'll show you again, just give us a chance.

What kind of life could they lead, with her always looking over her shoulder? Or waiting for the next bullet to fire? He'd never be safe with her. Like Sekoda, he'd want to keep her safe, and it would kill him.

A shrill whinny bounced off the canyon walls, jolting her. She whipped her upper body first in one direction, then the other, trying to trace the source. Prickles of anxiety broke out at the back of her neck.

She told herself there was nothing to be alarmed about. Maybe a wild dog had frightened a horse. Or a mare ran into a wall of vines.

But she couldn't erase the image of hundreds of mustangs being driven toward a cliff, or Emilio being towed on his belly by a panicked stallion. . . .

Annie wheeled Chance around and backtracked, knowing she'd not rest easy until she solved the mystery.

Trepidation mounted as Annie scanned the walls, unable to quell the sinking feeling that she was being driven toward a cliff of her own.

Then ahead, across the canyon, she spotted a pair of riders. Renegades from the looks of them, and in between them, the distinctive glossy blue black hide of Brett's stallion.

Oh, if Brett had any idea that they'd seized his horse, he would be fit to be tied. He wanted Blue Fire more than anything.

She hardened herself against the flare of pity for him. It was no longer her concern. Besides, she'd told him to let the stallion have his freedom and he hadn't listened. At least the Comanche would have sense enough to set him free if they couldn't tame him.

Annie's determination to remain indifferent vanished at the flash of a familiar gray Arabian and its broad-shouldered rider behind the tree line. A horrifying thought numbed her mind. If Brett was aware of the stallion's capture, he'd not stop until he claimed that horse. And she'd seen him in action: he knew little to nothing about controlling a mustang, much less stealing one from beneath the keen noses of the Comanche!

Without further compunction, Annie cut across the canyon, determined to catch the stallion once and for all. She couldn't give Brett herself, but she could give him something better. She could give him his dream.

Brett lay on his belly at the canyon's rim just above Annie's property, his attention trained on the only structure left standing—a slant-roofed stable with an open lean-to attached to one side. The Indians had hobbled the stallion within the crumbling corral, obviously not trusting the security of the fences, and with good reason. One man then went inside the stables, while the other paced in the shade of the overhang.

With only two guards, Brett could slip past them. He just needed to bide his time and wait for the right moment to slip down and get the stallion; he'd come too far now to leave without him.

What the Indians even wanted with the horse, he couldn't figure. Nor could he hedge a guess as to why they'd brought the steed to this particular section of the canyon. They gave the impression of waiting for something, and he hoped this wasn't to be a rendevous for renegades.

A jangle of reins drew his notice to the plains at his back at the same time he heard his name called. Flap Jack, Dogie, and Henry approached at a canter on horseback.

Brett climbed to his feet and walked toward

them. "What are you fellas doing here?"

"Me and Flap Jack got worried when you didn't come back," Henry answered, dismounting. "Didn't mean to bring the boy—he follered us and we didn't notice till we were halfway here."

Brett tried not to stare at Dogie standing beside the pinto with his hands in his pockets and his chin tucked to his chest. "How's Emilio?"

"Lucky. Busted his arm in two places and broke three ribs, but a circuit doc got him fixed up."

"I don't suppose you heard anything about the fillies yet?"

"Not yet, but I expect Tex got 'em back to the Triple Ace safe and sound by now." Henry scanned the level area. "Where's Annie?"

"She left," Brett replied in a flat tone.

Dogie perked up. "Left? Where'd she go?"

"I don't know."

"Did y'all get the stallion?"

"No, they did." He pointed to the camp below.

"Good glory, what are Comanche doin' with him?"

"I was just about to rope him when they managed to beat me to the punch."

"But why? They revere that horse—think it has special powers or some such."

"I've been trying to figure that out myself."

Henry rubbed his bristled jaw. "I got an uneasy feelin' about this, Ace. It ain't the Comanche way. Usually when they steal a horse, they do it and skedaddle. They don't pitch camp. It's too dangerous—especially with blue coats perching like vultures."

"Unless they're waiting for something. Something valuable."

"Like what?"

Brett paced the ground. "What do the Comanche want more than anything?" he thought out loud.

"Revenge," Flap Jack suggested.

"Freedom," Dogie offered.

"Their old way of life back," Wade Henry said.

"That's right—and they'll fight to the death for it. How better to fight than with guns? We know someone is supplying them; what if that someone is willing to exchange weapons for this horse?"

A troubled frown multiplied the wrinkles on Henry's brow. "Ace, it might not mean anything, but we ran into Rafe at the Silver Spur."

"Sure did," Flap Jack added. "He said he'd gone to work for Ike Savage. He was boasting about how he'd teach you who was boss."

"You think he's trying to steal the horse out from under my nose for revenge?"

"No, I think he's stealin' it for Savage," Wade Henry answered.

"But why would Ike want the stallion?"

The answer hit them both at the same time.

"Annie."

Chapter 24

Hands on his hips, Brett paced the ground. "What a tangled mess." This whole thing was getting more complicated by the moment.

The only reason Ike might want Annie was if he knew she was Mustang Annie. How had Ike discovered they'd be in the canyon, though? Brett had been very careful not to reveal Annie's involvement with the outfit, much less their direction. Now that he thought on it, it did seem odd for Ike to have shown up in Sage Flat at the same time as he had.

Rafe. He was the only one with grudge enough against Brett to alert Ike where to find them.

"When Savage heard the rumors of me hiring a female mustanger, he put two and two together," Brett said. "He's got two reasons to want her. One, she threatens his position and his life, and two, she escaped his wrath."

"Savage don't like being played for a fool."

"So he figures on catching the stallion to catch her. But there's one thing he didn't count on—Annie not going after the bait."

"Uh, Ace?" Dogie interrupted. "She is now."

Brett leaped to his feet and raced to the rim. Even without the scope, he could make out the familiar figure skulking around the perimeter of the pen, her blonde hair rippling in the sunshine.

So that was why she'd been so adamant that he not go after the stallion.

She'd planned on stealing it herself.

Betrayal clubbed into his chest with bruising force. He didn't want to believe it. Closing his eyes, Brett finally had to face the fact that any feelings from the night they'd spent together belonged to him and him alone.

Still, he couldn't just sit back and let her walk into a trap. He didn't know how many lies she'd told or how many times he'd been conned by her, but one truth he couldn't deny—Savage had used her brutally, and he couldn't bear the thought of her going through that ordeal again.

"I've got to stop her." Brett headed for the ridge of rock marking the downward trail.

Wade Henry turned him around with a gnarled hand to his arm. "Think about this—if you go racing down there half-cocked, what's gonna happen to Annie?"

"I'm not just going to let Savage catch her."

"We might already be too late," Flap Jack notified them in a grave tone. "Savage is riding in now, and he brought company."

Three additional men had joined the unit. Brett didn't recognize the two driving the buckboard wagon stacked to the hilt with crates, but the third horseman he'd have known anywhere. Rafe.

Three against six. Best to go for the leader, then the rest would fall out. Thinking quickly, Brett asked, "Flap Jack, did you happen to bring along your cards?"

"Never leave home without 'em."

Brett pocketed the deck, then started issuing orders. "First thing we want to do is get Annie out of there. I'll go down and create some sort of a diversion before he sees her. Meanwhile, Henry, I want you to come in from the north. Flap Jack, come in from the south."

"What about me?" Dogie said.

"Take Fortune. Ride into Tascosa, find Jesse Justiss, and tell him to bring his ass back here fast. No one else, just Jesse. Think you can handle that?"

"Sure thing, Ace."

He rested his hands on the boy's shoulders and gave him a stern look. "And when this is over, you and I are going to have a little discussion."

Leaving Chance tied a safe distance from the corral, Annie kept low as she made her way along the sagging fence to the gate closest to the stable door. A flatbed wagon pulled up and commanded the guards' attention. It was now or never.

Her sole focus on getting in and out before being caught, she didn't hear the approach of footsteps until it was too late.

"I knew you'd come for him."

Annie's hand froze on the latch of the gate. Her heart went solid in her breast, and every drop of blood in her body sank to her feet.

That voice had haunted her for four years, lying in the back of her memory like the shadow of a beast.

She turned slowly. The shadow detached itself from a tall cottonwood and the face of her worst nightmare appeared in the pre-dusk glow.

"How did you find me?"

"Haven't you learned by now that you can't escape the long arm of the law?" His mouth slanted in a smile that turned her stomach. "Actually, you can thank your friend Corrigan."

Brett? He wouldn't have told Ike where to find her.

"Never could keep your hands off the dark studs, could you Annie? Where is Corrigan, anyway?"

Annie refused to answer, afraid if he discovered Corrigan was roosting just above them, he'd send his men after Brett.

Instinct had her searching for an avenue of escape. In front of her, men crowded around the buckboard, indifferent to her plight. Behind her, the canyon wall loomed; to her left, the pasture, and to her right, a grove of cottonwoods.

"I wouldn't try it," Savage warned.

Gripping her hair tightly in his thick fist, he prodded her into the stables and gave her a shove. Annie stumbled but she reined in her panic, knowing she couldn't let him get her riled or she'd make a mistake.

Think, Annie.

She had her revolver in her boot. Did she risk shooting him and drawing the attention of his men?

Something else. Something quiet. Her knife!

Annie wasn't sure how much damage it would do to his thick skin, but if she caught him unawares she could jump on his back—slice his throat. . . .

"Oh, this place brings back memories, don't it?" He stood in the warped doorway, hands braced on either side of him against the frame. She kept the bile down her throat and her eyes on his back as she worked the knife out of her pocket. She could barely make out the stocky shape of one of the Indians inspecting the contents of a crate. "Looks like Ole Quanah is gonna be right pleased with the goods that stallion bought him. Poor bastards don't even realize all the guns in the world aren't gonna help them. But what can you expect from a bunch of dumb savages?"

Fury rose inside Annie, and without thinking, she went after Ike with teeth bared. For such a large man, he was exceedingly swift. He spun around, seized her by the wrist and flung her to the ground like a pesky fly. The knife skidded across the floor and landed beneath an old work table. He picked it up, then dragged the blade down his thumb with a smile.

Breathing rapidly, Annie realized too late that her attack had only incited the animal in him. She scrambled to her feet with a sense of déjà vu. Now she'd have to take her chances with the revolver. She could only hope his mass would muffle the sound. If not . . . she could always use the second bullet on herself.

"Ohh, sweet Annie, you just never learn, do you?" His fingers lightly grazed her jaw and she shied away from his touch. "What other weapons you got hiding under there?"

Annie fought for all she was worth as he roughly searched her. Her resistance only delighted him, but she could not let him find her revolver—

"Ah, what's this?"

She almost wept when he pocketed the Smith and Wesson. As her whole body went limp, he laughed a graveling, bottled sound. "Oh, Annie, *Annie*—you've become quite the little outlaw, haven't you?" His smell choked her, his body crushed her to the wall.

Without her weapons, Annie knew her only chance of coming out of this alive was to feign surrender and catch him unprepared. So when his hand glided down her throat, she forced herself not to cringe. She nearly lost her lunch, though, when his tongue paved a slimy path down her neck. Eyes closed, stomach churning, she inched down the wall . . .

"Looks like I'm interrupting something."

Her attention snapped to the doorway, where Brett strode boldly in. Annie nearly wilted with relief before fear soared inside as, in her mind's eye, she saw history repeat itself.

"Beg pardon." He tipped his hat. "Just wanted to thank you for catching my horse."

Annie could hardly believe her eyes when Brett started back for the door. He planned on *leaving* her? With Ike? Not doing anything to help her?

The incredulity must have struck Savage, too. "You must think I'm a real chump to fall for this act. I've seen the way you look at her."

"Her? She does look damn good—for a dead woman. But like you tried to warn me, Savage, once a thief, always a thief."

Brett swaggered toward Annie. Unlike Sekoda, who had let anger rule his actions, he remained dangerously cool and calm. When he drew his finger down her cheek, it was all she could do not to melt against him.

"She's very good at what she does, though. She woos you, wins your trust. Then the minute you turn your back, she sinks a blade into it."

At first Annie thought it part of some performance. But the cold glint in his eyes and the bitter note in his tone told her this was no act. He thought she'd been trying to steal the stallion. Her heart plummeted and to her shame, her eyes stung. She wanted to cry out, "How could you think I'd betray you?" She'd bared her soul to him. She'd shared her body with him.

She'd lost her heart to him.

But she kept silent, afraid if Savage learned how much Brett had come to mean to her, he'd kill him just to make her pay again.

"So, if you don't mind. . . ." Brett tapped two fingers to his hat. "I'll just take my horse and be on my way."

She watched as he backed out the door, still unable to believe he'd not even try to help her.

Savage slapped his palm against the door, hindering Brett's exit. "You aren't taking that horse nowhere."

"The thousand dollars I paid her for his capture says I will."

Annie perked up, alerted that this *was* some sort of a ploy: no fee had ever reached her hands.

"But Annie didn't catch it," Savage sneered.

Brett pointed out. "Neither did you."

"I made my own arrangements for his capture," Savage thrust out his chest as if to intimidate Brett with the badge pinned to his vest. "And if you try taking that horse, I'll string you from the nearest tree."

"Well, it seems you and I are at a standstill, Sheriff. We both claim possession of the same unmarked horse. In my mind, there's only one way to settle this." He reached inside his vest pocket.

In a the blink of an eye, Savage had the Colt drawn from his low-slung holster, cocked, and aimed at Corrigan.

With a flat smile, Brett extracted a worn deck of playing cards and held them up between his thumb and forefinger.

The sheriff's face turned a murky shade of embarrassed red, then he lowered the pistol to his side. Annie mentally timed how long it would take her to snatch it from his grip, only to realize that he was watching her.

"Care to make a wager?" Brett asked, removing the sleeve and ruffling the pack.

"What kind of wager?" Ike demanded.

"Five-card stud. Winner gets everything he deserves. And if you want to make the stakes more interesting, you could throw in the woman. I don't have much need for her, but she did have her . . . uses."

The deliberate journey his gaze took should have been as insulting as the remark. Instead, to Annie's shame, it coaxed a warmth low and deep in her middle. The fact that she could still respond to him humiliated her more than what Savage had done.

While Brett dragged the work table into the center of the floor and set up the game, Annie kept her eyes on Savage, unwilling to miss a chance to snatch his revolver out of its holster. At one point he turned his back toward her, but just as Annie leaned forward and her fingers closed over the handle, Brett caught her eye. An almost imperceptible shake of his head made her release the weapon. They just couldn't risk bringing on the rest of the men.

After the longest fifteen minutes, Brett smiled and splayed his cards. "Well, lookee there, Savage. Three aces."

Ike stared at the hand. Then a slow, nasty sneer pulled at his mouth. "You're good, Corrigan, but your aces don't beat my pretty ladies." He spread four stone-face queens atop the table.

Brett gaped at the cards for a moment. Then he leaped up from the stool. "You pulled that diamond from your sleeve!" His rage sounded so genuine that she almost believed the performance.

At least . . . she *hoped* it was a performance . . .

"You callin' me a cheat?" Savage asked in a threatening tone.

"Damn right," Brett shot back.

In one swift motion, the table flipped over; cards went flying everywhere. Ike trampled them beneath his feet he charged toward Brett and slammed head-first into his stomach. Both men crashed through the doorway, onto the dirt outside.

Savage's men instantly congregated, drawn by the entertainment of a good fight.

Brett got in a couple good blows as they rolled in the dirt, but within minutes, Savage clearly had Brett overpowered. The fingers pressing into

Brett's windpipe turned his face purple.

Annie snapped. She'd lost one man because she'd been submissive—she'd not lose another.

Spotting an old rope near the eave post, she fashioned it into a lasso; at the same time, Brett gained a surge of strength and shoved the three-hundred-pound man off him. Brett gasped and grabbed his throat while Savage staggered backward, only to have his own men push him back in the circle. Just as he reached back toward his holster, Annie's lariat looped around the nose of the revolver. With a yank of the rope she wrenched it from his hand, and in a movement that would have made Joe Flick proud, Annie had Savage's own weapon pressed against his temple.

Around them, the air went suddenly still.

"I've never killed a man before, but believe me, it would give me great pleasure to make you the first."

Sweat ran down Savage's face. She knew he was itching to knock her out of the way. She almost dared him to, because one slip of her trigger finger and his brains would be splattered from here to hell and back.

The sound of multiple hammers being drawn back sounded like cannon fire in the stillness.

Annie looked around her in astonishment. Henry, Flap Jack, Dogie, and a fair-haired man she didn't recognize circled Savage's men, who slowly raised their hands above their heads.

Brett advanced on Ike and grabbed him by the

collar, the veins standing out on his neck and arms. His cold rage finally erupted into blazing fury. "Remember the stakes of the game, Savage? Winner gets everything he deserves? Well, I'm gonna give you everything you deserve, you filthy sonofabitch."

A right-handed undercut to his jowls snapped his head back. "That's for what you did to Annie's grandfather."

A left-handed fist to the other side sent his head whipping the other way. "That's for what you did to Annie's husband."

Delivering the final crushing blow, Brett brought his knee up between Savage's legs with force enough to jam his balls into his windpipe. "And you know what that's for."

Savage turned green, dropped to his knees, and toppled over.

Brett scowled down at the badge on his chest. "Never did have much use for the law."

"I brought Mr. Justiss, Ace. Just like you said."

Brett layed a hand on the boy's shoulder. "You did real good, Dogie."

Amazing how a few words of praise could make the boy's face light up.

"Actually, he caught me less than a mile out of the canyon," Jesse said. "We've suspected Savage of running guns to the Indians for over two years. We just couldn't ever prove he was involved in it—until now."

Brett tilted his head and studied his friend.

"You really aren't the dumb-ass deputy you've been pretending to be."

"No, I'm the best damn Pinkerton detective you'll ever meet."

Brett grinned. He didn't doubt it for a second. Jesse and Flap Jack dragged Savage to the wagon, where a pair of Indians and Savage's cronies sat bound and tied on the tail gate.

"Rafe," he called out to his former wrangler, "you should have stuck to building fences. It's a lot easier than splitting rock—which is exactly what you'll be doing for the next ten years."

Rafe glared at him, and Brett's grin broadened. Then it faded as the sensation of being watched settled over him. He turned to find Annie standing beneath the overhang. Their gazes met across the distance, and their hearts beat in unison.

He lifted his hands. Annie took one step. Then another. Then raising her arms, she sprinted into his arms. For long moments she simply held on to him with a choking grip. Then she pulled back to press moist kisses along his jaw, his cheeks, his lips. He tasted her fear, her relief, and, dare he hope . . . her love.

Once more she buried herself against his chest. Brett clutched her to him, his nose buried in the sweet fragrance of her hair. "You're shaking."

"You damned fool," she sobbed. "You could have gotten yourself killed."

"Does it matter?" he asked quietly.

"Of course it matters," she whispered, looking at the ground.

"Let's get you out of here."

"Where?" she asked in surprise.

"Back to the ranch. We've got some unfinished business to settle. You do want your money, I assume."

"But . . . I didn't catch the stallion."

"No, you didn't." His tone went brittle.

She dug in her heels; the connection of their hands broke. "You think I was going to betray you."

He didn't need to answer; the truth lay in his eyes.

"Keep your damn money."

"Annie, what was I supposed to think when I saw you down there?"

"You could have trusted me! I've never lied to you, Corrigan. I've never cheated or conned you either, though I've had plenty of opportunity. In fact . . ." she choked on her own thick voice. "I've been more honest with you than with anyone . . . *anyone* in my whole life. And you still thought the worst. I wasn't trying to steal the horse away from you; I was trying to steal it *for* you."

"Why would you risk your life to bring me that horse?"

Annie swallowed. Her lips trembled. Her eyes glittered with tears. "Because it was the only thing I could give you."

Chapter 25

It was a somber procession back to the Triple Ace. Annie and Wade Henry kept exchanging glances, his reassuring, hers worried. She had no idea what awaited her. U.S. Marshals? A hangman's rope? Jesse Justiss with a jail cell ready and waiting . . . ?

If not when they reached Tascosa, then eventually. It was only a matter of time before she would be made to pay for her crimes.

So why was she risking her hide to collect a fee she'd not likely live long enought to spend?

Brett had to know that as well as she did, but he didn't say a word. In fact, he hadn't said more than two words the last forty miles, not even to his men. He didn't even seem to care that the stallion he'd wanted so desperately trotted behind them as meek as a lamb.

He merely rode ahead, hat low over his eyes,

jaw set, shoulders slouched with either weariness or resignation . . . she couldn't tell.

Annie wished for the anger she'd felt when she'd first realized he thought she meant to steal the horse, but in her heart, she couldn't blame him. She'd spent half her life relieving people of their horses and, she realized now, a portion of their pride.

He was better off hating her.

When they arrived at the ranch, Brett helped her off Chance's back. Lines of weariness fanned out from the corners of his eyes and had embedded itself in the grooves of his face.

He tucked a strand of her hair behind her ear. "I want you to go in the house and get a good night's sleep. No one will bother you."

Annie wasn't sure what surprised her more—the gentleness of the gesture or the compassion behind his words. A tiny voice inside her reminded her that she needed to get while the going was good, that the longer she lingered here, the shorter her chances of making a clean escape. But she was so tired. . . .

Sapped of energy, drained of emotion, she complied without argument, falling asleep almost before her head hit the guest room pillow.

Brett stared at her from the doorway, his throat so tight he could barely breathe. Annie lay across the bedspread, her hair all around her, her clothes dusty and shadows of exhaustion under her eyes.

He remembered the first time he'd seen her,

standing in front of him so tough and indifferent . . . no, not even indifferent. Dead, inside and out.

She'd gotten him his stallion. If he let himself think about how close he'd come to losing her, he'd come unhinged. Why had she pulled such a crazy, reckless stunt?

"It was the only thing I could give you."

Nothing had ever touched him more than Annie's simple declaration. He'd spent over half his life amassing *things*—money, property, livestock—in an effort to prove his old man wrong, and she, who had nothing but an inbred instinct for survival, had risked everything to give him a stupid horse. Didn't she know the stallion meant nothing compared to her?

Losing the struggle with himself, Brett pushed away from the doorjamb and crossed the carpeted floor. The bed dipped beneath his weight as he climbed in next to her. Brett curled his body around her slight frame, wrapped his arms around her middle, and inhaled the scent of her hair. It smelled of Texas plains, wild mustangs, and panhandle winds. After tomorrow, he'd never see her again. Once he paid her fee, there would be nothing holding her to him.

How was he supposed to let her go?

Sunshine streamed through the bedroom window as Annie slowly dressed in the split riding skirt and blouse Brett had given her, feeling as if she were donning armor. In a sense, she supposed she was. She'd leave here today after be-

ing turned inside out and upside down, and
have to pretend it didn't matter.

She descended the stairs, her saddlebags over
her shoulder. On the flagstone landing, she
paused to look around at the beautiful objects in
Brett's home. The colorful tapestries, the prism
lamps, the crystal decanter sets and leather
bound books . . . one day a woman would live
amongst all this finery. She'd keep his house,
cook his meals, sleep in his bed and bear his children. . . .

For a moment she allowed herself to wonder
what it would be like to be that woman. She
didn't fool herself into thinking objects brought
happiness; she'd spent some of the best years of
her life in a dark little cabin with nothing but the
basic essentials. But the idea of living out the rest
of her days safe in a home like this, with a man
who made her feel cherished and desired and
loved . . .

Annie closed her eyes. No, she'd given up the
right to such dreams the day she'd stolen her
first horse.

Tossing her head, tilting her chin, straighten-
ing her shoulders, she strode out the front foor.

She came to a stunned halt on the gallery.

Below, gathered at the bottom of the steps, the
men of the Triple Ace stood shoulder to shoulder, their hair slicked backed, Sunday suits crisp
and clean. In the center of them was a black-
coated man with a white collar and Bible. Her
stomach clenched.

"What is this?" she managed to ask.

Dogie, wearing a yellow shirt bright enough to make the flowers grow, stepped forward. "Miss Annie..." He sucked in a deep breath, then blurted, "I'd be right proud if you'd do me the honor of being my stepmother." He shoved a posy of yellow flowers and Indian paintbrush toward her.

Dumbly, Annie took the wildflowers. "Is this one of your pranks?" If so, it was unbearably cruel and humiliating.

Brett stepped up beside his son and laid a hand on his shoulder. "It's no prank," he assured her. He looked heartbreakingly magnificent in the silvery-gray suit and green silk shirtwaist that matched his eyes. His face was shaved smooth; his eyes glowed with an inner light. "Dogie and I had a long talk last night and laid a lot of cards on the table. One of them was deciding that we needed to make an honest woman of you. And honest men of ourselves."

In front of his men, he knelt on one knee and took her hand in his. "Annie Harper, would you do me the honor of becoming my wife?"

She could hardly speak for the emotion squeezing her chest. "Why are you doing this?" she whispered in agony. Here... now... in front of his men. . . .

"Because you amaze me like no one ever has, and I can't imagine living the rest of my life without you. Stay with me, Annie. Help me build this place. Spend the rest of our days chasing horses . . ." His voice dropped to an intimate, almost inaudible level. ". . . and our nights making love. Say you'll marry me."

The temptation to say "yes" was almost unbearable. There'd been a time when raising horses, building a ranch, and loving a good man had been her sole joy, comfort and purpose. It had also been her destruction. She'd not let it be his. "I can't marry you, Brett."

The silence lay heavy as lead around them.

"Can't, or won't?" he asked.

Even if she could find her voice through the thickness in her throat, she didn't know to answer. Can't implied cowardice; won't, willfulness. Neither really applied. She started past him, each step a brittle effort.

Brett's strong, solid hand on her arm stopped her in mid-stride.

"Is it because of the stallion?" he asked. "Annie, I was a fool to think even for an instant that you were going to steal him—"

She shook her head but refused to look at him. "I would have thought the same thing in your position."

"Then what is it? Give me one good reason why."

Tears stung her eyes. How could she tell him how afraid she was of losing him? How afraid it made her to think of the day he'd see her for the thief she was and turn away from her in loathing? Or worse, someone making him pay for her past sins? "Because some things just aren't meant to be." Knowing if she didn't leave now she'd disgrace herself in front of everyone, she pleaded in a whisper, "Let me go, Brett."

"Not on your life. I made the mistake of doing that once; I won't make that mistake again. I've looked for you in every woman I've met, and now that I've found you I'm not ever going to let you go."

She lifted anguished eyes to his. "You have no choice."

She rushed down the steps and past the men standing with hats in their hands and bare heads bowed, toward the stables where Chance would be waiting.

"Annie!" She heard Brett's boots hit the steps. "Damn you, don't do this!"

"Let her go Ace. She don't want to be with you."

"Get out of my way, Wade Henry."

"No. You'll have to go through me."

Dogie stepped forward. "And me."

Then Flap Jack. "And me."

Even Emilio joined them to stand up for Annie against him.

"Get the *hell* out of my way." He tried dodging past them. The strength of three men converged on him, grabbing each arm and hooking him around the waist. Annie kept walking, each step putting another crack in her heart.

Then softly, his voice carried across the distance. "He's gone, Annie."

She came to a sudden stop.

"He's not coming back."

She pressed her fingers to her mouth to stifle a sob.

"But I'm here, and I love you. And you love me. Stop punishing me for it. Stop punishing yourself."

Is that what she was doing? Punishing herself for falling in love again? For wanting to live again?

"Look at me," Brett beckoned.

Oh, God . . .

"Annie, look me in the eye and tell me you feel nothing for me."

Knowing she shouldn't, she turned around. The love in Brett's eyes reached out to touch her, to warm her, to fill her empty, aching, so desperately lonely heart with bittersweet longing.

And Annie was lost.

"Have you forgotten that there's a bounty on my head?" she asked.

"I haven't forgotten." The men released their hold on him. He gradually closed the distance between them, his eyes never leaving hers. "And I'll take care of it. Will you trust me to do that?"

Annie couldn't help a watery chuckle. Leave it to Brett to think he could dictate their way out this one. Then again, if anyone could, Brett could.

"Even if by some miracle you managed to save my skin, you have no idea what kind of trouble you're asking for. I can't cook. I can't clean. I can't even give you babies."

"We'll hire a cook, we'll hire a maid, and we've got Dogie." He brushed her hair out of her eyes, his touch so tender she nearly wept. "I don't deserve a beauty like you, and you don't deserve a bastard like me. But for as long as I live, I will need and cherish and desire only you. And you'll never be more loved by anyone, Annie. I'll remind you every second of every day."

It was all Annie could do to keep from throwing herself into his arms. Did she dare take such a risk?

Buck up, Annie; it's time to ride.

Her eyes clenched shut as Sekoda's voice echoed through her heart and caressed her soul. She could picture him shouting the words from the back of his horse, or from the corral fence, or in the privacy of their bedroom. . . .

And she realized that Koda never would have wanted her to deny herself happiness should she be lucky enough to find it again. He'd want her to seize it with both hands and hold onto every precious second it lasted. And if she didn't accept Brett's offer now, she'd spend every breathing moment regretting it. "Are you sure you're willing to take your chances on a woman willing to take a chance on life—and love—again?" she asked.

"Happily. As long as the woman is you and the man is me."

The simple ceremony took place on the front gallery, with all the Triple Ace hands in attendance. Dogie stood in as best man. Even Jesse Justiss arrived in time to hear the I-do's, and before she could say Blue Fire, she'd been pronounced Brett's wife.

No sooner were the vows spoken than Brett leaned down to whisper, "I need to talk to Jesse a moment. I'll meet you upstairs."

Standing at the window of the room she would share with Brett, Annie tried on her new name the way most women tried on dresses, turning it this way and that way: Annie Corrigan. Annie Harper Corrigan. Mrs. Brett Corrigan.

What in hell had she done?

Annie didn't fool herself into thinking that Jesse had ridden up from Sage Flat to attend their wedding, just as she knew that Ike Savage would not be the only outlaw under discussion. The impression was cinched when the door opened a short while later and a grave silence entered the room. She didn't have to look to know that her husband stood in the doorway, just as he didn't have to tell her of the outcome of his meeting.

Tomorrow, she would pay the piper.

Annie glanced down at the gold band Brett had placed on her finger barely an hour ago. A heart twined around a single diamond big enough to poke a man's eye out. "The ring is beautiful," she said in an effort to delay the inevitable news. "I've never worn one before."

"Not even Sekoda's?"

"Comanche don't exchange rings. He about pitched a fit when I wanted a preacher to marry us." She laughed at the memory. Astonishingly enough, for the first time in what felt like forever, it didn't hurt to think of him.

The laughter faded when Brett walked up behind her and wrapped his arms around her waist. "Jesse wants to arrange a meeting with the U.S. Marshals tomorrow."

Annie almost cried. "So soon?" But she held her tongue, and only nodded. "I guessed as much." She leaned back against Brett and absorbed the solid length of him. "If anything happens to me, I want Dogie to have Chance. He'll take good care of her."

His embrace tightened. "Nothing's going to happen."

"You don't know that, and neither do I." She fell silent a moment, then her fears spilled forth as if a damn had busted. "What if I hang? What if I go to prison? Or worse, what if by some cruel stroke of fate I get off scot-free, and someone comes gunning for you?"

"Don't, Annie. We are not going to start 'what if-ing' everything to death. We are going to take each moment as it comes, and live each day as if it's our last. And no matter what, there aren't going to be any regrets."

He was right, she admitted. What happened tomorrow was out of her control, so there was no sense borrowing trouble, as Granddad would have said. "You should have given up on me long ago."

"That's like asking me not to breathe. We belong together, Annie, like sunrise and sunset. Without you, I'm only half a man."

"And without you, I am nothing."

"Don't ever say that." He turned her in his arms. "You are *not* nothing. You don't need me to validate you. You are a strong, brave, incredibly passionate woman, with more honor in your little finger than most people have in their entire body. And you deserve to love and be loved. Don't ever doubt that, don't ever feel guilty for it, and don't ever deny yourself."

"But if anything happened to you—"

"Then you would go on. And you'd find happiness again."

He stared unflinchingly at her, his piercing gray green eyes driving his truths home. In that instant, a band snapped around Annie's heart, and she suddenly understood herself in a way she never had before. In an effort to bury the wild, reckless side of her character, she'd wrapped her own existence so tightly around Sekoda's that she'd lost herself in the process. By demanding that she allow herself feel, to dream, to live, and to love, Brett was encouraging her not only to find her own identity again, but also to accept whatever she found. With him . . . and without him.

No greater gift had she ever been given.

She touched her fingers to his cheek, her heart

so full of love that she wondered how it didn't burst. "I love you, Brett Corrigan."

His eyes closed, and he swallowed roughly. When he opened them again, they looked suspiciously damp. She was amazed that three tiny words could have such an impact on such a powerful, imposing man.

He took her hand in his and stroked the band around her finger. "No regrets?" he asked gruffly.

"Only one," she softly admitted. "I wish this was our first time."

It took only an instant for her words to register, and when they did, his silvery-green eyes darkened with an emotion that sent shivers dancing along her spine. Need. Raw, naked, desperate need. "*Every* time between us will be a first time."

He kept his gaze steady on hers as he loosened the black satin ribbon she'd tied around her collar. "For instance . . . tonight will be the first time we make love as husband and wife." His mouth curved in a sensuous grin that promised a night of unforgettable delights.

Annie couldn't help but smile. He always had the right words to banish her worries. She'd been unforgivably unfair to him before, using him in a desperate bid to put past ghosts to rest. But no ghosts hovered between them any longer, and no secrets. There was just her and Brett and a night of unexplored love ahead of them, and she wouldn't let a second of it go to waste. "It will also be the first time we make love in a bed."

His eyes darkened to slate. He clasped her face in his hands and guided her mouth to his. Annie's body responded to his kiss in ways that both thrilled and alarmed her. A liquid fire burned low in her belly, and her breasts swelled and grew heavy.

Then his lips left her mouth to roam down her neck, to the pulse at the base of her throat. Annie closed her eyes, let her head fall back, and moaned. Her hands clutched his arms as sensation rolled over her in waves. Tingling awareness, climbing need, dizzying desire ...

She was dimly aware of him unbuttoning her blouse, highly aware of his breath against her breast. Then his tongue flicked over her erect nipple, and Annie cried out as her knees buckled.

Impatient for the feel of his bare skin, she pushed his coat off his wide shoulders. Buttons pinged as she ripped his vest, and then his shirt, open. She nearly strangled him trying to unknot his tie.

"Maybe you better let me do that," Brett chuckled.

"Just do it quickly."

He tore out the starched collar and tossed it to the floor, then made fast work of removing his tie. Annie pushed his shirt down his arms, only to whimper in frustration when the cuffs got caught on his wrists.

He spared her the trouble of trying to remove

his trousers by shucking them off himself, and then . . . ahh . . . hot, smooth skin pressed against her. Annie swept her palms up the backs of his thighs, skimming over the dusting of hair to clutch his smooth, hard buttocks. Proof of his desire pressed long and thick against her belly. The thought of him inside her filled her with giddy anticipation, and she kissed him with savage need. Never before had she felt so weak and so powerful as she did in this moment, and when he gentled the kiss to taste her at his leisure, never had she felt so cherished and adored.

"Do you want me, Annie?" he whispered against her jaw.

"More than anything."

"Then come and get me." He stepped back and stood in all his naked glory just out of her reach.

Annie lowered her lashes to half-mast, and a saucy smile played on her lips. She took a bold, fearless step forward and ran her hand up his chest. "I've been bringing studs to their knees for a long time now, gambler. You sure you're up to the ride?"

He quirked one brow. "Is that a challenge?"

"Challenge, hell. It's a promise."

After kissing her senseless yet again, Brett lifted her in his arms. The mattress cushioned her fall as he set her on the bed, then braced above her, his arms locked on either side of her. Sweat beaded on his brow, evidence of the effort of his restraint. She knew he was giving her this last chance to back out, because now, it was all or nothing.

And damn, she wanted it all.

She took his face in her hands and whispered against his mouth, "Make me yours, Brett."

"With pleasure."

And he did. With his hands, his mouth, his body . . . there wasn't a part of her he didn't claim. He pleasured her in ways Annie had never imagined, and more times than she ever believed possible; and each time, her spirit received its long-denied freedom to soar.

And Annie in turn gave him everything of herself—her body, her mind, her soul, her heart; no restrictions, no regrets.

Only when dawn had begun to glimmer outside their window did she collapse atop him, her cheek to his heartbeat, so limp and sated and so completely at peace that if they came for her at this very moment, she couldn't bring herself to care. At least she'd die a happy woman.

Brett drew her tight against him, and in her ear he whispered, "I love you, Annie."

Her throat went tight.

He murmured, "Promise me that if I fall asleep, you won't run off again."

It seemed odd yet infinitely touching that such a powerful, commanding man might harbor such vulnerability. "I promise." She kissed the slick skin over his heart. "The only place I'll ever run is straight into your arms."

Epilogue

One year later . . .

She'd gone after the horses.

The stables were filled to brimming with steeds of every age and color combination. Arabians, Mustangs, and mixed breeds grazed in harmony on the lush grasses of the Triple Ace. Sophie's Star hadn't escaped the prowess of the stallion and brought forth a colt the next spring, but Liberty Loo was fast becoming a favorite purebred mare for area Thoroughbreds.

The rancher at the Bar 7 in Nevada had accepted Brett's offer of a Triple Ace horse in exchange for dropping the charges against Annie for the one she'd stolen. Of all the horses on Corrigan land, he'd chosen the black stallion called Blue Fire.

And thanks to Jesse Justiss, she and Henry had

received a Governor's pardon for testifying against Ike Savage, who would be spending the rest of his life in prison.

Brett had fired all his men the day they'd held him back on Annie's behalf, and she'd hired every one of them back directly after the wedding that put Mustang Annie to rest, and made her Annie Corrigan. Annie and the men all knew Brett had fired them to save his pride, when in fact he'd never respected them more for being willing to stand up for her—even if it meant standing up against him. He tried to pretend it drove him crazy that they took their orders from her, but one and all knew he was the worst of the lot.

Dogie bloomed into early manhood under Brett's guidance, and Annie feared for the young ladies' hearts when he realized the power of his own charms.

And as for herself . . . Annie caressed her swollen belly. It had come as quite a surprise to discover that she wasn't barren after all. In two months time, she hoped to bring into this world a little girl for Brett to cherish, as he cherished her.

Yes, she'd gone after the horses—but she'd found so much more. She'd found everything worth living for.

Author's Note

Authors are often asked where their ideas come from. This one struck as I was walking through my living room and heard the song Mustang Sally coming from the television. All day that song continued to play in my head, and I found myself humming it in my sleep.

The very next day, I met "Mustang Annie." I'd been working on another story when she appeared in my mind and said, "Either tell my story or I'm gone." Well, many a writer will tell you that if you don't get the story down when it hits, you won't get it back. Such was the way with this one: scene after scene showed itself to me, and as I scribbled notes on every napkin, notebook and grocery receipt, I feared if I didn't tell Annie's story then, she'd take it away.

What struck me most significant about Annie was her eyes. They were so flat and lifeless that it almost hurt to look at her. And I knew then, that she needed someone to make her feel alive again—and who better than a man who grabs hold of life with both hands?

I will always be grateful to my editor for tolerating the senseless telephone conversation she received shortly after, and for enabling me to temporarily put aside the other story so I could write Annie's, and for giving me and the characters the time needed to tell their tale.

I would also like to extend a special thank you to fellow author and dear friend DeWanna Pace for helping me "color" the Texas Panhandle; to my dear friends Jan, Debbie, Alexis, Patti and Peggy for encouraging me to take a risk with this book; and to Eve, Jamie and Kelly for introducing me to Brett. But most of all I'd like to thank R&B artist Wilson Pickett, who sang of Mustang Sally and unknowingly provided me with the inspiration, and to country artists Lone Star, whose beautiful delivery of the song "Amaze" was released right about the time Brett fell in love with Annie, and maintained a permanent spot in my CD player beyond the last page. Thank you, gentlemen, for capturing my hero's feelings so eloquently in song.

I've taken liberty with several facts in the story. My research proved conflicting on when Tascosa was actually founded, so I chose to leave the year up to the reader's discretion. Sage Flat is a completely fictional town. Also, though the scenario and the characters are also completely fictional, the scene where Annie saved a herd of mustangs from being driven over a cliff is based on a true incident when the military drove 1,400 head of wild horses over the side of the Palo Duro Canyon in an effort to eradicate the Comanche and their way of life. And finally, although details on the setting and time period are based on research, any discrepancies are mine alone.

I hope you find Annie as compelling and Brett as irresistible as I did. May all your risks be fruitful, and all your rides be wild.

Rachelle Morgan

PO Box 1217, Hughes Springs, TX 75656
http://www.angelfire.com/tx2/RachelleMorgan

If You Enjoyed *Mustang Annie*,
Then Take a Sneak Preview of
Rachelle Morgan's Sensuous New Romance
Coming Soon from Avon Books

Last Hope, Colorado
1886

She didn't know who looked worse: the man, or the horse he rode in on. Both carried the mark of miles of weather in their slouched postures and dust-caked hides: both looked as if they hadn't seen a meal in ages, and both seemed incapable of taking another step without toppling over.

From her room above the saloon, Honesty McGuire watched the lone rider as he drew closer, stirring up dust on a street that hadn't seen traffic in months. She couldn't see much of his face past the heavy growth of whiskers around his mouth and jaw. Rust-brown hair fell past the collar of the duster covering him from neck to spur. He was a bit too thin for her tastes, too, but a girl in her position couldn't afford to be too choosy.

As much as she wished otherwise, Honesty needed a man. One capable enough to withstand the rigors of travel yet obedient enough to do her bidding without question. At least he was sober. And young. And breathing.

So that left only one question: since the ore mines had been stripped, only two kinds of people showed up in Last Hope anymore—those looking for someone or running from someone. Which was he? The hunter? Or the hunted?

A drink, a meal, and a bed. Jesse Justiss craved all three so badly he'd have given up his four-dollar boots for just the sight of them.

He navigated his horse around a pot hole to the warped hitching rail and dismounted. A spear of agony shot through him the instant his boots hit the ground. Knees on the verge of buckling, he leaned his sweat-drenched forehead against the saddle and cursed ten ways to Sunday through gritted teeth. He'd taken bullets twice before, and hadn't taken this long to recover. Maybe he should have heeded the doc's advice and given his shoulder a couple more weeks to mend before tearing up one side of the Rockies and down the other. Maybe then he wouldn't be feeling as if hot railroad spikes were being driven through his chest. But then, Jess never had been very good at taking advice.

Once the pain had subsided to a tolerable ache,

he pushed away from Gemini's side and circled the horse, inspecting him carefully. The mustang had been a gift from the prettiest horse thief he'd ever had the pleasure of knowing. Jesse had laughed when Mustang Annie told him he'd never find a finer mount or more faithful friend, but over the last eight years, he'd lost count of how many times Gem had proved her right.

The sight of blood on Gem's front foreleg caught Jesse's eye. "Hell and damnation," he swore under his breath. "What have you done to yourself this time, old pal?" He knelt and ran his hand along Gem's leg, careful to avoid the ragged gash just below his knee. A fresh cut, probably from the trip down the mountain. No swelling, and no limping—both good signs. But that didn't mean the animal hadn't pulled a muscle or suffered an even more ruinous injury. It just meant Jess had caught it in the early stages.

Jess wiped his hand down his face. The last thing they could afford was another delay. But until he knew for certain that Gem hadn't suffered a serious pull, he'd not take any chances.

Through weary eyes, Jess gave the town—if it could be called that—a full sweep. The windows of the false-fronted structures that weren't busted or covered with boards wore grime so thick you couldn't even see through them. Paint peeled from signs that creaked on rusty chains. Patches of weeds had sprung up between cracks in the boardwalk and had begun taking over the packed dirt road, and a general air of defeat had settled over the area.

"You sure picked a helluva place to pull up lame," he muttered to the animal.

With a sigh as dismal as his surroundings, Jesse turned to the only open establishment. THE SCARLET ROSE GAMBLING PARLOR AND SALOON was painted in bold, sweeping strokes of red across a whitewashed backdrop. It couldn't have been more appropriately named, for the building stood out from the others like a perfect blossom in a row of tumbleweed.

He started toward the front door, but a sudden sense of being watched stopped him. Prickles danced up Jesse's spine. He glanced up and searched each of the four windows set into the false front behind the second floor balcony. A flutter of curtains made his sight hone in on the corner window.

Jess froze. His right hand shifted to the holster at his hip and, with one deft flick of his finger, he popped the safety strap. Though he hadn't seen anyone watching him, that sixth sense had saved his hide too many times to mistrust it now.

Several seconds passed with no further movement. He stepped onto the boardwalk and cautiously pushed the door open, standing half inside the double wide doorway, his nerves tight as sunbaked rawhide, his senses alert as he scanned the interior of the Scarlet Rose.

A woman in red silk appeared in a doorway to the right of the bar. Upswept blonde hair frizzed around an oval face lightly powdered with rouge. Mid-twenties, curvy in all the right places.

Then she caught sight of him.

"Land's sakes, you scared the fooley out of me!" she cried, slapping one hand over her ample bosom.

The genuine surprise in her soft brown eyes made it obvious that she hadn't been the one spying on him. Jess tipped his hat. "My apologies, ma'am." He kept his hands in sight and a good distance between them, letting her know he posed no threat. "Are you Scarlet Rose?"

"The one and only. Who's asking?"

Still wary. Smart woman. "Nobody important." Jesse scanned the rest of the saloon. A stage skirted in worn red velvet was the main attraction, flanked on either side by tall windows draped in a red velvet print. The balustrade rimming the staircase and the second floor wore the same red velvet bunting, and red mats covered a dozen tables scattered about the room.

Satisfied that no danger lurked in the corners, he strode to the polished mahogany bar that ran the length of the north wall. Shelves climbing to the ceiling framed a mirror scrolled with gold woodwork that many a poker player no doubt used to his advantage.

Scarlet Rose, recovering her surprise, brushed her hands down the red cotton fabric stretched tight across her midriff, and took up her position behind the bar. "Now that I've got my heart back in my chest . . . what's your pleasure?"

Jesse hooked one heel over the brass foot rail. "Whiskey—if you've got it."

"That's about all I've got—five cents a shot." She plucked a bottle from beneath the bar and poured him a shot.

Jesse plopped down a few nickels, then tossed back the whiskey. Blissful fire burned down his throat and into his belly, washing away weeks of accumulated dust.

"We don't get many visitors around here since the mines played out."

He didn't miss the inquisitive gleam in her green eyes or the subtle question in her statement. He knew the game; he'd played it for years. "My horse pulled up lame. Any idea where I might find a good hostler?"

"In Last Hope? You'd have better luck finding gold." She tipped the bottle and refilled his shot. "Folks expected this to be another Leadville. Miners hit color twice, but the shafts played out within a year. Then everyone pulled up stakes and moved on to richer pickings."

"You're still here."

One shoulder lifted in a shrug. "Stubborn, I guess. There's still a couple of prospectors up in the hills who swear they won't leave till Last Hope becomes Lost Hope." A crooked smile played on her rouged lips. "I guess I can't bring myself to give up till they do."

"Persistence." Jesse saluted her with his shot

glass. "Now, that's a quality worthy of admiration."

The blush that stained her cheeks confirmed his belief that even such a worldly woman wasn't immune to flattery.

"Actually, I'm headed toward Leadville myself to meet up with a pal of mine," he told her. "He might even have passed through here in the last couple of weeks. Big fellow, red hair, thick Scots brogue . . . ?"

"Sorry, sugar, nobody like that's come through here."

Jesse resisted the urge to ask her if she was certain. Scarlet was a shrewd woman who had doubtless seen it all and forgotten nothing, and the fastest way to raise her hackles was to press her with a bunch of questions. Jesse hadn't reached the ripe age of thirty by making stupid mistakes.

It had been a long shot, anyway. Duncan McGuire was known to frequent larger towns that provided a variety of opportunities to either load or lighten his purse—depending on which way the wind was blowing. McGuire would have avoided this place like smallpox.

"Look, I've got a stable in back where I keep my mule," Scarlet said, breaking into his thoughts. "If your horse don't mind putting up with Bag-o'-bones' brayin', he's welcome to rest up there for twenty-five cents a night."

Jesse couldn't blame the woman for trying to make extra coin, despite the steep price. "Much obliged. It looks like I'll be needing a room for myself, too, if you've got one to spare."

"Got half a dozen empty ones upstairs. Fifty cents a day, including meals."

Jesse almost choked on his whiskey.

"You pay whether you eat or not, so you might as well eat. And no one goes upstairs without a bath first."

"And I suppose you know just where a man can find a bath hereabouts?" Jesse asked with a lifted brow, fully aware that it, too, would come with an outrageous price tag.

"Bathhouse closed a few months back, but I've got an old tin tub in the pantry. A dollar a filling—a dollar fifty if you want hot water."

"That's robbery!"

She gave him a mischievous smile that shaved years off her features. "There's always the creek."

That ribbon of mud and muck just outside of town? At this rate, he'd be flat broke by nightfall. "You drive a hard bargain, Scarlet."

"So I've been told. But I make it worth every penny."

The smokey lilt of her voice left no mistake that they weren't just talking a room, a meal and a tub of water. "How much more for personal treatment?" he couldn't resist asking.

"Depends on how personal."

"A back scrub and hair washing—for starters."

"Well, normally that would cost an extra ten

cents, but for you . . . it'd be on the house." Her
voice dropped a notch. So did her gaze. "Anything more will be up for negotiation."

The first genuine smile Jesse had felt in months
tugged at his mouth. If he looked half as bad as
he felt, it was a wonder any woman would look
twice at him, much less flirt with him so bra-
zenly. But then, women of Scarlet's profession
would flirt with a fencepost if it meant adding
to the till.

Suddenly, warning prickles once again danced
up the back of Jesse's neck. His hand slipped to
his holster even as Scarlet called out, "There you
are, Honesty. We've got us a visitor."

The guarded glance Jesse cast over his shoulder became an eye-popping double-take as his
sights filled with the most stunning vision he'd
seen in years. She stood halfway down the staircase, one hand on the banister, the other propped
lightly on her hip. A mass of ebony hair that con-
trasted with her porcelain skin tumbled down
her back in loose ringlets and framed a delicate
face that belonged on a cameo pin. Dainty brows
arched over wide, round eyes with impossibly
long, sweeping lashes that, though Jess couldn't
swear to it, looked natural. Her nose was small
and narrow, and her mouth . . . God, lips that
ripe and full had been *made* for kissing.

Desire slammed into him with the force of a
lightning bolt. The low-cut, red satin dress hugging her curves from bodice to knee left little to
the imagination, but a whole lot to temptation,

as if it had been designed solely for the purpose of driving a man crazy. At that moment, Jess would have sold his soul to explore the black lace edging lining the slopes of her breasts, to run his hands down the matching ruffle attached to the swell of her bottom, or to slip off off the dark stockings hugging the most shapely calves he'd seen in ages.

"Why don't you show him to a room while I scare up something for supper?" he dimly heard his hostess tell the woman.

"Sure thing, Rose," she said. "Follow me, cowboy."

Anywhere, Jesse thought, her spun velvet voice wrapping around his vitals, while a familiar fever surged through his blood stream and settled below his buckle. As he numbly watched the twitch of red silk and black lace across her bottom, he couldn't decide who deserved his thanks more—Rose for employing such a prize, or Gemini for getting him stranded with her. Even from a distance, he could tell she was tall for a woman, just a few inches shorter than his own five-feet eleven, which meant their bodies would fit together like two pieces of a puzzle. Images that would have made even the most seasoned harlot blush sliced through his mind.

She paused at the top of the steps. "Are you coming?"

Not yet, but he would if he stared at her much longer—right here in the middle of the Scarlet Rose.

Jess thanked the beard for hiding the color he felt heating his cheeks. It had been a long time since he'd felt such a swift and immediate response toward a woman, and he knew it wouldn't be wise to go anywhere near her until he got himself under control. "I'll be along after I've seen to my horse," he said.

With a tip of his hat, he strode out the door, leaving Honesty to stare after him with her mouth agape and her heart in her throat. Never in all her born days had a man looked at her like that. Every inch of her skin tingled, and a strange, faintly wicked sensation stirred deep in her belly.

"You gonna give me a hand or are you gonna stand around gawking all day?"

Snapped from her musings by Rose's humor-filled question, Honesty followed the woman into the kitchen. "I wasn't gawking."

"You were. Not that I blame you—that one's got the makin's of a true Lothario."

Warmth flooded Honesty's cheeks. "If your tastes run toward the scrawny desperado type."

"You just ain't opening yourself up to the possibilities." Rose opened the door to the cast iron stove and started shoving chunks of pine into its mouth. "Fetch those kettles out of the pantry, will ya, hon?"

Honesty moved to the pantry and brought out a pair of banded wooden buckets and two huge copper kettles. She caught sight of the man leading his horse across the back yard with the straight-shouldered, loose-limbed stride of a man at ease with himself and the world.

Possibilities? Good gravy, he looked as if he'd been dragged through a riverbed and hung out to dry. It wouldn't surprise her if his face was plastered on wanted posters from here to Mexico. All those whiskers, that long, matted hair . . . Hadn't she heard somewhere that long hair often hid the cropped upper ear marking a horse thief?

"So what does he want?" she asked, hoping Rose read nothing more into the question than idle curiosity. She'd done her utmost to hear the conversation between the two of them, but the stranger's voice had been too low timbered to make eavesdropping possible.

"Same thing as every other man. Good whiskey, a hot bath, a soft bed, and willing woman to share it with."

She should have guessed. Why should he be any different? "He didn't have to make a trip all the way out here for that."

"He didn't. Apparently he was heading for Leadville when his horse went lame."

"Do you believe him?"

"Why shouldn't I? No one comes to Last Hope willingly anymore."

That was an understatement. Even she wouldn't be here if fate hadn't stepped in.

"Water's just about ready, hon. Go on and take him his bath while I put a stew on for supper."

A sudden flurry of panic erupted in Honesty's middle at the idea of being in the same room with the stranger. "How about if I cook the stew and you take him his bath?"

Rose laughed. "I want the man pleasured, not poisoned." Then she glanced over her shoulder, and her face softened. "Honesty, are you afraid of him?"

"Of course not!" she hastily denied. Cautious, yes. And why not? Three months ago her father had been shot down in cold blood. Who wouldn't be wary after that? "I just can't shake the feeling that his showing up here isn't as innocent as he wants us to believe."

"That may be true, but his reasons aren't any of our concern. He's the first customer to walk through those doors in weeks, and as long as he's got the coin, we'll oblige his every whim."

That thought made the disturbing sensation in her middle return full force. She couldn't forget the hungry look he'd given her, and his raw, naked longing had stirred something inside Honesty she'd buried long ago—a desire to belong to a man. To be his alone to honor, cherish, and protect till their last breath.

Honesty glanced down at her hands, the nails short and chipped, the fingers conspicuously bare. "Rose . . . don't you ever dream of something more than this?"

She set down a sack of flour she'd taken from the cupboard. "What, like prince-charming, castles-in-the-sky, people-throwing-flower-petals-at-my-feet kind of dreams?"

At Honesty's nod, she confessed, "I used to have that dream all the time."

"But not anymore?"

An unladylike snort blew through the air. "Dreamin' is for pretty young skirts like yourself, not frayed old garters like me."

"You're not old, Rose."

"I'm twenty-five and I've done a lot and learned a lot and lived a lot in those twenty-five years."

More than most, Honesty suspected. Though only five years older than herself, life had hardened whatever soft edges Rose might once have had. Once again, Honesty was reminded of how much her father had protected her over the years. "What about love, Rose? Did you ever love during those years, too?"

She looked suddenly ancient and weary. "More than any woman should have to, darlin'." With a sigh, she said, "Look, take Jesse his bath. If he wants more than a good scrubbin', turn him over to me."

That Rose would make such a sacrifice touched Honesty more than she could say, but she knew good and well that she hadn't been hired as decoration. Rose could no more afford to lose a customer, than Honesty could afford to lose a possible means of solving the mystery her father had left her. If the man wanted more than a good scrubbing, well . . . Honesty hadn't reached womanhood without a few tricks in her pocket.

With a brave smile, she patted Rose's arm.

"Don't worry about me. I can take care of myself." She'd had plenty of practice in the last three months.

All right, she thought, grabbing the tub by its handles, so he wasn't exactly the knight in shining armor she'd been hoping for.

Come to think of it, his scruffy appearance could play to her advantage. No one would expect to find Deuce McGuire's daughter with such a disreputable person. He might even provide opportunities to search places normally forbidden to her. And if Honesty had learned anything in her twenty years, it was never to overlook an opportunity.

No matter how pitiful it appeared.

Jesse took his time tending to Gemini, bathing the wound, bandaging his leg, doing his best to apologize for causing the injury in the first place. But even if the mustang hadn't needed the extra attention, he'd have used it as an excuse to get himself under control.

What had come over him? So Rose's girl was a looker.

The last thing he had time for was a sable-haired, misty-eyed temptress distracting him from his assignment.

Then, with a grimace, he realized that until Gem's leg healed, all he had was time. Too much of it.

"What kind of trouble have you landed me into this time, huh, Gem?"

The horse looked at him with soulful brown eyes, then turned to the bucket of hay Jess had filled for him. With a sigh, Jess gathered the strips of cloth and tin of ointment he'd used to doctor the horses leg.

Once he had Gem settled in the rickety stall next to a bony, dark-hided mule, Jesse returned to the saloon, mounted the steps, and let himself into the first open room.

The accommodations weren't much to boast about. Plain walls, an iron bedstead and side table, two chairs tucked under a supper table, and a claw-footed wardrobe that smelled faintly of cedar. The red calico screen in the corner probably hid a commode and wash stand. He'd slept in worse places, though. It came with the territory.

As promised, a tin tub sat waiting in the center of the room. All it lacked was water.

Jesse lowered himself onto the bed and the ropes strained and screeched in protest under his one hundred seventy pound frame. The spread was a bit frayed, but at least there weren't fleas jumping at him or questionable stains.

Jesse discarded his duster, pulled off his boots, draped his gun belt around the foot-post, and topped it with his hat. The few shots of whiskey had his head pleasantly buzzing. As soon as his bath showed up, he'd indulge in the first good soaking he'd had in weeks. And after a good night's sleep, he'd start scouring this two bit town for clues leading him to Duncan McGuire.

A floorboard squeaked under his stockinged feet as he crossed to the window overlooking the empty street. It still amazed him that the case had been open for sixteen years. A kidnapping wasn't his usual taste. Cattle rustling, train robberies, stagecoach heists and horse thieving ... those were the cases that he fed on.

Had fed on, Jess corrected. After twelve years, he was just fed up. He wouldn't even have accepted this assignment if he could have avoided it. But what's a fellow to do when the man who saved his life asks for a favor? McParland wouldn't even have asked him to take the case if the agency wasn't running so short-handed. But with a majority of the agents tied up with the McCormick strike and the Denver Branch just getting on its feet, Jess knew his old friend hadn't had many options. Nor could Jess have turned him down.

He rubbed his shoulder and continued staring out the window as a setting sun cast the deserted road in shades of red and black.

Damn, but he wished he had more to go on than the scanty information in the file. Duncan McGuire had stolen the daughter of a San Francisco shipping magnate, then absconded with the ransom.

The child, unfortunately, was lost to her family forever; a few weeks after the ransom had been paid, the clothes she'd been wearing washed ashore of San Francisco Bay. Jess didn't hold out any hope of recovering the money, either;

McGuire was a notorious con-artist with a penchant for gambling. But he'd find "Deuce" McGuire eventually—and once he did, he'd be done with the Pinkerton Detective Agency. A man could only spend so many years being shot at and beat up and left to rot in places unfit for the human race. . . .

Jesse pushed back the incident chewing at the edge of his memory. Yeah, the faster he found McGuire, the sooner he could hang up his badge and get on with the rest of his life. Maybe buy himself a plot of land, find himself a wife, have a couple of kids.

Unfortunately the hot lead he'd been following had grown colder than a Montana winter.

"If I were a Scotsman, where would I be?"

A rap on the door interrupted his musings.

At his call, Honesty walked in, balancing a stack of towels and soap in one hand and a yoke of water buckets across her shoulders. As before, the sight of her chased conscious thought from his head. Belatedly Jesse realized he should have offered to relieve her of her burden, yet he seemed incapable of moving.

What was it about her? She wasn't the first sightly woman he'd seen and no doubt wouldn't be the last. And yet, she carried herself with a regalness that made him want to touch her and keep his distance at the same time.

She set the towels on the table, then poured the buckets into the tub. "Do you plan on bathing with your clothes on?"

Jesse pushed away from the wall and unfastened first one shirt cuff, then the other. "Honesty. An unusual name."

"My father was an unusual man. You might want to test the water before you get in."

Ahh, a no-trespassing subject. He could respect that. He didn't much care to discuss his father, either.

After scooping his hand through the water and finding it to his satisfaction, he finished unfastening his shirt and tossed it carelessly on one of the chairs.

"Good gravy, what happened to you?"

Jesse didn't have to look at the web-like scars above his heart to know what she was referring to. "I had a fight with a Winchester and lost." He unbuttoned his trousers and she whipped away to face the wall. Jess paused for a second and quirk his brow. Hell, she acted as if she'd never seen a man undress before.

"Does it hurt?"

"Only when I breathe."

"You're lucky you're able to do that. An inch lower and you'd be dead."

"That was the plan." He shucked his pants, then lowered himself into the steaming water with a sigh. The tub was almost too small to hold him; Jess had to fold his knees to his chest just to fit. "You can turn around now," he told her with a chuckle.

Honesty peered over her shoulder, as if checking to see if it was safe, before lifting her chin and approaching him. She knelt behind him, and he heard her lathering her hands. He nearly melted when her soap-slick palms glided across his upper back.

"So what brings you to Last Hope?"

"Nothing in particular. Just passing through."

"Unless I miss my guess, you do that often."

She must take fishing lessons from Rose. "Often enough."

"Are you a miner?"

"Not hardly."

"An outlaw?"

"No."

"A gambler?"

That one made him smile. "Sometimes. Are you always this nosey?"

"Sometimes."

The sideways grin she gave him stole the breath from his lungs. It struck him as so pure and innocent that a moment passed before Jesse remembered that purity and innocence were hardly words connected with a women of her profession.

"Close your eyes so I can wet your hair."

Jesse did as she bade, and groaned with pleasure when the warm water tumbled over his head. Damn, but that felt good. The scouring of her fingers against his scalp felt even better.

He leaned back and allowed himself to enjoy the full extent of her ministrations. Lilac perfume and a woodsy scent he recognized as patchouli wafted around him as fingernails gently scored his scalp from brow to nape. Her hands then circled his neck, ran across his shoulders, and down his chest, taking extra care around the puckered scar born of McParland's exceptional aim. . . .

Remembering his cravings when he first arrived in town, he amended them. To hell with the meal—this bath was heaven itself.

When he opened his eyes, he was treated to the delicious sight of Honesty's breasts trying to push their way out of their tight confines. Yep, definitely heaven.

Just then a glitter of gold caught his eye. Languidly, he slid his forefinger beneath the chain and lifted an object from the valley it called home. The size of the ruby set into a gold ring raised his eyebrows. "What's this?"

Soapy hands gently extracted the jewelry from his grip and dropped it between the pale swells. "A gift."

"You must be quite talented."

"From my *father*."

Even if her correction had called for a reply, the appearance of a straight blade in her hand would have warned Jesse against voicing it.

"I hope you aren't too fond of that scruff on your face, because you and it are parting company." She gripped his chin between her thumb and forefinger. "I can't abide whiskers." Only then did Jess realize how deep a blue her eyes were, and right now, they glittered with a determination that set his nerves on edge.

Biting her lip, she tilted her head first one way,

then the other. The sight of those pearly whites nibbling on pink flesh made Jesse's mouth water.

"Have you ever shaved a man before?"

Perfectly arced eyebrows shot upward. "Do I *look* like a woman who has never shaved a man?"

Put that way, shaving was no doubt a drop in the bucket of services she offered.

She did that thing with her lip again, and the images that arose in Jesse's mind would have made even the bawdiest harlot blush. His skin became suddenly overly sensitive to the water, his senses acute to the woman beside him. The rasp of steel scraping away beard and her gentle breaths were the only sounds in the room.

Normally he avoided bedding saloon girls. He knew the kind of men who paraded in and out of their beds each night, and had no desire to take with him any souvenirs gained from a few minutes of pleasure.

So his swift, gripping desire to bed this one struck him as odd—and a little unsettling.

It had to be the whiskey dulling his wits—not her sweet, fresh fragrance, so out of place among the pervading smells of spice and whiskey and sweat. Not the glossy black curls piled atop her head. Not the beads of bath water dotting her skin.

Closing his eyes, Jess forced himself to concentrate on something other than Honesty. He'd just about succeeded when her soft cry echoed through the room.

"Oh, my lands . . . !"

His lids slowly lifted. He found her staring at him through eyes wide with astonishment. "What?"

"You're beautiful!"

The remark shouldn't have sent a spear of pleasure through his chest. It sounded far too feminine, and brought back the derogatory names thrown at him all his life by his own gender. Angel-face, pretty boy, buttercup . . . And those were the polite ones.

She swiftly busied herself with wiping cream off his face. "I expect people tell you that all the time."

"Not if they want to live." And not exactly in that manner. But as Jess had gotten older, he'd learned to close his ears to the names and use his looks to his own advantage: women seemed to appreciate them, and men were so busy underestimating him that they never realized how much danger they were in until it was too late.

But strangely enough, when Honesty said it, instead of feeling that familiar surge of resentment, he'd felt a surge of power—as if she could pay him no higher a compliment. Hell, for all he knew, it could be part of her "routine." All harlots had one; some were just better than others.

Honesty was infinitely better than most, he decided when her hand delved beneath the water and her fingertips grazed his hips. He couldn't decide if it was a move designed to arouse him, or an innocent mis-aim. Either way, hot blood centered in his groin. He seized her hand under the water. "Do you tend to all your customers so thoroughly?

She blinked. "Rose said to oblige your every whim."

His every whim, huh?

A wicked grin tugged at his mouth. What the hell was wrong with him, anyway? When a man found himself stranded with a beautiful, willing woman, he shouldn't complain; he should fall on his knees and thank the gods.

So what if he didn't have time for the distraction? After two months of diligent tracking, he deserved a night off. And if that night included being pleasured by the prettiest harlot this side of the Rockies, he'd consider himself richly rewarded.

"Honesty?"

She swallowed heavily. "Yes?"

"I've got a whim that needs obliging." He dragged her hand to his shaft. Blue eyes widened in alarm, and for a moment Jess wondered how much experience she had in pleasing a man. She looked as if she'd never touched one before.

Then her fingers tightened around him and he couldn't think at all.

"My, my, that's quite a loaded weapon you're packin'," she drawled in that red-velvet voice.

Jesse inhaled sharply. "You keep touchin' me like that and it won't stay loaded long."

Her lashes fell and she licked her lips. The sight of her pink tongue sliding across the seam of ripe flesh proved his undoing. With a half growl, half-groan, he cupped his hand around the back of her neck and dragged her face down to his.

The instant their lips met, sensations swirled through Honesty in kaleidoscopic colors—the blue of desire, red of fire, purple of need. . . .

As his tongue delved into her mouth, she thrust back, tasting whiskey and soap and man . . . oh, so much man. And as the shock of him filling her palm wore off, it gave way to glory. Honesty whimpered, suddenly unable to get enough of him. Her hand moved up his stiff organ, past the soft hair that nestled the core of him to a stomach rigid with muscle, then glided up to the tight wall of his chest. How could she ever have thought him scrawny? Lean, yes, but hardly scrawny. There was no mistaking the solid muscle beneath her fingers.

"Damn, but you taste sweet," he murmured against her lips.

Dizzy from his assault on her mouth, Honesty's head felt too heavy to support and fell back. He seemed to take that as an invitation to blaze a hot path down her neck with his mouth. Her limbs turned to liquid, her blood to lava. Her breathing grew so ragged she feared she would faint.

"Your skin is so soft. . . ."

And his was so . . . hot. Honesty knew she'd go up in flames if he kept this up.

She'd die if he stopped.

Only when his hand slipped under her skirt and slid past her stockings, over her garters to her bare thigh, did she come to her senses.

Breathless, she pulled back, knowing if she didn't put some distance between herself and this tub full of temptation, she'd never regain control of the situation. "How about if we take this to drier ground?" she suggested in a ragged whisper.

Eyes impossibly thick-lashed and so green they'd have put jade to shame studied her with a twinkle of mischief. "Don't tell me you're afraid of getting a little wet?" he dared.

Honesty pushed away from him with a strength she wouldn't have believed herself capable of, and hastened on weak-kneed legs to table. She pressed her hand against her breast, closed her eyes, and released a slow, pent-up breath. This had gone much too far.

She slipped a trembling hand inside her skirt pocket, where she kept the "secret to a man's greatest pleasure." The packet had come in handy more times than Honesty cared to remember. "Would you care for another drink?" she asked, half amazed that she could even talk.

"I've had enough, thanks."

"Well, I haven't. And I think there's a rule somewhere that a lady isn't supposed to drink alone."

She poured them both a glass of whiskey from the bottle brought up earlier, then watered down the contents in her glass. She'd never had much tolerance for spirits, and getting soused would defeat her purpose.

Then she unfolded the packet and lifted it to the rim of his glass. Instead of pouring the powder into his drink, though, she paused, tempted for a moment to toss it aside. To take what he offered and to hell with the consequences.

Then Deuce's face appeared before her, with laughing Scottish eyes and stern father's mouth, and she knew she had no choice.

Honestly pressed her lips tightly together and quickly finished her task. When she turned around, she nearly dropped their drinks.

Jesse stood in a ray of setting sunlight in all his naked glory. Every inch of his tall, bronzed body was corded with sinew. With the grime washed away, his hair was the light blond of a sunbeam. Darker brows arched above eyes the color of spring grass, and a slight indentation channeled from the straight-bridged nose to a set of perfect, perfect lips; the whole masterpiece was framed by a sculpted jaw. She hadn't imagined he'd turn out like this!

Speechlessly, she watched him cross the room, flip the sheets over on the bed, and climb in. Seconds later he was propped against the headboard, arms winged behind his head, a devilish smile on his fallen-angel face, and wicked promise in eyes that glittered with a raw, aching need that matched the one pulsing through her veins.

Oh, lands, she was in trouble.

Aware that he was waiting, Honesty forced

herself to walk to the bed. She handed him his glass of whiskey, lifted her own, and, hoping he never knew how dearly she regretted what she was about to do, proposed a toast: "To an unforgettable night."

He couldn't remember a damn thing.

With his elbows propped on splayed knees, his head cupped in his hands, Jesse sat at the edge of the bed, naked as the day he was born. Around him, the scent of lilacs swirled erotically.

His gaze turned to the woman in his bed. Her hair fanned across the pillow slip, silky black tangles against pristine white. A vague image of burying his fingers in that hair stirred at the back of his memory, yet he couldn't quite grasp it.

She rolled onto her side. Her eyes were closed, her lashes casting a shadowed crescent on her cheekbones. Her lips curved into a smile of wistful bliss that had his gut knotting as she nuzzled the sheet as if inhaling its scent.

Abruptly she stilled. A frown creased her brow. Then she shot up off the bed, giving him nothing more than a glimpse of bare back and curvy bottom before snatching a blanket over her nudity. Eyes as wide and frantic as a stormy sea searched the room. "Oh my gosh," she whispered. "Oh my *gosh*!"

Through bleary eyes, he watched her throw a wrinkled chemise over her head, then wriggle into a pair of ruffled pantaloons. Seeing her in the undergarments had as much an impact on him as the red corset he'd taken off her last night.

At least, he thought he'd taken it off her.

Jess frowned and strained to put the night in order in his mind. He distinctly remembered soft skin and hot kisses that could turn a man inside out. And he remembered laughing when Honesty spilled whiskey on his chest, then moaning when he made her lick it off. . . .

It got a little hazy after that. Nothing more than sensations of heat and dampness, and the most insane need to possess that Jesse had felt in his life.

The last thing he could recollect with any clarity was climbing atop her soft and willing body, feeling her arms wrap around his back and her legs around his waist, and hoping like hell to not explode the minute he buried himself inside her.

But then . . . nothing. Not even a glimmer to tell him what transpired next.

"What . . ." He licked his lips, then glanced around for something to get rid of the chalky taste in his mouth. There was half a glass of whiskey on the table. It tasted watered down and stale, but it was wet. "What happened last night?"

She paused in the act of tying her chemise to look at him. "Last night?"

Was it his imagination or did she look as confused as he felt?

"Yeah. Did we . . . you know . . . finish?"

"What kind of question is that? Of course we did!" She bustled about the room, plucking her dress off the chair and a petticoat from the floor. "Twice, in fact! We might have gone for a third time, except you had me so plumb wore out . . . well, let's just say that now that I know the extent of your talents, I'll be more prepared next time. Have you seen my shoe?"

Something about the way her words gushed out and she kept avoiding his eyes struck Jesse as odd, but his mind was too damned fuzzy to sort it out. How much had he drunk? Surely not enough to wipe his mind clean. Hell, he could out-drink an Irishman.

"Gosh, I can't believe I fell asleep in your bed. First time I've ever done that."

It was the first time he'd ever *had* a woman fall asleep in his bed. That was one thing Jesse had always prided himself on—and what had always made him so good at his job—clearing himself of the scene before it became incriminating.

"By the way, you owe me three dollars."

"Three dollars!" he cried, then immediately regretted raising his voice when a thousand ice picks seemed to stab themselves behind his eyeballs.

"Surely you didn't expect a poke for free."

No, but he expected to at least remember it. How did he know he'd been given his money's worth?

Yet how could he prove he hadn't?

"Aw, hell and damnation." Jesse ripped his trousers off the floor and plunged his hand into the front pocket. Pulling out a handful of coins, he blinked, then narrowed his eyes. Was this all he had left?

She snatched the required amount from his hand so fast his head spun, then dropped the coins into the valley between her breasts before heading for the door. She paused with her hand on the knob. "Thanks, cowboy. You really were incredible."

At least one of us enjoyed it.

Coming in September from
Avon Romance
Two historical love stories you'll never forget . . .

Much Ado About Love
by Malia Martin

What if the greatest male writer the world has
ever known was really . . . a woman? And what
if the man who uncovered her secret was the
only one who could set her heart free?

Always and Forever
by Blackboard bestselling author
Beverly Jenkins

Grace Atwood was desperate for a man . . .
to lead a wagon train full of brides out west.
Jackson Blake took one look at Grace and
decided to help her . . . and to keep her by his
side—always and forever.